I0776654

The Suit

a 509 Crime Story

by Colin Conway

The Suit

Copyright © 2019, 2023 Colin Conway

Original Cover Design by Zach McCain
Updated Cover Design by Rob Williams

First Edition – 2019, Second Edition – 2023

ISBN: 978-1-961030-08-4

Original Ink Press, an imprint of High Speed Creative, LLC
1521 N. Argonne Road, #C-205
Spokane Valley, WA 99212

Visit the author's website at www.colinconway.com

What is the 509?

Separated by the Cascade Range, Washington State is divided into two distinctly different climates and cultures.

The western side of the Cascades is home to Seattle, its 34 inches of annual rainfall, and the incredibly weird and smelly Gum Wall. Most of the state's wealth and political power are concentrated in and around this enormous city. The residents of this area know the prosperity that has come from being the home of Microsoft, Amazon, Boeing, and Starbucks.

To the east of the Cascade Mountains lies nearly two-thirds of the entire state, a lot of which is used for agriculture. Washington State leads the nation in producing apples, it is the second-largest potato grower, and it's the fourth for providing wheat.

This eastern part of the state can enjoy more than 170 days of sunshine each year, which is important when there are more than 200 lakes nearby. However, the beautiful summers are offset by harsh winters, with average snowfall reaching 47 inches and the average high hovering around 37°.

While five telephone area codes provide service to the westside, only 509 covers everything east of the Cascades, a staggering twenty-one counties.

Of these, Spokane County is the largest with an estimated population of 506,000.

For Mr. Bryan Whitaker and Mr. Keith Pursch

*Everyone has a plan until
they get punched in the mouth.*

– Mike Tyson

The Suit

ROUND ONE

Chapter 1

Andrew Miller stood at the corner of Wall Street and Sprague Avenue, waiting for the traffic light to change. The late morning sun bounced its rays off the surrounding buildings. Downtown was sure to be hotter than the predicted eighty-eight degrees.

Across the street was the Spokane Transit Authority's bus plaza, the central hub for riders coming and going through the heart of the city. Along with its vital mission, the plaza also acted as a central point for low-level crime. Trespassing, loitering, and panhandling were daily irritants for surrounding businesses. Over twenty-five years, the community had grown immune to the weirdness the plaza attracted.

Andrew smoothed his tie with his right hand while in his left, he held a soft leather briefcase. His blue suit, white shirt, and gray Hugo Boss shoes made up his favorite ensemble; his girlfriend nicknamed it his power outfit. He was ready for the afternoon presentation that he and his assistant had spent three days assembling. He closed his eyes and lifted his face to the sun.

"Walk. Walk," repeated the audible signal in its robotic tone.

Andrew opened his eyes. From the opposite side of the street, several people moved into the crosswalk.

An older man, bent over from age, scurried forward as if late for an appointment.

A husky woman pushed a baby stroller.

Two teenaged girls, oblivious to everyone except themselves, giggled as they approached. One of them filmed the other with her cell phone.

A man in his late twenties wore an *Independent* hooded sweatshirt and stood on the edge of the sidewalk.

Andrew's eyes scanned them all, but it was the man in the sweatshirt that caught his attention.

He stepped into the crosswalk. *It's too warm for a hoodie*, he thought.

The hooded man walked slowly now, as if purposefully separating himself from the others.

Andrew stepped out of the way for the older man, then the woman with the baby stroller.

Across the street, the crosswalk's indicator now flashed red.

The teenagers were at Andrew's shoulder when he noticed the blade in the hooded man's hand.

Andrew stopped in the middle of the crosswalk.

"Gimme some money," the man said. His hand shook slightly as he raised the knife. He blinked several times, and his left cheek twitched. He was unshaven, and his eyes appeared tired, as if he hadn't slept in some time.

"What are you doing?" Andrew asked, pointing to the cars across the intersection. One of them honked in protest. When he brought his right hand back down, his left lifted the briefcase in front of his chest. He now held it with both hands.

"Hey!" the man yelled, his face scrunching in anger. He lunged with the knife, burying it into the soft leather.

Andrew released the briefcase with his right hand and punched the man. This caused the attacker to stumble backward and lift both hands to his face. Then Andrew dropped the briefcase, which still had the knife in it and stepped forward. He twisted quickly and struck the man's upper left leg with a roundhouse kick.

In agony, the hooded man crumbled to the ground. He grabbed his upper thigh, and fear flooded his eyes.

Andrew leaned over him, his fist clenched, ready for another strike. Adrenaline coursed through his system, and blood pounded in his ears. His vision had tunneled onto the fallen man.

Several cars now honked.

Andrew Miller stepped back from the man who lay sprawled on the ground, picked up his briefcase, and yanked the knife free. He dropped the weapon before walking away.

If he hurried, he would still be on time for his appointment.

Chapter 2

Senior Patrol Officer Leya Navarro arrived at the bus plaza and parked her car in the designated location for law enforcement vehicles. She'd been dispatched to the call and sighed after it came through.

No one liked being sent to The Pit—the nickname patrol officers had given to the bus plaza. The place stunk like desperation mixed with body odor, and every incident involved a dirtball. Citizens didn't cause trouble in The Pit. Therefore, the call wouldn't be worth an officer's time nor the paper it would likely incur. But respond, she must.

According to dispatch, the plaza security team had an individual in custody for assault. The suspect, Craig A. Taylor, also had a Failure to Appear in court warrant from a previous arrest.

No need to hurry, Leya thought. Taylor was going to jail one way or another.

Leya grabbed her phone, opened her Facebook app, and messaged her sister about joining the family for dinner. When she was done, she slipped out of her car and headed into the plaza.

People made a path for her as she walked. Leya wasn't a big woman, standing 5'8" and weighing 125 pounds, but it was the uniform and attitude that made people take notice. She knew that was the real weight. Let them see the badge, the gun, and the look that she wouldn't accept any of their nonsense—nine times out of ten that would set things correct from the beginning.

A heavy-set security officer met her outside the safety office. He wore a black security vest with a full complement of goodies—badge, radio with earpiece, notebook, pen, handcuffs, telescoping baton. The vest was too small for his frame and appeared uncomfortable. His name badge read *Jenkins* and was Velcroed to the vest. He looked silly—like an earnest child wanting to play police officer.

When she neared, Leya nodded as a way of introduction.

"You here for our guy?" Jenkins said with a smile. For a man in his mid-twenties, his face was already jowly.

"Guess so," Leya said, failing to match his level of enthusiasm.

"You're gonna love this." He yanked open the door to the security office. "I've never seen anything like it."

They walked through a short hallway into a back room. It smelled like disinfectant had been recently applied.

A man in a hooded sweatshirt sat on a wooden bench with his hands cuffed behind him. Even though he leaned his head back against the wall in a show of calm, his legs jumped in small, jittery jerks. His nose was swollen and crooked, and blood covered the lower portion of his face.

Leya leaned into Jenkins and whispered, "Craig Taylor?"

"Yup."

"You do that?"

Jenkins raised his hands in mock surrender. "Most definitely not."

"What happened?" Leya asked, her voice returning to normal.

Turning to look at them, Taylor said in a nasal voice, "I got jumped."

Leya asked, "Who jumped you?"

"A suit."

"A suit?"

"That's what I said. Guy punched me in the face. For no reason."

Leya glanced at Jenkins and raised her eyebrows. He smiled.

She turned back to Taylor. "What did you do?"

"Nothing. I didn't do nothing. I was minding my own business, and this guy hit me. You ask me; the guy must hate poor people. It's the one percent rising up against us."

"The one percent?"

"That's what it is," Taylor said. "And we gotta stick together against them. You're one of us, Officer. You're part of the ninety-nine."

Leya faced Jenkins. "You guys have video around this place, right?" She twirled her finger for emphasis. "Did you get the incident on camera?"

"Oh man, that's the best part," he said with a chuckle. "Follow me."

In the camera room, Jenkins introduced Leya to Camille Evans. The female security guard stood and shook hands with her. She was a slender redhead who wore the same type of security vest that Jenkins did, but it didn't fit nearly as awkward as it did on the big man.

"Cammie, show Officer Navarro the footage of the fight."

Evans nodded and turned to the wall of cameras. She pointed to a screen and said, "It'll come up here. Gimme a sec."

In a moment, the screen flickered as time changed. Cars passed intermittently through the intersection at Sprague and Wall. Evans pointed to a man wearing a hooded sweatshirt on the screen and said, "There's our boy, Craig Taylor."

Jenkins tapped the opposite side of the screen, calling attention to a suited man with his face lifted toward the sun. "Watch this guy."

As the traffic light changed, the people around Craig Taylor stepped into the crosswalk. The suited man delayed moving. When he did, Taylor made his way directly toward him. The suit appeared to notice and slowed his gait.

"They know each other?" Leya asked.

"Dunno," Jenkins said.

The suit pointed off-screen.

"Why's he doing that?" Leya said.

"Don't blink," Evans said.

On the screen, Taylor lunged forward in a stabbing motion. His hand landed on the briefcase the suit carried. The well-dressed man then punched Taylor, which caused the hooded man to step back, covering his face. The suit dropped his briefcase, stepped forward, and kicked Taylor in the leg, dropping him to the ground. The well-dressed man stood over Taylor for a moment with his fist readied for another strike. Then he stepped back, picked up his briefcase, yanked something out of it, and walked away.

"The hell was that?" Leya asked.

Evans reached around the officer and picked up a plastic baggie with a knife in it. "Our boy tried to stab that suit. Got his butt handed to him in return."

Leya pulled a small knife from the plastic bag and opened the blade. It was only a couple of inches long, but still a knife. She put the weapon back in the clear bag and said, "Play that again but slow it down. Can you do that?"

"Sure," said Evans.

Leya watched the video once more, concentrating on every detail. When it was done, she said, "Play it again. Regular speed."

After her third viewing, she asked, "How long did that entire exchange last?"

Evans said, "From the time the crosswalk indicator said, 'Walk' to the end of the fight, eleven seconds."

"How long was the actual confrontation?"

"From the moment he lunged, to the time he hit the ground, two seconds."

"Wow," Leya said. "I can't wait to talk with this guy. Where's he at?"

Jenkins shrugged. "Not here."

Leya glanced at Evans, who shook her head.

"He didn't stick around?" Leya asked.

"No."

"You get his name?"

"No," Jenkins said. "He never talked with us. Just went on his merry way."

Evans nodded in agreement.

"The hell?" Leya said. "The guy was attacked with a knife, but didn't stick around to alert the police? Who does that?"

Jenkins and Evans glanced at each other before shrugging in unison.

Leya studied the knife in the plastic bag. Her eyes jumped to the paused image on the video screen, then back to the weapon. "I don't believe this."

"What's wrong?" Jenkins asked.

"There's no victim," Leya said. "I can't arrest a guy for First Degree Assault with no victim."

Leya shoved the camera room door open, banging it against the wall. She stalked into the small room where

Craig Taylor waited in handcuffs. He looked up, and his eyes rapidly blinked. "You find the guy who did this to me?"

"You tried to stab a guy. We've got it on camera."

Taylor turned away and lowered his head.

"Why did you move on him?"

He looked back up with anger in his eyes. When he spoke, his words came out in a slow staccato rhythm. "I ain't sayin' shit."

"Did you know the man you attacked?"

"I attacked *him*? He attacked me! I'll tell you something, lady. I'll never forget that guy. I'm gonna find him and make him pay."

"You really just make a threat against him? In front of a police officer?"

Taylor rolled his head around. "My head hurts. I think I got a concussion. And I'm coming down. I can't be held accountable for what I say."

Leya smirked. "Right. You're a victim."

Taylor nodded. "That's what I'm saying. I'm a victim of the brutality of the one percent."

Leya's eyes flicked to Jenkins, who grinned like a kid on Christmas morning. She turned her attention back to Taylor. "It's your lucky day, Craig."

"It don't feel so lucky. Did I tell you I got a concussion? I probably should go to the hospital."

"The guy you attacked didn't stick around to press charges."

Taylor's eyes focused on Leya. "Then, I wanna press charges." His legs bounced wildly, but his voice remained steady. "I want to get that—"

"For what?"

Taylor blinked several times. "Look what he did to my face. I know he broke my nose. I can barely breathe out of it."

"The guy defended himself against *your* attack. Therefore, you're not pressing anything except your luck. However, I can show you the video we got. It's impressive. Unless you're you, of course. I bet if we got it on Facebook, it would go viral. People all over the world would laugh at how you got your butt whipped by some guy in a suit. The one percent would eat it up."

Taylor shook his head. "I forgot. You work for them. How could I ever think I'd get an even break?"

"But you are, Craig. You are. I'm not arresting you for the assault. That's the bright side. Unfortunately, you've got a warrant, so you're still going to jail."

"What?"

"Stand up, tough guy. You know the drill."

Taylor slowly rose to his feet and stared at Leya. "I got beat up, and I still go to jail?"

"Funny how life works."

Taylor snickered. "Ain't no thing. I've been there before. I'll be out tomorrow."

"Don't count on it."

Chapter 3

"It's called the knockout game."

"Dude, that shit's old. Muthafucka's been playin' that game for years. It's dumb, yo."

Matt Taylor silently stared at Rabbit until he became visibly uncomfortable.

"I mean," Conrad 'Rabbit' Anderson said, sitting up as straight as he could in the blue bean-bag chair, "I'll play if you want to play. I was only saying that the game's been around for a while."

Matt loved it that Rabbit's vocabulary cleaned up whenever he felt like he was in trouble. He only talked street when he was lying or pretending to be tough.

"Conrad," Matt said, knowing full well Rabbit hated his first name even more than his nickname. "I know the game has been around a while. I'm not an idiot."

"But why?" Rabbit asked. He must have heard the whine in his own voice because he cringed.

"For kicks, man. Times are lean, and the boys are anxious. Since the drugs have dried up, everyone's living off their old ladies or their moms. Some of the boys are even talking about pulling a rip to make ends meet, and you know that'll end badly. What we need is a distraction until the pipeline gets reset, and we're back in the game. Otherwise, they're going to get their dumb asses into some trouble they can't get out of."

"Why don't we do that? Pull a job, I mean. A real job."

"You got an idea for one? If you got a job for us to do, then do spill." Matt stared at him, challenging him to speak up. When he didn't, Matt continued. "That's what I thought. I don't have any original ideas either. Besides, we sell drugs, Rabbit. Pulling a job isn't our thing. We don't have any skill at ripping or hijacking, and none of us has ever pulled a strong-arm job."

"It was just an idea."

"So is getting a regular nine-to-five, which ain't my style—"

"Mine neither," Rabbit interrupted.

"I'm looking for something to distract me from the woes of today. Bingeing Netflix and video games doesn't do it for me. I want action, *real* action. I haven't had anything since I left the Corps."

"What about Ronnie?"

Matt shook his head. His girlfriend, Veronica, had gotten increasingly hooked on OxyContin and spent most of her days in a stupor, lying in his bed. She was in the back room now. A year ago, he couldn't believe his luck when he first started sleeping with her. Now, he couldn't believe what she'd turned into. Still, she could be attractive if cleaned up, and he didn't have to work hard to get at her. Besides, the house belonged to her parents, and they let her live there rent-free. It was worth that alone to keep her around. Of course, he had to keep her stocked in Oxy, and he had to keep the house somewhat clean for surprise parental visits. Overall, the pros outweighed the cons when it came to her.

"What about Ronnie?" Matt repeated. "That ain't the type of action I'm talking about. I mean, if you want me to talk about what we do, I'm happy to tell you, since I know you're all head over heels for the girl."

Rabbit lifted his hands in surrender. "All right, I get it. You sold me on doing something, but why this? Why the knockout game?"

"Because it never seemed like it was really done right before. You know? It was like one jerk over here would do something, and then another jerk over there would do something, but there was never a real game being played. Know what I mean?"

Rabbit shrugged. "I guess."

"What I'm saying is we make it official. We set up…" He struggled for a word before settling on "…perimeters."

"You mean parameters?" Rabbit asked.

"That's what I said. And a goal. Money for the winner. I'll put up five hundred bucks as a bounty."

Rabbit's eyebrows lifted at the mention of five hundred dollars. "Really?"

"Why not? I've got to keep the boys motivated, especially now."

Rabbit's eyes stared off into the distance.

"What's going on in that head of yours? You're scheming. I can see it."

The smaller man refocused on Matt and said, "We should get the guys to toss in a hundred each. Get their buy-in, so to speak. My stepdad used to say it was important for people to have skin in the game. They'd be more motivated that way."

Matt pointed at his friend. "See, Rabbit? That's why I like you. You're a thinking man, not just a pretty face. Let's do that. I'll put in the first five hundred to get the juices flowing, and the other guys will each bring an extra hundred to the table. That could easily bring the pot to over a grand. That's some decent cheddar."

"The guys will definitely throw hands for that kind of money."

Matt clapped, excited by the vision. "I know, I know. To make it official, we'll need some rules to keep the game in order. I mean, even the UFC has rules, right?"

Rabbit nodded. "I see what you're saying. Something like, the knockout has to be witnessed to count."

Matt slapped the back of one hand into the palm of another. "Recorded, man. Videoed. That way, everyone can see it. That's beautiful, Rabbit. You're a genius!"

The smaller man grinned widely for a moment, but it slowly faded. "Wait. Can't we get in trouble if we have it recorded?"

"Can't we get in trouble if we have it recorded?" Matt mockingly repeated. "And here I just said you were a genius."

Rabbit lowered his eyes.

"C'mon, man, don't you want your greatest hits recorded?"

The smaller man looked up.

"Don't you want people to know you brought the thunder on some unsuspecting fool?"

"I see it now," he said.

"All right, that's better. Man, I don't know why it's so hard to bring you around sometimes."

"I'm just cautious."

"I know. That's why I need you. We make a good team."

Rabbit nodded in agreement. He said cautiously, "Rule number one: it needs to be recorded to count. Rule number two?"

Matt stood with his hands on his hips as he thought. He looked up suddenly and said, "One punch, and they need to go down. If they don't go down, you don't score."

"What about a second punch?"

Matt mimed throwing a roundhouse punch. "Pow! It's called the knockout game, son. In other words, one… knockout… punch. You only get one to score. If you miss or you don't land, you're done. Sorry, Charlie, sit your ass down." Matt hopped around the living room in excitement.

"What happens if the person wants to fight?"

Matt stopped moving and snapped his fingers. "Good question. That's a good question, indeed. I like that. What should we do? I mean, if you hit them and they don't go down, but they decide to mix it up, should you get any points? That's like overtime, right?"

"How about this? If the person doesn't go down, no points," Rabbit said. "That's clean and simple. But if that person decides to fight back, we should get at least one point, right? I mean, I'd want a point. Maybe we give two points for a knockout and one point if they fight back, but you still have to knock them out. You can't attack them if they're not fighting."

"I like it. Rabbit, you've got a flair for this."

The smaller man beamed at his friend's praise. "What's the third rule?"

Matt looked up at the ceiling and thought. "We can't overregulate this thing. This shouldn't be too complicated. A minimum of rules. Kind of like *Fight Club*. Ever seen that movie? No? What's wrong with you? Anyway, I think only one more rule."

"What's that?"

"The victim has to be chosen at random."

"Aren't they always?"

"No, no. You don't get to pick your own victim. That would make the game too easy."

"Random how? We walk up to a street corner and have another guy pick someone?"

Matt shook his head. "More random than that. Let's make it like a game show. Add some *theatricality*." He had spread his hands wide, like a circus ringmaster, when he said theatricality.

"How do we do that?"

Matt lowered his head and thought for a moment. He soon walked around the room, murmuring to himself. Suddenly, he opened his eyes and clapped his hands several times. "I've got it. We'll put the guys' names in one bowl and victim descriptions into a different bowl. Then we'll start the game. We draw one name, and that's the contestant who's up for the day. He then pulls a victim description and goes hunting."

Rabbit smiled for a moment before laughing. "Oh, man, that's beautiful."

Matt joined in the laughter. "This is some Joker-style shit."

"Only there ain't no Batman coming to the rescue."

Chapter 4

When Andrew Miller landed on his back, he slapped the floor with an open palm as he hit. The woman standing over him held his left arm pinned under her right armpit. She punched toward his face, stopping less than an inch from his nose. Then she dropped a knee into his rib cage, forcing an expel of air from him.

"I'm sorry," Haley Reynolds said as she released Andrew's arm. He rolled over and stood.

"Don't be. You did fine. Do that next month, and you'll pass your test."

Haley said, "Thank you, sir," and bowed slightly.

"Join the rest of the class. It's about time to close."

Haley hurried over to the rest of the group while Andrew stepped to the back of the mat. He followed along with the bowing-out ceremony led by the school's instructor, Mr. Daniel Shaw. As the class dispersed, Andrew tidied up around the mat and watched his instructor interact with the other students. When he was done, Mr. Shaw approached Andrew.

"Mr. Miller," he said, as it was appropriate to call black belts in the American Kenpo system by their gender titles.

"Sir?"

"How did Haley do tonight?"

"She did well. She's ready for the forms and technique portion of the test. We should spar over the next couple of weeks, though. She needs confidence in her fighting skills."

"Noted. What would you like to work on tonight?"

"I'd like your opinion on something."

Mr. Shaw smiled at his highest-ranking student. "What's bothering you?"

"I was attacked today."

The instructor's smile faded. "You okay?"

"Yes, sir. I'm fine. A man came at me with a knife."

Mr. Shaw studied Andrew.

"It wasn't that big of a deal. I blocked his lunge with my briefcase. Then I counterattacked and knocked him to the ground."

"Only you would think a knife attack wasn't a big deal."

Andrew shrugged, slightly uncomfortable with his instructor's praise.

"What's the problem, then?"

"I wanted to hit him after he was disarmed and disabled."

"He had a knife, Mr. Miller. With what you've been through, that response is understandable."

"But he was down and defenseless. I wanted so badly to hit him again. Even now, I can feel that hate inside. That anger is sitting at the top of my chest."

Mr. Shaw nodded. "Did you hit him while he was down?"

Andrew shook his head.

The instructor put his hand on his student's shoulder. "You were attacked, and you responded. With adrenaline flowing through your body, you had the opportunity to attack further, but you chose not to. It sounds like you did a fantastic job of controlling yourself."

"I wanted to hit him. I mean, I *really* wanted to hurt him. It's still running through my mind."

"Mr. Miller. *Andrew*. You're a fourth-degree black belt, not a robot. You've experienced a lot in your life, more than most people can imagine, yet you managed to control yourself in this situation. Look for the positive."

Andrew nodded slightly.

"Are you going to talk with her about this?"

"No, sir," he said, knowing that his instructor was asking about his therapist. Mr. Shaw was one of the few people who knew about his past. "We haven't talked in a while. It's not necessary."

"What happened to your attacker, by the way? Was he arrested?"

Andrew shrugged. "I don't know. I didn't stick around long enough to find out."

"Why not?"

"If I dealt with the police, I would have been late for a meeting. Besides, I was safe, and he was hurt. I don't need the police to protect me."

Mr. Shaw patted Andrew's shoulder firmly. "Mr. Miller, you really should learn to trust other people."

ROUND TWO

Chapter 5

Matt stood in the corner of the room, beaming. The game was about to begin. Besides Rabbit and him, there were eight other guys in the house. Earlier in the day, they had assembled to explain the rules of the game.

His crew was a ragtag following of high school friends and friends-of-friends. After returning from the Corps, Matt hooked up with them. They were aimless, with no motivation. The majority had sold weed in high school when it was illegal and dreamed of going into business for themselves when it was legalized. However, none of them had any experience with a business or knew how to raise money. When it was legalized, their opportunity decreased lessened due to state-approved competition. They could still sell illegally grown marijuana, but most buyers preferred the safety of purchasing from a state-sanctioned store.

It was Matt who suggested they all had great skills in sales and that they just needed to find a new product. He hustled and found a connection. He bought the coke, and the guys sold it. Developing new customers was the challenge. It was slow going, but they were learning and growing. He firmly believed they were developing into a good organization. Unfortunately, it felt like they had just started to gain some traction when the supply dried up.

Matt was frustrated. It felt like the Corps again. Needing supplies and not having them. Wishing they would arrive and making do until they did. He hated that feeling. It made him feel powerless, and that was something he had promised himself he wouldn't feel again.

At first, the guys were lukewarm about the idea of playing, but when Matt said he was putting five hundred bucks into the pot to start the game, everyone else got excited. Each man went home and returned with their hundred-dollar entry fee.

Not one of them had that kind of cash readily accessible, though. One of the guys donated plasma for a portion of his fee. A couple of others stole money from their family members. The stories about raising the entry fee were tossed around and laughed over. No one asked how Matt raised his five hundred. They knew he had money coming in from Uncle Sam. He had been shot and would forever receive a disability payment from the U.S. government. If he had coin in his pocket, it was assumed it was because of that safety net. No one questioned him.

The pot for the game was now officially fourteen hundred dollars. Everyone played except Matt. He said he'd stay out of it since it was his idea, and he was the leader of the crew. This was for them. The guys nodded at his announcement, loyalty burning in their eyes. It made Matt happy to see that look again, just like he had from the team he'd led in the desert.

Rabbit lifted a ceramic bowl above his head. "Who wants the honors?"

Joel 'Stick' Murphy, a tall, thin young man, stepped forward and put his hand in the bowl. He pulled out a strip and opened it. "Henry," he announced. The group cheered as Henry stepped forward.

Rabbit next held a metal bowl into the air as the group looked on. The room became hushed.

Henry Ramos was the only one in the group who was never given a nickname. Every time someone tried to give him one, he'd punch them. Eventually, everyone stopped.

The closest nickname anyone ever hung on him was when Matt called him Hank. No one else could call him that, though. Henry stuck his hand into the bowl and pulled out a slip of paper. After he opened it, he read it aloud. "Man in Seahawks shirt."

The group emitted a mixture of laughs and groans.

"The hell?" Henry asked.

"Who wrote that?" Rabbit asked, putting the bowl to the side.

"I did," Shaggy said. Jay 'Shaggy' Walsh ran his fingers through his long, scraggly hair and tossed it back out of his eyes. "I hate the Seachickens. I was hoping I'd get to pull my own paper and punch one of their fans in the face."

The men in the assembled group chuckled at Shaggy's comment. It was evident they anticipated what was about to happen.

"Doesn't matter who wrote what," Matt said, pushing off the wall to clamp a hand on Henry's shoulder. "The game is starting. Ol' Hank here has until midnight to find a victim and take a swing. One more time, so we're clear. It's two points for a knockout. He gets nothing if the person doesn't go down. If, and *only* if, the victim fights back, can he take another swing. He must knock them out then to earn a single point. Everyone understand?"

Billy 'Bam Bam' Bell asked then, "Can I do more than one at a time? Like this guy in a Seahawk shirt. If there was a convention of them, could I knock them all out and win the game right then and there?"

"Yeah!" a couple of guys hollered.

"That wouldn't be much of a game, would it?" Matt said. "You get only one chance, so make it count."

A young man fiddling with his cell phone spoke up then. Barry 'Gadget' Wilkerson was easily the smartest guy in the group. "Dudes, this is like a lot of people getting knocked out. Two points per knockout. That's five knockouts to win the game. There's nine of us playing. That's like forty-five knockouts."

The room became suddenly quiet.

Matt stared at Gadget. "Okay, *mom*, what's your point?"

"I'm just saying that's a lot of people."

"Are you pussing out before the game even starts?"

Gadget glanced around the room. When his eyes settled back on Matt, he softly said, "No."

Matt looked at the rest of the men. "Anyone else pussing out?"

The rest of them hollered some version of "No."

"Ready to go out there and knock some bitches out?"

A unanimous "Yes!" was yelled.

When the group settled down, Rabbit added in, "The first one to get ten points earns the title of baddest mother on the block and gets fourteen hundred bones!"

The group cheered again. Matt let the excitement rumble for a few seconds before raising his hands to let everyone know to quiet down.

"Once we start," Matt said, "you need to keep this on the down-low. Don't tell your family or girlfriends. Don't gossip about this on Facebook."

"Facebook is for senior citizens," Gadget mumbled.

"You know what I mean."

"But it sure will be fun," Rabbit said.

The laughs were loud and raucous in the small house.

Matt waved down the noise again. "Who volunteers to follow Henry while he searches to destroy?"

Trevor 'Denver; Bowers and Chester 'Critter' Scott raised their hands.

"All right. Remember, it gets videoed, or it doesn't count. You understand?"

The group nodded.

Matt looked at the small clock on the wall. "It's three thirteen, boys. Time for mayhem."

Henry, Denver, and Critter left the house. Rabbit and Matt huddled together, leaving the remaining men to talk amongst themselves excitedly.

"I can't believe we're actually doing this," Rabbit said.

"Why not?"

"It seems reckless. It's definitely going to attract the attention of the cops."

"Of course it will," Matt said.

"And you're okay with that?"

"It's low-level bullshit. You think the cops are going to devote that much time to it? Besides, I'm bored, and it's hot out. I just want something to happen in our lives. Don't you?"

Chapter 6

Even though it was mid-July and the height of baseball season, it didn't take long to find a Seahawks shirt.

Critter spotted it before Henry did. "There," he said, smacking his friend with the back of his hand and then pointed to the overweight man across the street.

"What's he waiting for?" Henry asked.

"He's standing at the bus stand," Denver said.

The man was in his early forties and had his head bowed as he played with his phone.

Henry smiled. "Too easy. Get ready."

Critter and Denver both nodded and hurriedly pulled out their phones. Henry trotted down the sidewalk and crossed the street so he could circle back behind the man. He didn't want to confront him directly. That would ruin what Henry saw as the biggest advantage of the knockout game: surprise.

As cars passed by on Main Avenue, their drivers were unaware of what was about to occur. The heavyset man smiled as he repeatedly tapped something on his phone. He never bothered to look up. Instead, he focused his attention on the device in his hand.

As soon as he was within a couple of feet of the man, Henry swung his right fist with all his might, hitting the man in the jaw. The man in the Seahawks shirt never saw it coming. He collapsed to the sidewalk. His head bounced on the concrete while his phone skittered away.

Henry turned to Critter and Denver. He triumphantly raised his fists in the air.

Critter yelled, "Big hitter!"

From down the block, a female voice screamed, "Hey!"

Another female voice yelled, "You can't do that!"

Two professionally dressed women hurried Henry's way. For a brief second, he thought about hollering back at them.

How dare they yell at me?

He turned to check out Critter and Denver's reactions, but they were already sprinting away.

That pulled Henry from inaction, and he ran in the opposite direction. He didn't worry where Critter and Denver were headed. He knew they'd meet him back at the hangout.

Henry laughed as he ran. A renewed purpose in life surged through his heart and soul. Life suddenly felt good again.

He was going to win the game and that fourteen hundred bucks.

Chapter 7

Officer Leya Navarro responded to the report of an assault at the corner of Main Avenue and Howard Street. A female caller witnessed an attack, and the victim was currently on the ground.

When Leya arrived, Officer Ken Jarvis was already on the scene. As she approached, she heard Jarvis say into his radio, "Adam one eleven, we've got one mid-forties male, conscious and breathing, but he was rendered unconscious from the assault. Has medical been started?"

Leya nodded toward Jarvis. When he finished his interaction with dispatch, she asked, "What's up?"

"Victim here, Archie Holloway, was assaulted waiting for the bus. No prior communication with his attacker. Guy just walked up and *boom*."

"No provocation?"

"None."

"What did the suspect look like?"

Jarvis shrugged. "No description. Victim was fiddling with some slot machine game on his phone, and the next thing he knows, he's on the ground waking up. He has no idea who or what hit him. The only way he even knew he was assaulted was from witness descriptions."

Leya studied Holloway as he sat on the curb with his head in his hands. The man appeared to be in shock.

"Witnesses are over there," Jarvis said, pointing out two females standing at the edge of the sidewalk. Both were in their early thirties and dressed in business attire. "Mind getting their statements? I'll take lead on the paper."

"Done."

As she stepped away, she heard the whine of a large truck from down the street. Leya knew better than to start an interview as the fire department arrived, so she waited a few moments. A large red engine pulled up to the curb. A handful of firefighters jumped from the truck and hurried to the victim.

Leya continued to the witnesses. After introducing herself, she asked what they saw.

The first woman, Helen Gardner, held herself tightly as she spoke. "It was terrible. This bully, he was big. He crossed the street, ran up to that poor man, and hit him so hard. I mean, really hard. He crumbled to the ground so fast. It was like I couldn't believe what I was seeing." Her eyes widened as she retold her story.

"Did the guy say anything before he punched?"

Helen shook her head. "I don't think so, but we were down the street, so he might have said something softly. It looked like that bully hit that man without a word. It was so… brutal."

"What did he look like?"

"White with dark hair. Blue jeans and a white T-shirt. I think the jeans were dirty, but, again, we were down the block. He seemed kind of average-looking is the best way I could describe him."

"Would you be able to identify him if you saw him again?"

Helen nodded. "I'm pretty sure. I don't think I'll forget that face."

Leya looked to the second woman who had introduced herself as Amy Jasper. "Can you add anything to what she said?"

"After he knocked that man down, the guy turned to his friends across the street and posed for them."

"Posed?"

Amy lifted her arms and flexed her biceps. "Like a bodybuilder."

"Or a boxer who just won a fight," Leya said.

Amy lowered her arms. "That probably makes more sense."

"Wait. You said he had friends across the street?"

"They were recording it."

"Like a video?"

"Definitely. They both were holding their phones up," Amy said, miming the action of recording a video with a cell phone.

"One of the guys yelled something." Helen turned to her friend. "What was it?"

"'Big hitter,'" Amy said.

"'Big hitter'?" Leya repeated.

Both women nodded and repeated together, "'Big hitter.'"

After completing the interview with the two women, Leya returned to Officer Jarvis. He said, "He's going to be okay. Unfortunately, he's worthless as a witness to his own assault. I tried encouraging him to remember his surroundings, but all he could recall was that stupid game. He said he was on a run, that he was going to beat his high score. That's what he remembers about the incident. Crazy, huh? Hopefully, you got something better."

Leya relayed the interviews to Jarvis. When she was done, she said, "It's all good info, but there's almost zero to go on for suspect descriptions."

"If we put out 'white guy in jeans and a white T-shirt,' we'd drag in half the population of Spokane."

"So, we write a report and move on with our lives unless that video shows up somewhere."

"Unless that video shows up," Jarvis agreed.

Chapter 8

"Have you seen this video?" Kelly Hall asked Andrew Miller as he walked by the receptionist's desk.

"What's that?"

The receptionist pointed at her computer monitor. "It's going viral on Facebook. Some girl posted it last night. A suit was attacked near the bus plaza by some dude with a knife. Guy kicked the crap out of his attacker, then took off."

Andrew moved behind Kelly's desk to watch the video play but never saw his face on the screen.

"People online are saying the suit might get charged for assault."

"Unlikely," Andrew said.

"For real."

"But the guy had a knife."

"I don't know," Kelly said. "It looks like this guy might have used too much force. You know what I mean? Anyway, supposedly, the cops are looking for him."

"How do you know?"

Kelly shrugged. "That's what people are saying."

Andrew stepped back from the computer.

"That looks like you," she said.

"I wish."

"No serious. I've seen you walk away a lot. That's your back." Kelly blushed. "I mean the back of your head, anyway. And your... well, your suit."

"We all look the same in a suit," Andrew said.

"Not even close," Kelly said. With a small, embarrassed laugh, she studied the frozen image on the computer screen. "I'd swear that's you."

He turned to leave.

"I guess you'd have to know how to kick some butt," she called after him.

Andrew stepped into his office and closed the door. He sat at his desk and opened Facebook. His account was private, and he rarely used it. It was primarily a tool to connect with a few friends from his time in the military. He didn't even have a picture of himself on the account, and it didn't include his last name.

It didn't take long to locate the video. This time, he closely watched it. The angle the footage had been taken was from behind him. His face was never on the screen, but it definitely looked like his body and his movements. It wasn't that hard to make out. Even Kelly thought it looked like him.

The girl who made the video had focused on the attacker as opposed to him. When the cars honked, she turned the camera toward them, then back to the attacker on the ground.

Andrew watched the video once more before closing Facebook.

Chapter 9

"Holy shit!" Matt called out.

The group had been huddled around Critter's cell phone, watching the video he took of Henry's punch.

Several of them broke away and danced around in exhilaration. Henry smiled as a couple of guys shook him by the shoulders and excitedly slapped his back.

"Straight baller," Shaggy said as he lightly punched Henry in the chest. "Dude hit the ground like a sack of potatoes."

"Like an extra-large sack of potatoes," Henry said.

"Like an extra-fat sack of potatoes," Critter added, eliciting howls of excitement from the group.

Matt waved for everyone to quiet down. "Well, well, well, one pull of a card and a man is already on the board. That didn't take long to get things started. Two points for Hank," he said, pointing at Henry. The young men in the house bayed in delight.

Matt looked at the small clock on the wall. It was almost six o'clock. "Is it too late to go again?"

The group hollered "No!" in unison.

Matt laughed and then said, "Who's the next man up?"

Rabbit lifted the bowl and waved at Critter. The younger man stepped over and reached into the ceramic bowl. He pulled out a piece of paper and read it. "Stick."

Joel 'Stick' Murphy, the tall, razor-thin man with a red shock of hair, whooped in excitement. The guys nearby patted him on the shoulder.

Matt said, "Stick, your window is small for this challenge. Midnight is the cutoff. Are you willing to accept? You can wait until tomorrow if you want."

"Nah, man, I want to go now."

Matt smiled. "The man wants to go now!"

The group cheered again.

"Bring the bowl, Rabbit."

The smaller man stepped over to Stick and lifted the metal bowl above his head. Stick put his hand in, swirled it for a moment before selecting a piece of paper. "A dude with red hair," he said, running his hand through his own ginger locks. "What the hell?"

The guys laughed with delight, and Henry smiled. "I wrote that one hoping someone would turn around and knock you out."

The laughter increased in volume as Stick flipped off his friend.

"Maybe you can knock yourself out," Denver hollered over the laughter.

"Oh, God, please do that," Henry said.

Matt waved down the noise. "Who is following Stick? Hank should stay off the street for a bit, so any two others will do."

Bam Bam and Gadget raised their hands. "I'll go," they said in unison.

"Okay, but Gadget is definitely running the camera," Matt said, eliciting more laughter from the group.

Bam Bam shrugged. Everyone knew his specialty, and it wasn't playing with toys.

"You're on the clock, Stick," Matt said, "and you're two points behind Henry."

Chapter 10

Arnold Farris stood outside Mootsy's Bar, smoking a cigarette. He'd just finished his third Pabst Blue Ribbon and was on his sixth cigarette since arriving. Two to one, he thought and then chuckled to himself but stopped when he realized it wasn't as funny as he first hoped.

He promised himself to quit smoking today. That lasted about three hours until his boss fired him for swearing at a customer. It wasn't his fault, really. The guy was an asshole, and Arnold held his tongue as long as he could. Unfortunately, the customer kept needling him until he couldn't take it any longer, and Arnold finally told him what he could do with his complaint. It was anatomically impossible and grounds for immediate termination.

Arnold smiled to himself and leaned his back against the building. He watched two pretty girls walk by. They didn't even glance at him.

Stuck up bitches, he thought. *Too good to even look at ol' Arnold.*

He inhaled on his cigarette, then pushed the smoke out through his nose in a slow exhale.

Across the street, a couple of guys watched him.

The hell are they doing? he wondered.

One was a beefy sort of fellow, and the other was kind of small. They just stared at him. They weren't anything special, so why the hell were they looking at him?

Arnold yelled, "What?"

The two men laughed but continued watching. He waved them off dismissively.

Arnold turned to the bar's yellow front door and examined his reflection in its window. The years hadn't been kind to him. His face had wrinkled, and his skin had darkened like old leather. At least his red hair had held on to most of its glory. He ran his fingers through it, spat on the ground, and put his back against the wall again.

He looked down the street after the two girls who had walked by. Back in the day, his day, he could have had women like that. He had a good job, the respect of men, the adulation of high-class women. He took another drag on his cigarette.

Where did it all go wrong? he wondered.

Was it the ex-wife? Or the booze? Probably both. Deciding that, however, left him questioning which was the chicken and which was the egg. Arnold chuckled to himself again. They were one and the same, both at the same time. Yeah, that made sense. He nodded, feeling satisfied he had solved one riddle for the day.

He looked back across to the street, and the two guys were still standing there, but the smaller one was taking his picture now. Arnold took a drag on his cigarette, smiled, and extended his middle finger. He moved off the wall into the center of the sidewalk.

"You want some of this?" Arnold yelled, spreading his arms wide. "Why don't you come and get some?"

A flash of color passed him just before his world went dark.

Chapter 11

Leya Navarro sat at the dining room table just as the telephone rang. Her husband, Ernie, made a *What can you do?* gesture and smiled at their two girls. In their years of marriage, Ernie had never gotten a call on the home line. It was exclusively for Leya and almost always work-related.

Leya pushed back from the table and hurried into the living room, picking up the telephone receiver by the fourth ring.

"Navarro," she said.

"Leya, it's Josh." Sergeant Josh Holtz was a swing shift leader and a former academy buddy.

"Joshua, it's enchilada night. This better be good."

"Sorry, pal. One of the guys told me you caught an assault today."

"I did."

"Reminiscent of the knockout game?"

"Yeah. Guy at a bus stop. Knocked out cold."

"You get a suspect?"

"No."

"The victim remember anything? Or did a witness see anything unusual?"

"There were a couple guys with the suspect."

"What were they doing?"

"They stood across the street from the attack. Witnesses believed they were recording it. You know, video."

"Damn," Josh said.

"Why?"

"We've got another assault. Exact same M.O."

"How's the victim?" Leya asked.

"He'll survive."

"You catch the guys?"

"They're in the wind."

"I wrote my report with Jarvis," Leya said. "You should be able to find it."

"Thanks, Leya. We'll link the reports together and get them to a detective."

She ended the call and returned to the dinner table. Ernie had waited for her, but the girls had already started eating.

"Everything okay?" he asked.

"It's fine," she said. "Something's brewing, but I'm not exactly sure what."

ROUND THREE

Chapter 12

Craig Taylor walked through downtown, once again a free man. He'd gone before the judge, set a new court appearance, and was kicked loose. He told that bitch cop he'd be out in a day, but it took a day and a half. Two nights.

It was enough to remind him how much he should enjoy the simple things in life—the fresh air, the sun, revenge.

Craig thought about the man in the suit and how the guy had sucker-punched him when he wasn't expecting it. He reached up to touch his nose. It was broken. The jail doctors had reset it and then put a strip of white tape over the bridge to help it stay in place. Now, it was sensitive to the touch, and his eyes were blackened like a raccoon. He looked like he lost a five-round fight to Conor McGregor, the wily Irish bastard he still idolized.

As he walked, Craig let a fantasy pass through him. It was the idea of going straight, not drugging, and drinking anymore. He played with the idea of being a square, not chasing whores, and settling down with a wholesome woman. He'd also quit smoking and gambling to avoid the prospect of landing in jail again. Maybe he'd even try to reconnect with his mother.

The farther he got away from the concrete hotel, though, the more distant that fantasy became. The reality was he didn't like wholesome women. He liked whores and loved smoking and gambling. He also didn't want to reconnect with his mother. She was a miserable, overbearing shrew who chased his brother into the Marine Corps so he could escape her clutches. Craig knew he was too scared to leave town, so he put up with her occasional bullshit. As far as drugging and drinking went, those were the things that held him together in this miserable life. Jail was the cost of doing business.

He chastised himself for losing control and attacking the suit. That was stupid, he knew. He'd never done that before, and with a knife, no less. Jonesing was bad enough. Adding a large helping of stupid on top of it made it worse. He needed to get control of himself.

When he finally arrived at the small brown house on Fifth Avenue, Craig walked up the steps and entered without knocking. No one was ever awake at that hour. It was shortly after nine and quiet as a morgue. He knew there wouldn't be any food in the refrigerator, so he didn't bother looking.

Black letters were written on a piece of paper tacked to the south wall. The top entry said *Henry – 2*. Underneath was written *Stick – 2*. He stared at them for a moment, trying to understand what they meant.

On the cluttered coffee table, a red bong stood with a Bic lighter near its base. Craig picked them both up. After inspecting the bowl and finding it still filled with some previously smoked bud, he lit it and inhaled deeply.

"Turn around," a voice behind him said.

Craig did as ordered and slowly lowered the bong. He stared at the man who held a gun pointed directly at his face.

The man curled his lip and said, "If you exhale, you die."

Craig laughed, expelling the smoke he had held in his lungs. This began a coughing fit for several moments. Once he regained control of himself, he threw the lighter at the man with the gun. "The hell, Matty? You could have killed me."

"How? Death by inhalation?"

"The gun."

Matt stared at the gun in his hand. "I wouldn't have shot you. You're my brother."

"Those things can go off without warning."

"No, they can't. It only goes off when I want it to go off. There's nothing to be scared of."

"Not all of us were Marines."

Matt tucked the gun behind a seat cushion on the couch before turning back to his brother. "You don't look so good, Craiger."

"I'm not. You got anything better than this?" he asked, lifting the bong for emphasis.

"Got some kickers, if you want 'em, but I was talking about your face."

Craig lifted his hand toward his broken nose but stopped. He knew what it felt like without touching it. "I'll take the pills. Then I'll tell you about my face."

Matt walked to the back of the house, and Craig followed along silently.

Veronica, Matt's girlfriend, slept on top of the covers. She wore only panties and a bra. On the nightstand were a half-empty bottle of OxyContin and an opened can of beer. Matt sat on the edge of the bed and removed a pill from the bottle.

She mumbled something Craig couldn't understand. He didn't think Matt could understand it either, and his brother didn't investigate what she wanted. He put the bottle of pills back on the table, squeezed her butt once, then patted it.

Craig stepped out of the doorway and returned to the living room. Matt came out a second later and handed him the pill, along with the opened can of beer. Craig popped it into his mouth and washed it down with the warm liquid.

"Haven't seen you in weeks. Where you been?"

"Here and there, you know."

Matt nodded. "What's up with the face?"

"Landed in jail couple nights ago."

"For what?"

"Made a move on a guy while I was out of my mind. He kicked my ass."

"What were you on?"

"Peyote. It was the only thing I could score."

Matt pointed at Craig's face. "And that's how that happened?"

"Guy was a stone-cold fighter. It was like I took on the Notorious."

"McGregor, huh? The guy was that good?"

"Two moves, and I was on the ground. It was embarrassing."

"You were jonesing, right? You weren't at your best."

Matt shrugged. "Not at my best, right. Man, I haven't trained since high school. Even if I was now, it wouldn't make me as sharp as that guy. He was something."

"What are you going to do?"

Craig sat on the coffee table and looked up at his brother. "I'll lie low for a bit. Either get really high or maybe work on leveling out. Neither one sounds appealing, though."

"What does sound appealing?"

Craig held back his thoughts, took a deep breath, and shrugged.

Matt grabbed the can of beer from his brother and took a sip. He crinkled his nose at the taste of warm beer.

Craig pointed at the names on the wall. "What's that?"

His brother glanced at the paper. "It's a game me and the boys are playing."

From the smile on his face, Craig could tell his brother was excited about it. "Tell me."

Chapter 13

General Detectives' Office Lieutenant Clay Larkins sat behind his desk and leaned toward the computer monitor, concentrating intently. His glasses were pushed up on his forehead. His attention was so diverted that he didn't hear Leya Navarro enter his office.

"Lieutenant?" she said finally to get his attention.

Startled by her voice, Larkins jumped in his chair. "Damn, Navarro. Make some noise next time."

She apologetically held up her hands. "Patrol walk, sir."

He waved her in. "What do you want, Leya?"

After roll call, Leya used one of the computers in the duty room to print the report Sergeant Holtz had told her about. She read it carefully and confirmed the similarities between the two assault calls. Feeling confident about the relationship, she approached her supervisor and explained the situation. Her sergeant suggested she meet with the general detectives' commander to see if the cases had been assigned.

She laid the two reports on the lieutenant's desk. "Yesterday, there were two assaults downtown. Both were random attacks, but they share the same M.O. Have you assigned these to a detective yet? Nothing popped up in the system when I checked."

"I'm reviewing reports now," he said. He pulled his glasses down from his forehead and settled them in place. "I'll assign them when I can."

"Patrol has already linked these two," Leya said. "Can you assign someone now? That way, I can talk with them? Maybe start working on locating persons of interest."

A pained look crossed Larkins's face. "That's not how it works. Once I review a case, I need to determine caseloads, who is going on vacation, who is attending classes, et cetera. You get the point, right? Then that detective will review the reports when they have time. This isn't Major Crimes, where they run out and deal with a body on the scene. This is the General Detectives' Office. This is the grinder. Everything shakes out here, and we're buried. Give it time, and I'll get the reports to someone. Then you can talk with them."

Leya stared at him, disapproval seeping through her mask of professionalism.

The lieutenant, obviously not appreciating a junior officer's disrespect for the reality of life in his division, said, "Of course, you can always work these if you're so motivated."

"I think I'll do that," Leya said and picked up her copies of the reports. She wanted to make a biting comment about things getting worse while some lead-assed lieutenant sat around waiting to assign a report when he *felt* like it.

However, she did the smart thing, stayed quiet, and walked away. Engaging in a losing battle with a superior officer would not help her today nor her career tomorrow.

Chapter 14

Andrew Miller left his office and walked to the Rocket Bakery for coffee. Usually, he was alert to threats from others. It had been ingrained in him from years of training and experience.

He never looked at his cell phone while he walked. Instead, he kept his head up and made eye contact with others around him.

He also never listened on music in his headphones while moving through the city. This action took away his sense of hearing and put him at a disadvantage.

As far as consuming alcoholic beverages, Andrew refrained from doing so while in public places. He would occasionally drink a beer at home, but never out in the world.

Andrew wasn't necessarily paranoid, but his past had taught him to be prepared for certain things. Attacks could come at any time, from anyone, and in any direction. He needed to be in a constant state of vigilance.

It had been several years since he'd dealt with anything similar, but the attack in the crosswalk had him questioning himself. Could he have spotted the threat sooner? Should he have attacked before the lunge made it to him and struck his briefcase?

He pushed the questions from his mind as he walked. Those thoughts were clouding his attention to the moment. He needed to focus on the *now*.

As he walked, he was keenly aware of men and women standing on the sidewalk. Some watched him. Why did they look at him? Were they threats? Were they there to do him harm?

He didn't fear them, knowing he would and could protect himself, but he was wondering if another attack could come without warning. Why had that man with the knife chosen him? Was it random? Or was it purposeful?

His heart began to race. Another adrenaline rush, just like before. It had been some time since these were trained into submission.

Andrew looked around, knew he was being ridiculous, but he broke into a trot, nonetheless.

If his heart was racing, anyway, he might as well take advantage of it.

Chapter 15

The crew was at the house on Fifth Avenue. The anxious look was there, and Matt gave the same answer as before. "Nothing."

A collective moan went out among the men. The streets were still dry when it came to powder. Matt had heard the nineties went dry for a period, but he couldn't have imagined it was as long as this. Regular customers were searching for a new high, moving to prescription pills, meth, and even heroin, which was the exact opposite of cocaine. People would do anything to kill the pain, Matt knew.

The boys needed something to distract themselves.

"Enough bitching and moaning," Matt said. "Who wants to play?"

The nine assembled men made various noises to show their excitement. Matt had spent some time that morning with his brother, telling him about the game. Sharing what they were doing had excited him even more, and Matt wanted to get back to it. When Craig left, he called the guys immediately.

"Let's get going. Until the snow arrives, it's game on. Henry and Stick are on the board, both with successful turns. Rabbit, grab the bowl and get the next man up."

Rabbit held the white ceramic bowl above his head and pulled out a name strip. "Gremlin," he said.

Several in the group voiced their disappointment at not being chosen.

"Gremlin!" Matt yelled with excitement. "The man of the hour. Get up and pick your poison."

A wisp of a man with big ears, Glen 'Gremlin' Kaiser stepped forward. He wore a baseball hat with the brim curled up. It was pulled down so far that his ears pushed outward, giving him a strange, creature-like appearance. This was how he always wore his hats and how he had earned his nickname. Several of the guys clapped him on the back as he moved toward Rabbit.

Gremlin reached his hand into the metallic bowl and pulled out a strip of paper. He unfolded it and moved his lips as he read to himself. "What the hell?" he muttered.

Critter snatched the paper from his fingers. "A woman in a red dress," he said loudly.

The men laughed in unison.

"A woman," Denver howled. "You gotta hit a broad!"

"I ain't hitting no lady," Gremlin said. His eyes pleaded with Matt. "That's disrespectful."

Matt stepped forward and grabbed the piece of paper from Critter. "Then, forfeit your turn and get zero points."

Gremlin crossed his arms and set his jaw. The guys intently watched him.

"What's it going to be, man?" Matt asked. "You drew the paper. This is your assignment. You either—"

"Fine."

"Fine, what? Fine, you'll do it, or fine, you'll forfeit?"

Gremlin lowered his head. "I'll do it."

The group cheered its approval.

Chapter 16

Craig Taylor stood across from the bus plaza and studied the building. He knew better than to cross the street. He had been banned after his recent confrontation. Just walking onto their sidewalk would get him arrested again. He wasn't scared of the rent-a-cops, but it was a hassle he could do without.

Instead, he stood on the corner where the other man had been, the man who attacked him when he least expected it. Where had he come from? Where was he going?

Craig replayed the moment in his head.

Was he on his way to a meeting? Or from a meeting?

To lunch? Or from lunch?

Craig turned in circles, looking upward at the tall buildings surrounding him. A guy like that could be anywhere downtown.

Was he even from here? Maybe he was from out of town, just here to do some business, then go back to whatever godforsaken place he was from.

He shrugged finally and moved farther down the sidewalk. He sat on a bench in front of the Bank of America building and thought. The stomach cramps were getting to him again. He'd have to take another pill soon to take the edge off, or the pangs would grow continually worse.

At some point, Craig realized he should try to kick. Life might be better without the monkey on his back.

As he shook in the sunlight, men in suits continued to walk by, ignoring him, or worse, totally oblivious to him. He watched the nameless, faceless corporate robots go about their self-important business—God, how he hated them. The more anger he pushed their way, the more they seemed to be unaware of him.

Craig recalled that he was something special in high school. He had trained in both Judo and Hapkido at the Boys Club, and what's more, he was good at both. He even wrestled with his high school team. He was varsity good. Of course, his school sucked, but that didn't mean he wasn't good. He won more matches than he lost. And when he fought in the alleys after school, he won more of those than he lost. Craig developed a reputation around the school to be feared.

It irked him that these suits could walk by him as he shivered in the morning sun, not even looking at him, not even acknowledging his existence. He was virtually nonexistent to the one percent, and that pissed him off.

As a thirty-something male in a blue pinstripe suit walked by, Craig yelled, "Hey!" as loud as he could. The man jumped several feet to the side, holding his hands up in a submissive gesture. The look of fright was priceless, and Craig laughed so hard it soon turned into a coughing fit.

When he finished hacking, Craig chuckled at the memory of the suit's fear. A smile soon grew, along with a renewed sense of purpose. The stomach cramps didn't seem so bad anymore.

Chapter 17

A woman with a short red dress walked into the Starbucks on Main Avenue right across from the downtown mall. Gremlin watched her until she disappeared inside. "That's the one," he said. "I'm gonna do her."

"I don't know, man," Stick said, looking up and down the street. "There's a lot of people around here." His eyes scanned the block for cameras. "I'm sure they got cameras over at the mall. You shouldn't go anywhere near there."

Denver agreed. "We should move elsewhere. There are a lot of eyes around here."

Gremlin listened to them both but kept his focus on the Starbucks entrance. "I hear ya. How about this? Let's set up down the block, where there's not as many people. If she comes out and heads our way, I do it. If not, we find someone else. It's not like bitches in red dresses are fallin' outta the sky."

Stick and Denver glanced at each other before shrugging.

Gremlin hurried away while the other two men walked casually behind him.

Five minutes passed. Three hundred seconds never seemed so long to Gremlin. "Shit," he said, hopping around. "You think she went out the back?"

"Chill out, man," Denver said, "There ain't no back exit. Maybe she's drinking her coffee inside. Maybe someone's chatting her up. This ain't no dine and dash. Learn some patience."

Gremlin nodded and stopped jumping, but his hands continued to fidget. He shoved them in his pockets to hide his anxiousness.

Stick laughed. "You look ready to pop out of your skin."

Gremlin pursed his lips and kept his focus down the street. "I wanna get this done and get on the board."

"Relax," Denver said, "or you'll do something stupid."

"Got it," he said, mostly to himself. "Calm down. Deep breaths."

Stick said, "Red dress is coming out."

The woman had exited the Starbucks and was headed their way.

Gremlin yanked his hands from his pants. "Is the camera ready?"

"Gimme a second," Denver said.

The woman sipped from a paper cup and read her cell phone as she slowly walked toward them.

"Shit," Gremlin said. "Can she move any slower?"

"Relax," Stick said, motioning downward with his hands. "She'll be here soon enough."

The woman stopped walking. Her interest was captured by whatever was on her phone. She sipped from her cup yet remained still. Several people on the sidewalk moved around her and made irritating faces at being forced to redirect their paths. She never once looked up at them as they passed.

"This is bullshit," Gremlin said. "I'm going."

"Don't," Stick said, but it was too late.

Gremlin ran. His black Converse high tops slapped the sidewalk as he sprinted toward her. The adrenaline pumped in him as he got closer. He knew he would knock her out, since she would be unaware he was even there. That's how it was for both Henry and Stick, right?

In anticipation of a strike, he clenched both fists. He hadn't run since PE in high school, so even the short sprint suddenly had him breathing hard. Running was a lot harder than he remembered it. He also recalled being faster.

The rubber soles of his Converse smacked the concrete, and he sucked deeply for air. He realized too late how much noise he was making by sprinting straight for the woman.

As she raised the cup to her face, the woman looked directly at Gremlin. Her eyes widened in fear.

She moved then, but it was too late. Gremlin's punch whipped out, clipping her nose. The woman spun around, tossing her coffee and phone in opposite directions. It was a wild pirouette, but she never lost her footing. When she stopped spinning, she immediately brought her hands up over her face.

Gremlin stopped and waited for the woman to collapse. When that didn't happen, he stood dumbfounded and unsure of what to do next.

It was an awkward moment, Gremlin staring at the woman as she stared back.

When she finally screamed, he quickly glanced around and became suddenly aware of the various strangers on the sidewalk with him. They watched him with horror. A couple of men moved toward Gremlin.

"I'm sorry," he mumbled, then sprinted toward his friends.

The embarrassment rising in him was worse than the burning in his lungs.

Chapter 18

Officer Leya Navarro heard the call dispatched over the radio and put herself on it. Stranger-on-stranger assaults in downtown were rare. Three in two days, during broad daylight, was an apparent trend.

She pulled up to the corner of Post Street and Main Avenue and turned off her emergency lights. Another officer was already on scene with the victim. The Fire Department was there tending to her. A group of people surrounded the scene.

Leya approached Officer Rodney McCrea, a patrol lifer with a genial disposition. McCrea stood by as a couple of firefighters tended to the victim, a woman in a red dress. Blood covered the lower half of her face.

"What happened?" Leya asked.

"Her name is Tammy Vincent. She was on the sidewalk when some street turd ran up and punched her in the face. When she screamed, he ran away."

"Anyone see what happened?"

"Several," he said and pointed to the crowd.

"Any video of the assault?"

McCrea's eyes swept the buildings in the area. "I've looked but haven't seen anything. No one in the crowd has rushed forward to say they recorded it."

"I'll interview the witnesses," Leya said. "If you want me to take the lead on this, I'll do that too."

Suspicion flooded McCrea's eyes. "Why?"

"Why what?"

"Why would you offer to take the paper?"

Leya shrugged. "Because there are two other cases that match the M.O., and no detective has been assigned yet."

"I get it. You want to break the big case and rub somebody's nose in it."

"That's not true."

"Don't bullshit me, Navarro. If I was still young, that's exactly what I would do. Now, I'm content to let someone like you have all the self-satisfaction you can handle."

Leya clucked her tongue before heading toward the crowd to begin the slow, methodical process of interviewing witnesses. Most saw only a white male running eastbound along Main Avenue. A couple reported three white males were running. Descriptions were varied. Leya dutifully asked questions and made the appropriate notations. When it was done, however, she didn't have anything of value. She stared at her notebook for a moment before shutting it.

Officer McCrea leaned against the door of his black-and-white patrol car, watching citizens pass by. Leya approached him and leaned a hip against the car.

"What'd you get, kid?"

"I got bupkis," she said.

McCrea watched a particularly attractive woman exit a nearby yoga clothing business. She smiled at him, and he watched her walk away for some time.

"You're a dirty old man," Leya said, knowing that McCrea was a lifelong bachelor.

He shrugged. "Meh. I'm looking, not buying. Anyway, you still want the paper? I've got the victim's statement. I can still take the lead on assembling the report."

"I'll do it," Leya said. "She give you a description of the man who hit her?"

"White male. Baseball hat with that stupid brim curl, you know what I'm talking about? Blue jean shorts and black high-top Converse. Real fashion plate, this one. She said he looked excited.”

“Excited?”

“And short.”

“Excited and short?”

McCrea nodded. “That’s about it. No real features to go on. It may not be bupkis, but it’s pretty damn close.”

Leya slapped the side of the patrol car as she walked away.

Chapter 19

"You hit a woman, and she didn't go down?"

Gremlin nodded as the guys laughed.

Matt said, "Oh, man, I've got to see this. Someone show me."

Denver stepped forward and started the video on his phone. The other guys crowded around.

Gremlin dropped onto the couch and held his head in his hands.

"Oh, man, look at him run," Matt said, which set off a bunch of guffaws.

Someone said, "Play it again," and Matt replied, "Yeah, yeah."

The second viewing got more laughter as the group anticipated Gremlin's sprint, the strike, and his look of confusion.

"Wait, wait," Matt said, pointing at the video on the phone. "What did he say there? He said something."

Denver and Stick looked at each other and shrugged.

"What did you say?" Matt asked.

Gremlin leaned his head back on the couch and stared at the ceiling.

"What did you say?" Matt's voice hardened.

"I said I was sorry," Gremlin whispered.

The room erupted in laughter again. They moved away from the video on Denver's phone and formed a semicircle around Gremlin.

"What the hell happened?" Henry asked.

"Yeah, what the hell?" Bam Bam said.

Gremlin started to say something, but the group burst out in laughter again. He flicked his hand at them. "Aww, shut up." That brought more laughter.

Matt calmed them down by lifting his hands. "All right, all right. Gremlin had his chance but came up short. No points."

Rabbit grabbed a pen and wrote on the paper stuck to the wall. *Gremlin – 0.*

"Fourteen hundred is still up for grabs, boys. We need the next contestant."

Matt picked up the ceramic bowl and held it in front of Gremlin. "Come on, man. Pick the next guy. Maybe he'll have the same luck you did."

Gremlin smirked, but still reached into the bowl and pulled a strip of paper out. "Shaggy."

The thin, scraggly haired man hopped up and down in excitement before stepping forward. Matt picked up the metal bowl and held it in front of him. He carefully extracted a piece of paper. He playfully held it far away from him as he slowly opened it to reveal the next victim.

"A doctor," Shaggy said.

"A doctor?" Matt repeated.

"Yeah, a doctor," Critter spoke up from the other side of the room. "I hate those bastards. Go punch one of them in the mouth for me."

The room burst into laughter.

Matt shrugged and looked at Shaggy. "I guess you're going to the hospital."

Chapter 20

Craig Taylor walked south until he found an affluent neighborhood, and then he headed east. As he went, he paid attention to the lawns of the homes. It was nearly eleven in the morning, and most of the houses were silent, but some had activity to support the manicured lawns and flower beds. If the attending person was hired to help, Craig moved on, not giving any further consideration to the house. If it might be the actual homeowner, he slowed.

If it was a man tending the flower bed or the lawn, even if he was elderly, Craig scratched the house from being a possibility. He knew what he was looking for and was willing to take his time until he found it.

Back at Matt's house, Craig watched the scene play out with Gremlin. His body felt on fire, and his stomach burned, but he controlled himself because he had a new mission. He would share his vision with Matt when the time was right. Until then, he had to control himself and his pain. He had to take care of one other thing first. If he looked weak and out of control, Matt and the others would never buy into his plan.

He finally found what he was looking for. She was bent over at the hips, pulling weeds from the flower beds at the front of the house. When she stood, she loudly sighed, then dragged her bucket a couple of feet farther along the bed to start the process over again. Craig was never good with guessing ages, but she reminded him of his grandmother before her passing, and she was almost eighty. The woman wore a sunbonnet kicked back on her head.

In the driveway was a single car—a late-model Toyota. The garage door was open, revealing a clean interior, but no second car.

He passed her house, never making eye contact with the woman, and continued several houses to the end of the block. He then turned the corner and walked into the alley. Reminding himself not to be too excited, he paid attention to the possibility of neighbors observing him as he walked calmly but with purpose to the back of the yellow house, second in from the end of the block.

There was a gate to the backyard with no lock. Craig opened the gate, stepped through, and quietly closed it behind him. He scanned the neighboring yards and didn't see anyone who would notice him. He hurried straight toward the rear of the house, pulled open the back door, and entered the kitchen.

A small, puffy dog barked at him, causing him to jump. Craig shushed the dog, but it continued to yap.

"Buster," the woman yelled from the front of the house.

Not afraid of the size disparity, the little dog continued its barking and skittered across the linoleum in front of Craig. He kicked the dog once, eliciting a yelp before it ran and hid in another room.

"Buster?" the woman called again, this time with concern in her tone.

Craig found a block of knives on the counter and slid out a large one. He turned to face the opening of the kitchen when the screen door at the front of the house opened. In a moment, it slammed shut.

"What happened, honey? Did you get hurt? Come here."

Holding the knife in front of him, Craig stepped around the corner.

The woman saw him and clutched the dog to her chest. Her eyes widened, and her mouth opened and closed several times without a sound. A fish gasping out of water.

He motioned for her to move away from the door, and she obeyed his silent directions.

"What do you want?" she finally asked. The little dog shivered in her arms.

"Money. Cash."

"Of course you do."

"You old people always have funds squirreled away somewhere."

She stared at him.

"If you don't get me some money, I'll hurt the dog. Then I'll hurt you."

"You'll hurt us anyway," the old woman said.

"Look, lady, I'm not into the kinky stuff. I just need some money, and then I'll leave."

She thought about it for a minute and said, "There's money in the bedroom."

Using the knife, he waved her deeper into the house. "Let's go."

Inside her bedroom, she put the little dog on the bed. Buster shook and stared at him. "Be brave," the woman whispered.

"C'mon," Craig said.

The woman turned to a dark wood dresser and opened the top drawer. She pulled out an envelope and handed it to him.

"How much is in here?"

"Three hundred dollars."

"Why keep that much money with your panties?"

She shrugged. "If I ever run out of checks ..."

"Checks? You have checks?"

Her shoulders lowered, deflated by the realization she had said too much.

"Get 'em."

She scooped up the dog and left the bedroom, shuffling her feet as she went. Craig followed her into the living room. Her purse was next to a leather recliner. She pulled out a checkbook and handed it to him. "That's the last book. I ordered a new box, but it hasn't arrived."

Craig opened the book and flipped to the last number. He decided what she said seemed reasonable. "What about credit cards? You've got to have one of them."

She put her hand back into the purse and pulled out a small leather wallet. From the wallet, she removed two credit cards, which she handed him—a VISA and a Nordstrom card. "This will ruin my credit."

Craig yawned while tucking the cards and checkbook into his back pocket. "Where's your telephone?"

She pointed to a slim phone hanging on the wall. Craig walked over to it. Using the knife, he cut the line to the wall.

"Was that necessary?" the woman asked.

"I could kill you instead."

The dog yelped as she pulled it tighter to her with a single arm.

"What about a cell phone? Got one?"

She reached back into her purse and pulled out a small flip phone.

Craig took it from her. "This is ancient." He stuffed it into his pocket. "Final question," he said, "and you're going to have to really participate in this one. I'm going to leave now, and I need to make sure you won't call the police."

"I won't call them," she said. "I promise."

"I need to make sure. Like super sure. So either I kill you—"

Another yelp came from the dog as the old lady's eyes widened, and she tightened her grip.

"Or you show me a place I can lock you in."

"The basement," she blurted. "The basement. There's a little lock on the door. You can lock me in there until my son comes to check on me tonight."

"Good," Craig said. "That sounds like a good idea."

She led him to the basement entrance, opened the door, and stepped in. She paused at the top of the stairs as she prepared to take the first step down.

For a second, Craig reached out, and his hand hovered over her back. It would only take a small push to send her down the stairs. He had never killed anyone before, and it seemed like it would be easy, especially this way.

The elderly woman took her first, tentative step down the stair, grabbing onto the railing for support.

When the moment passed, Craig lowered his hand and shut the door. He didn't want to kill someone that reminded him of his grandmother. She'd always been good to him. The old broad was lucky she didn't remind him of his mother, though.

He pushed the lock into place, wiped down the few places he touched with his hands, and hurried out of the rear of the house.

Chapter 21

There was security everywhere.

Shaggy, Denver, and Critter walked around the outside campus of Sacred Heart Medical Center, their eyes always in motion for not only a doctor but security.

They didn't find many doctors, but they found countless nurses and a lot of security guards.

"What if I did a nurse?" Shaggy asked.

Critter chuckled. "Go ahead, but you ain't getting points for it."

"Shit," Shaggy muttered and hurried ahead of Denver and Critter.

"I don't like this place," Denver said.

"Bad memories?"

"Too many witnesses. Too much security. You know, there've gotta be cameras everywhere, right?"

Critter stopped walking and turned around. He watched the activity of people amongst the buildings. "Where else could we find a doctor besides a hospital?"

Denver pulled his phone from his pocket and activated the screen. "It's almost noon. Do doctors take a normal lunch?"

Critter shrugged. "I don't know. Maybe."

"Get Shaggy. I got an idea."

***

Near the hospital campus, there was a small building with a couple of national fast-food restaurants—a Subway and a Qdoba. The three of them hurried across the street. In each restaurant, though, were only families and nurses.

Not one person resembled what they thought a doctor should look like.

They walked back into the parking lot and huddled.

"I thought this is where the doctors would eat," Denver said.

Critter shrugged. "I don't know, man. Doctors might as well be aliens for all we know."

Shaggy ran his fingers through his long, unkempt hair. "Shit, I didn't think this one would be so hard."

Across the street was an older bar, The Park Inn. Its parking lot was full for the lunch hour. "Why don't we try that place?" Denver said. "My mom goes there with her friend after work."

"It's an old person's bar, right?" Shaggy asked.

"How the hell do I know?" Denver said. "I'm trying to help you out because I'm getting bored watching you not make a decision."

Shaggy grabbed his crotch, then ran across the street, dodging cars until he made it to The Park Inn parking lot.

"That boy's an idiot," Critter said.

"He's taking forever. You think I'd get penalized if I punched him?"

Critter playfully slapped Denver on the back before sprinting across the street to join Shaggy. As they watched the front of the bar, a couple of neatly dressed men walked in.

"There's got to be a doctor in the house," Shaggy said and headed toward the front door.

The bar was dark inside. It took a moment for Critter's eyes to adjust to the new level of light. After they did, he stood near the front as Shaggy walked through the establishment, looking for a doctor.

Shaggy made it to the rear of the building, and then he looped back to the front on a different path. He stopped near a waitress who was placing a pitcher of beer on a table full of older men. Shaggy glanced at Critter and Denver, then back to the table.

With a final glance over his shoulder, he hurried to where his friends were waiting. "I found one," he said.

"Where?" Denver asked.

"The white-haired geezer in the light blue shirt. The one with the collar."

"He doesn't look like a doctor," Critter said.

The waitress walked up to the three of them. Her name tag read *Marnie*. She checked the three of them out before saying, "Take a seat where you like."

"We're waiting for a friend," Critter said. "He's parking the car."

Marnie eyed him. "That's fine. I'll bring you menus after you're seated."

They watched her as she walked away.

Shaggy leaned in and said, "That waitress called the geezer 'Doc.' They're not gonna come in here in their surgery uniforms, right?"

"Scrubs," Critter said.

"What?"

"Their uniform is called a scrub. I saw it on TV."

Shaggy waved him off. "I don't care. He's a doctor, okay. He's the one. Do you agree?"

Denver and Critter glanced at the older man for a moment and then at each other.

"If it gets him to hit someone, I'll agree," Critter whispered.

"Me too," Denver agreed.

"Then get ready," Shaggy said. He walked toward the back of the building, making no move toward the doctor.

Both Denver and Critter pulled their phones out. They took up positions at different points in the bar to record Shaggy surreptitiously.

"Is your friend still parking his car?" Marnie was clearing a nearby table.

"Uh… yeah," Critter said, glancing at the waitress, "he… uh, said he would be right in. He had to make a call or something."

"Isn't that how it always goes?" she said, picking up a couple of plates with a single hand. "What are you watching?"

Critter's stomach twisted. He couldn't lower the phone any further since he needed to record Shaggy's moment. His eyes flicked down to the screen to make sure the camera was still pointed toward his friend. Shaggy had made it to the back of the building and was now coming back toward the front. His path would take him right past the doctor.

"YouTube," Critter said, feeling his stomach turn again.

Marnie placed the plates down and moved toward him. "What is it?" she asked with a smile.

Critter turned his body slightly, but he held his hand steady. Marnie tried to step around him and said, "Why won't you let me see? Is it something dirty?"

A loud crash and scream came from the other side of the restaurant. Marnie took a quick look at Critter's phone before running toward the noise.

Shaggy sprinted to the front of the restaurant. His shoulder collided with Marnie's, which sent her spiraling into an empty table.

Denver was close on Shaggy's heels as they burst through the front door.

Critter slowly lowered his phone and walked outside. As soon as he was in the sunlight, he ran like his life depended on it.

Chapter 22

"I still say that doesn't look like a doctor," Gadget said after his third viewing of the recording.

"It was!" Shaggy yelled, his face reddening.

Gadget lifted his hands in mock defense.

The assembled group in the Fifth Avenue house argued amongst itself whether it was a good score or not. Shaggy had most certainly knocked the old man out with a single punch, but whether it was the right target was up for debate. Half the guys wanted a doctor to look like one portrayed on television: a guy in blue surgical scrubs. The other half agreed with the assessment that a doctor off the medical campus was still a doctor.

Matt sensed an uneasiness in the group. He couldn't tell what was occurring or why, but something had changed. Perhaps it was that the initial excitement of the game had worn off. He raised his hands to calm the group.

"Listen up," he said, and the crew became silent. "It's clear there's a disagreement, but Shaggy's backup said it was a doctor."

Both Denver and Critter glanced at the other guys but eventually nodded in agreement with Matt.

"He gets the points. Shaggy's on the board."

Several guys groaned at that proclamation.

Rabbit pulled out a pen and wrote Shaggy's name on the paper stuck to the wall.

The front door opened, and Craig Taylor walked in, making quick eye contact with his brother. Matt noticed he stayed near the back.

"When are we getting the drugs?" Henry said. "I need money."

"Me too," Gremlin chimed in.

Matt shook his head. "Your guess is as good as mine. It's a desert out there. The Sahara. But I'm trying to find us a source."

"This is bullshit," Henry said. "I can't keep bumming off my mom because you're too scared to approach the man."

Matt stared at Henry until the entire room fell silent. The rest of the guys knew Henry had gone too far. When Matt spoke, his voice was calm, belying the anger he now felt.

"What do you want me to do, Hank? Want me to go further up the food chain to piss and moan? What do you think that'll do for us? You think they'll appreciate that? Or do you think we'll get even less when the time comes?"

The guys watched Henry shrink before their eyes. Only Matt could make Henry and Bam Bam toe the line. They knew what he'd experienced in the Marines. Even though he was slender, everyone knew not to challenge Matt. He was the only one in the group to have truly killed a man. Half a dozen to be correct. He was also the only one in the group to have been shot. Of the men assembled, he was the only one to have been to war, whether it be for country or crew. As far as they were concerned, Matt was the only true warrior in the group.

"Anyone else got a problem with how I lead?"

Each man looked down, not willing to meet Matt's gaze.

"When times became lean, I came up with a game for us to play. For *you* to play, I mean. I put up five hundred dollars of my own money to start the pot. I'm not playing. There's no chance of me getting my money back."

The guys looked at each other.

Matt continued, "I'm not playing, and neither is Rabbit."

Rabbit's eyes widened. When Matt glared at him, the smaller man nodded in agreement.

"That's six hundred in the pot that we used to fuel the fire," Matt said.

"Why not just split that money between us?" Shaggy asked.

Matt snapped his fingers. "That's a good question, Shag. Rabbit, what's six hundred divided by eight?"

"Seventy-five," Rabbit said quickly.

"Seventy-five," Matt repeated. "Seventy-five bones. If I gave you seventy-five bones, that wouldn't change one thing in your life, would it?"

"I could fill my gas tank," Shaggy said.

"But would it change your life, man?"

Shaggy shook his head.

Matt looked at the rest of the guys, and they, in turn, shook their heads.

"Six hundred bucks started the pot, then you all added a hundred. Now, there's a fourteen-hundred-dollar pot waiting at the end of the rainbow. Someone has the opportunity to earn that money." Matt pointed to Shaggy's name on the wall. "Wouldn't it feel better to earn that money, Shag? To beat the others to the pot of gold? Fourteen hundred dollars could change your life, wouldn't it?"

A smile grew on Shaggy's face.

"He's not beating me to that money," Stick said. "Fuck that noise."

The group laughed as the tension began to lift from the room.

Matt caught Craig watching him intently from the corner. "What's up, brother?"

Craig held up a handful of cash. "I'd like to join the game."

"The pot can grow to fifteen hundred," Matt said, eyeing the group. "But the group votes to let a new player in. Is he in or is he out?"

There was a unanimous cheer to allow Craig into the game.

"Welcome to the game," Matt said.

Craig walked across the room and handed the money to Rabbit. Then he turned to Matt and said, "Can I make a suggestion?"

Chapter 23

Captain Gary Ackerman of the Spokane Police Department strode down the hallway. Patrol officers and detectives moved out of his way. No one bothered to say good afternoon or even nod in his direction. The look on Ackerman's face told everyone to stay away. Today was not the day to engage in frivolous chatter.

He ran up the stairs to the office of the patrol lieutenants. He had called both on-duty lieutenants back to their office and asked to be notified once they arrived at the station.

Lieutenants Brenda Brady and Caleb Mitchell were seated in their office, heads bowed over paperwork. Both looked up when Ackerman entered, and each noticed the papers the captain held in his hand.

Ackerman ignored any pleasantries and asked, "Brenda, are you aware of the assault at The Park Inn?"

Brady nodded.

"The press is there now," the captain said.

"Sergeant Thomas has it under control," Brady said. "Stranger-on-stranger assault."

"How many have you had this week?"

Brady glanced at Mitchell, then back to the captain. "Sir?"

"It's a simple question, Lieutenant. How many stranger-on-stranger assaults have you had this week?"

Brady opened her mouth to answer, but the captain cut her off.

"If you're going to guess, this will be a different conversation than what I originally came up for."

She closed her mouth, thought for a second, and then said, "I don't know how many, sir. I know there was at least one other, but I'm not sure if there are more."

Ackerman tossed the papers on the desk. "There are four reports so far—random attacks. However, three of them look like the knockout game. Do you remember that? The knockout game?"

Both lieutenants nodded.

"This time it's different, though. Each attack looks like a concentrated effort due to the presence of a camera team."

Looking to distance himself from his counterpart, Lieutenant Mitchell said, "This appears to have been contained to downtown, well, close to downtown with the proximity of the hospital."

Ackerman said, "I get that, Lieutenant," making sure to call both by their rank, giving neither preference nor a break. "The problem is the news made the connection before the department. They're running it as the return of the knockout game. What happened when this stupid thing got traction last time?"

"Copycats," Mitchell said.

"Exactly. And then it's not going to be contained to downtown. It'll happen in a bar on the north side or in the valley. It won't matter. Some jackass will think it's a neat idea, and he'll copy it."

"Fuck me running," Brady said.

Ackerman grimaced. Brady was known for her overuse of a particular four-letter word.

"Get your teams on this. Inform them of the possible existence of extra players with cameras. This will get worse if those videos show up online. Also, Leya Navarro seems to have been on a couple of these calls. She's even written in the latest reports that they might be connected. Keep her involved. She's got good instincts on this. While she's on shift, make sure she responds to all calls that might fit this profile."

"Yes, sir," Brady said. Mitchell nodded in agreement.

"Now, I'm going to meet with Lieutenant Larkins and chew his ass for not assigning these cases to one of his detectives yet." Ackerman hesitated near the door, then said, "Maybe we need a new crop of lieutenants who can start moving to where the puck is going instead of where it's been."

Chapter 24

"I'll make it up to you," Matt said, his voice smooth.

After the guys had left the house, Rabbit turned to Matt and asked why he'd been forced out of the game. Matt explained he needed to sweeten the pot to keep the guys motivated. Pulling Rabbit from the game seemed the best thing to do.

"How are you going to make it up to me?"

Matt dropped onto the couch and put his feet up on the coffee table. "I don't know. What do you want?"

"I wanted a chance to win that money. I could use that cheddar."

"You wouldn't have won, Rabbit, you're not a fighter. You should be thanking me. I saved you from embarrassing yourself."

"Fuck you."

Matt chuckled, enjoying the irritation he caused Rabbit. It had been that way ever since middle school when Conrad followed Matt around like a yappy little dog. Even in high school, when Matt pinned the nickname Rabbit on him after Sally Goodwin said he was quick as a rabbit in bed, Conrad wouldn't stop hanging around him. Matt knew Rabbit was one of those guys you could manipulate as long as they were getting some attention. As a result, Matt loved coming up with ways to tease his friend.

Clearly irritated, Rabbit walked in circles with his hands on his hips.

"I'll come up with something that'll make you happy. I promise."

"How?" Rabbit asked, not looking at Matt.

"What about Ronnie?"

Rabbit stopped and turned to Matt. "What about her?"

"You want a turn?"

The smaller man didn't answer.

Matt thumbed toward the back of the house. "She's in the bedroom, flying high. If I give her to you, just this one time, will that make us even? I couldn't do it more than once, though. She's my girlfriend, you know, and that wouldn't be right. I mean, I love her, and more than once, well, that would just be wrong, wouldn't it?"

He kept his face flat, letting Rabbit work things out in his head. Rabbit probably knew he was being set up, but there had to be a glimmer of hope somewhere down deep that maybe Matt might let him have a go at her.

Matt admitted to himself long ago that he truly loved Veronica. He also admitted it was weird and abnormal. He supplied her pills to keep her high, but that didn't mean he didn't love her. Matt also knew Rabbit had had a crush on Veronica that went back to high school. Rabbit would have done anything for the former captain of the cheerleading squad, just to have one moment alone with her. Hell, Matt thought the same way, which is why he kept her in pills and took care of her now, even if she occasionally seemed not worth the cost of some of her baggage.

Rabbit blushed.

Matt grew a malicious smile. "You dirty bastard. I see how you are. I wouldn't let you sleep with my girlfriend. Just for that, you've donated your money to the cause. I'm not making anything up to you."

Before he turned away, anger flashed across Rabbit's face.

"Now that we've settled things, what do you think about the new rules of the game?"

Rabbit sat on the end of the coffee table, his back to Matt. "I don't know," he said, his voice sullen.

"I like them," Matt said. "Actually, I like them a lot. It'll make the game better, and it's going to add a little more anarchy to this city, don't you think?"

"It's dangerous."

Matt shrugged, but Rabbit couldn't see the movement. "Life is boring. Let's liven it up."

"I guess."

Matt stood, stretched, and rotated his neck, eliciting several pops. "Hey, Rabbit."

"Yeah?" Rabbit looked up, renewed hope in his eyes.

"I'm gonna ball Ronnie now." The hope faded in Rabbit's eyes. "You can come back and watch if you want. She might even dig that."

Matt laughed as he walked down the hall.

Chapter 25

The rules of the game had changed.

Craig had pitched an idea to the guys, and they bought it. After the contentious interaction between the crew and Matt, they were looking for any new idea to rally behind. Craig gave them something to build on, but it was Matt's buy-in that sealed the deal.

Even though Matt was younger, Craig admitted his brother was the smarter one. Now, many years after high school, Matt still read books when no teacher was making him. When Craig laid out his idea, Matt grabbed onto it and ran.

"What Craig is describing," Matt had said to the fellas, "is the archetype of our oppression—hell, it's the oppressor of our society." Of course, Matt had to define *archetype*, but once he did, he really got rolling. "Let's use this game of ours to fight back. No longer will we target women. We won't target men who, like us, are struggling to make ends meet."

Craig thought Matt sounded like a politician or worse, a salesman, but the guys bought it, just like those old women at church bought whatever the preacher said. Hook, line, and sinker. He used to watch that silver-tongued salesman with fascination whenever his grandmother made him tag along. That preacher was so smooth with those old broads, and his brother had the same effect on the crew at that moment. It was a different Matt than the one whose back was against the wall earlier. This one was confident and inspired.

Matt led the group to the new idea, and they followed with nodding heads and big smiles. They were now going after suits. Specifically, white males in suits and the attacks had to be limited to the downtown area. They were going after the one percent. Not only was it a game, but it was a statement against oppression. Matt said society would be forced to sit up and take notice. The guys ate that up. Craig knew Matt hated the one percent, just like he did. It was one of the few things the brothers had in common.

The guys were also now going out two teams at a time. This would increase the rate of the game and lead the police in different directions, in case anything went wrong. Matt came up with that strategy on the fly. The guys loved that idea, too, but Craig knew it was to keep the guys distracted a little longer from the real problem: the lack of drugs to sell.

Regardless, Craig smiled as he stood on a street corner with Henry and Bam Bam. The latter's name had been drawn, so Craig was there only to witness. He didn't care, though. He had an ulterior motive, and his eyes consistently scanned every face in the crowd.

"Where to start?" Bam Bam said.

Henry smirked. "They're all the same. Soulless, dead-eyed bastards. Like fish in a barrel. That one." Henry pointed down the sidewalk.

"Fine. Start filming," Bam Bam said.

Henry pulled out his phone and started the camera. Bam Bam walked toward an older white male reading something from a manila folder. The man had silver hair and was impeccably dressed in a dark suit with tan dress shoes. They were on a collision course, but the older man never looked up.

Bam Bam stopped walking, waiting for the man to get to him.

When he realized he was about to collide with Bam Bam, the businessman looked up, said "Excuse me," and moved to the left.

The big man swung his fist and caught the man in the temple. He was unconscious before he landed face-first on the concrete.

Bam Bam jogged back to Henry and Craig. Both stood there wide-eyed, watching the motionless man on the ground.

"Well?" the big-shouldered man said, "should we go?"

Chapter 26

Officer Leya Navarro stood at the corner of Lincoln Street and Riverside Avenue, just outside the offices of *The Spokesman-Review*. A crowd had gathered twenty feet away. Officer Lee Sheets was interviewing additional witnesses. A newspaper reporter and photographer stood nearby, anxiously waiting to talk with someone about the assault. A supervisor had already been requested to respond to the scene.

Paramedics treated a man in his early fifties. According to witnesses, he'd been struck by a young white male as he walked down the sidewalk. When he fell, he collided with the building, which resulted in a nasty scrape to his bald head. Blood remained over his lip and chin, the result of a bloody nose.

When he was done bandaging the wound, the paramedic looked at Leya and nodded. She stepped forward and introduced herself.

The man gave his name as Duane Violette and provided his birthday, address, and phone number.

"Mr. Violette, can you tell me what happened?"

He nodded, then looked down at his white shirt and multicolored tie. There was blood on them. He looked at the lapel of his gray suit and moaned. It was darkened as well. "These are ruined."

"Mr. Violette," Leya said, bringing his attention back to her.

"Yeah," he said, "I know. It's just that I liked this suit. The kid, right? That's what you want to know about. Yeah, well, I was returning from a meeting with my architect over near Browne's Addition." He looked back in the direction from where he'd come. "Anyway, I saw this runt of a kid walking sort of toward me."

"Sort of toward you?"

"Not directly in my path, but in my direction. He kept watching me, real alert like, you know what I mean?"

Leya nodded.

"When he got near me, he hit me."

"Where did he hit you?"

"Right there," Violette said, pointing to a spot on the sidewalk.

Leya smiled. "I mean, where did he hit you on your body?"

"Oh," he said. "He hit me on the nose. Mostly it missed me. Just sort of pissed me off. Guess it must have been enough to make me bleed, though."

"What happened then?"

"Well, I was pissed. He took a swipe at me, so I went after the little prick." Violette's eyes widened. "I'm sorry for swearing, Officer."

"You're fine, Mr. Violette. Just tell me what happened."

"I swung at him. I guess I missed him badly, though. I haven't been in a real fight since I was in junior high school. That's maybe forty years or more. I only proved I think I'm tougher than I really am."

Leya patiently waited for him to continue.

Violette shrugged. "Anyway, the kid hit me on the side of the head. I woke up with a bunch of people around. I didn't understand what was happening until the firemen arrived."

"The witnesses described your attacker as a short, white male wearing a Pittsburgh Steelers T-shirt."

"Sounds about right."

"Can you remember anything else about him?"

Violette shook his head. "Not really. I mean, I thought I could take the little bastard. He hit a lot harder than expected. That probably doesn't help, does it?"

"Adam one eighteen," called the dispatcher through Leya's shoulder microphone.

She keyed the mic. "Adam one eighteen, go ahead."

"Adam one eighteen, when you're clear of the call, you're requested at the corner of Washington and Riverside."

"One eighteen, copy. What about the supervisor to respond to media?"

"Adam one eighteen, supervisor is at Washington and Riverside. He requests your presence there."

Before leaving, Leya turned to Officer Sheets, but he'd already heard the radio traffic. He waved at her and turned back to the witness he was interviewing.

After she climbed into her patrol car, she pulled up the call on her mobile data computer (MDC). The call at the corner of Washington and Riverside had initially come in as an assault with eerily similar details to the one she was just leaving. They occurred a few minutes apart. *Much too close to be a coincidence*, Leya thought.

Deeper into the call log notes, the original assault report had been modified to a homicide.

Leya realized things had just gotten worse.

Chapter 27

Detectives Quinn Delaney and Marci Burkett stood near the body. Marci was in a black pantsuit with a red blouse. Her badge and gun were hidden beneath a matching suit coat. She wore high heels that were against the dress code of the department. For several years, she'd been in and out of trouble for violating the policy, but she hadn't conformed yet. Quinn was in a dark blue suit, light blue shirt, and red tie. His gun and badge were clipped to his belt and hidden under his jacket.

An outer and inner perimeter had already been established around the crime scene. The block had been cordoned off, with patrol cars diverting vehicle traffic and officers sending pedestrians in different directions.

The body of an older, white male lay face down on the concrete. The midday sun shone overhead, but the sky was bright blue, and the temperature wasn't supposed to exceed the mid-eighties.

Looking up, Quinn said, "Beautiful day."

"Not for him."

"What's with you? You skip breakfast or something? Is your blood sugar dipping?"

Marci raised her eyebrows, apparently not appreciating her partner's concern.

"Boyfriend problems?" Quinn asked.

"Things are fine. Why is it every time I seem a little grouchy, you ask about my boyfriend?"

Quinn chuckled. "Then what is it?"

"I skipped breakfast, and I'm not going to get lunch because of this," Marci said, pointing at the body on the ground.

"Run and get a sandwich. He's not going anywhere."

Marci shook her head. "I'm fine. I'll get something later."

"I should start carrying a granola bar in my pocket for you."

"Dude, I'm not a puppy."

"If you're not going to eat, can we begin?"

Marci bowed and gestured toward the body. "By all means."

Quinn bent over and, with his gloved right hand, pulled a wallet from the victim's back pocket. "Arthur McKee. Sixty-eight. Lives on the South Hill. Member of Snap Fitness."

Marci made several entries into her notebook while Quinn dropped the wallet into a plastic evidence bag, then stood.

"We know what killed him," Marci said.

"We do?"

"Some dirtball walked up and hit him. He fell and hit his face on the pavement."

"Was it the punch that did it?" Quinn asked. "Or hitting his face on the concrete? Maybe he had a heart attack."

Marci tilted her head. "Are you trying to test my nerve? Some kid hit him, and, as a result, this dude is dead."

"We don't know who the attacker was, and we don't know why."

"At least we don't have to wait around for some autopsy or ballistics," Marci said and walked toward the outer perimeter. "This is going to be about old-style police work."

"Your favorite."

Marci stopped at the yellow *Police Line—Do Not Cross* tape that indicated the inner perimeter. "You best watch your step until I get something to eat. Unlike you, I don't bring my lunch in a brown paper bag."

Quinn shook his head. That comment was not going to get under his skin.

Chapter 28

Officer Leya Navarro saw them approaching from the outer perimeter. Detectives Delaney and Burkett, along with Captain Gary Ackerman, were headed directly toward her.

Ackerman was dressed as sharply as ever in a custom-tailored suit. His haircut was perfect, and his walk was one of a man looking to ascend the next rung on the department ladder.

"Navarro," Ackerman said, "Do you know Detectives Delaney and Burkett?"

"Yes, sir."

"You've been keeping tabs on the recent outburst of stranger-on-stranger assaults, correct?"

"The knockout game? Yes, sir."

Ackerman winced and took a quick look around. "Let's not call it that while in public."

Leya looked to the detectives, then back to the captain. "But that's what it is."

"We don't know that for sure. Besides, that kind of talk brings out the crazies and copycats. Let the media give credence to the term, but we're not going to give voice to it, okay?"

Leya nodded. Marci and Quinn glanced at each other.

"Got a theory?" Ackerman asked. "We haven't had anything like this in years, and suddenly we've had four incidents—"

"Six, sir," Leya said.

"Six? Damn. Six incidents in three days." Ackerman looked at the news crews at the end of the block. "The press is going to have a field day with this. You've been out in front of this before anyone else. What do you think?"

"I believe it's the same group of guys," Leya said. "I don't know the reason they're doing it, but it's a concentrated effort."

"Why do you say that?"

"We have different descriptions for each attacker, so it's a larger group. I haven't figured out how many there are involved yet. Until today, the victims have been of various types, but the same M.O. has been used on every attack."

"Which is?" Quinn jumped in.

"One attacker and two acquaintances standing off to the side. Always recording it."

"Recording it?" Marci asked.

"Multiple witnesses have described associated males using their phones to record the attacks."

Quinn looked at the captain, his partner, and then back to Leya. "Has any of it appeared on social media?"

"Not to my knowledge," Leya said, "and I've been watching for it."

"What does that say?" Quinn asked. "Why film it and not put it up on some website?"

"Maybe it's a trophy," Marci said, "but more likely it's proof."

"Of what?" Ackerman asked.

"That they actually knocked someone out," Marci said. "Look at it this way. You've got a bunch of guys who are going around trying to knock people out. Nowadays, just saying you did something isn't enough. You need some sort of proof. You need video evidence. At least, pictures. Otherwise, no one will believe it happened."

"Makes sense," Quinn said.

"I'll buy the theory," Ackerman added.

"Then the question is why," Marci said. "Why do any of it in the first place?"

"That's a question we can answer at another time," Ackerman said. "But I think you just added a big piece to the puzzle. Here's what's going to happen. Navarro, you're going to take all the knowledge you've got so far, and you're going to work directly with these detectives. Until further notice, you *only* work these cases. All the knockout cases fall under this homicide. Understand?"

"Yes, sir."

"I'll notify your sergeant as well as your chain of command. Work the street for answers, but you're on this team, got it? No calls for service. No traffic stops. If you need to be in plain clothes, so be it."

Leya nodded.

Ackerman turned to the detectives. "I'm pushing all the other assault files under your umbrella. The homicide made this your territory. Any questions?"

Marci started to say something, but Ackerman held up his hand, then pointed to her high heels. She understood the implied threat and remained silent.

The captain looked to the eager press corps at the end of the street. "Now, I've got to go give them something that won't further inflame this situation."

Chapter 29

The laughter in the house woke Veronica Schuster. She lay in the bedroom, the real world slowly returning.

Her stomach hurt. She couldn't tell if it was from constipation or lack of food. Either way, it pushed her past the dreamy world into the reality of pain.

She reached over to her bottle of pills and discovered it was empty. There had been pills in it before, she was sure of it. She shook the container for good measure, but no sound came. In a fit of frustration, she threw the small bottle across the room.

As she lay there, she noticed a funky aroma and realized it was her.

I smell, she thought.

It took some additional thinking, but she calculated it had been almost a week since she'd showered. She knew she was going to need more medicine, and to get it, she would have to give Matt what he wanted. Matt had already visited her several times that week. Soon, he'd get mad and force her to shower. Better to do it before he got upset. Veronica pushed off the bed and padded into the bathroom.

She took a quick look at herself in the mirror. It was only a few years ago that she was the captain of the high school cheerleading squad. She was really something then. Straight As, perfect attendance, and the secret desire of every guy on every team—not so secret for some of them.

Then college came, and she found out that she was just like everyone else: nothing special, just another pretty girl, and those were already a dime a dozen. If that was the case, then what was she now? In a moment of clarity, Veronica Schuster admitted what she really was: a junkie living in one of her parents' rentals, screwing a sort-of boyfriend so he'd keep her stocked in Oxy.

Veronica pulled the skin down on her cheek, exposing an eye. She looked terrible.

Maybe I should clean myself up, she thought.

She could go home and get checked into a rehab program. Maybe make a real life for herself and find someone decent—someone better than Matt.

Her parents never accepted him, and why should they? He was exactly what they told her he was: a drug-dealing lowlife. He had reached his peak when he was in the Marines, and she wasn't with him then. His best years were already behind, yet she'd hitched her wagon to him.

Veronica softly laughed to herself. Sometimes, clarity was a bitch.

Stabbing pain in her stomach doubled her over. It felt like multiple knives being stuck in her stomach at once. She held on to the counter until it passed. When she stood upright, she saw her reflection again. Her face was bright red, and tears streaked down her cheeks.

"Damn," she muttered.

She lifted an arm and sniffed herself.

"It's not that bad," she said and returned to the bed, doubled over and clutching her stomach.

Chapter 30

Gadget and Bam Bam were on the game board, although Gadget had earned only a single point. The group was happily toasting both, and the videos of their deeds had been repeatedly watched. The group was even watching the videos of the previous knockouts and comparing who'd had the best one so far.

Craig pulled Matt aside. "I'm going to take off for a bit," he said.

Matt patted his brother on the back and said, "Where are you staying? If you need a place to crash, you're welcome to stay here."

"I appreciate it, but I'm going to wander a bit. See if I can score some cash somewhere."

Matt shook his brother's hand and told him to be careful.

Craig slipped out of the house without the other guys noticing. When Craig was on the street, he pulled one of the three Oxy pills he'd taken from Veronica's bottle and popped it into his mouth. He dry-swallowed it. He had slipped into the bedroom earlier and stolen the pills while she slept. He knew Veronica would be without, but he figured Matt would have additional pills stashed elsewhere. Matt was good that way.

As the pill took hold, Craig's world calmed itself. The pill didn't kill all the pain, and sure as hell wouldn't put a dimple into the thoughts running through his head, but it helped. He had to ration them. If he ate all three immediately, he'd be in a worse situation.

Craig wandered through downtown. Once, at a street corner, a nice older man grabbed him by the arm to stop him from stepping in front of oncoming traffic. Craig's thoughts were elsewhere, and he wasn't paying attention. The elderly man smiled kindly at him.

"Whaddya want? A medal?" Craig asked.

The old man shook his head and shuffled on.

Craig scanned the face of every man in a suit. He couldn't find what he was looking for, and he was getting increasingly agitated.

He fumbled with the pills in his pocket. *Maybe a second one would calm me down*, he thought.

The internal argument lasted for only a minute before he pulled a second pill from his pocket. He turned it over in his fingers as he continued to watch people on the street.

He lifted the pill to his mouth and froze when he saw a familiar face. The guy walked into the Western Bank building.

Craig shoved the pill back into his pocket and ran.

Chapter 31

"Where are your pills, Ronnie?" Matt asked.

Veronica was curled on the bed, crying. She held her stomach as she wept. She pointed to the bottle lying on the floor.

Matt picked it up and looked at it. "You had some left. Where are they?"

"I don't know," Veronica said. "Maybe I should go to the ER."

"You're not going to the hospital," Matt said. "You've got cramps because you're jonesing."

"It hurts."

"No, shit. You're taking too much." Even though her eyes were closed, Matt waved the empty bottle in front of her. "You took the last of these, and it didn't even make a dent, did it?"

"I didn't take them. I swear."

"Whatever," Matt said.

Wearing only panties and a bra, Veronica lay shivering in a fetal position. Matt grabbed the top cover and pulled it over her. He smelled how funky she'd become, and he turned away. Veronica grabbed the blanket and wrapped it tightly around her. Tears ran down the side of her nose.

"Can you score more?" she asked.

Matt looked at the bottle. The pills cost him, but they'd always been worth it before. He would never have gotten close to Ronnie if he hadn't gotten her the pills at first. She was gorgeous. *Was* being the operative word. Now, she was a shell of the girl she'd been in high school, a husk of the woman she was just a year ago. He'd idolized her since her junior year, even though she didn't know his name.

Now, her life was in his hands. Matt knew they would have to get her off these pills at some point, but he dragged it out because it meant she would still be his. Maybe today was the day.

"Ronnie—"

"Please!" she screamed.

Matt put the empty bottle of pills on the table and caressed her sweating forehead. "I'll get your medicine."

She forced a smile and mumbled, "I love you."

"I love you, too," he replied, even though he knew full well she didn't mean it.

Chapter 32

The three of them sat in the police department's conference room. Various assault reports were spread out on the large table.

Marci Burkett had a yellow notepad near her and was listing the various descriptions of the attackers. "These are horrible," she said.

"We took what the victims and witnesses gave," Leya Navarro said.

"I'm not pointing the finger at you," Marci said, "so relax. What I'm saying is, what the hell are we going to do with these descriptions? They're all white males. The only difference in descriptor we have is height and clothing style. Clothes change. And most people can't describe height and weight with any accuracy, so we're up a creek."

Quinn Delaney leaned back in his chair and looked at his notebook. "We might not have the actual motive, but I feel like we've got a pretty good handle on this."

Marci smirked.

Leya noticed her response. Marci shrugged when they made eye contact.

"This," Marci said, drawing an air circle around her face, "is me calling out my partner on his overt positivity."

Quinn dropped his chair forward. "It's a group. Leya said as much, and I believe she's correct. I've been thinking about that. If they *are* a group and they're planning these assaults, they must be meeting somewhere."

"Like a clubhouse?" Marci asked.

"Something like that. They meet and plan before going out. Doesn't that sound reasonable?"

Leya and Marci looked at each other and nodded.

"So we're looking for a group of white males, either loosely or tightly affiliated, known to congregate together."

Marci laughed. "Dude, you just described both the Mormons and the Hell's Angels."

"It's still something."

Leya said, "I agree. It is something."

Captain Ackerman walked into the conference room. Without a word, he turned on the television at the end of the table. As he selected a channel, he said, "The various news teams are running with the knockout game as the lead story. They alerted our public relations officer to give him a heads up."

The clock above the television clicked to five, and the Channel 6 news started.

The group sat silently as the reporter showed the scene of the recent homicide. Ackerman was interviewed, as were several witnesses. Archival footage from several years ago popped up on the screen as the reporter prattled on about the previous trend of the knockout game.

Ackerman glanced at Leya. She shook her head and pulled out her cell phone to call up the Facebook app.

When the on-scene reporter finished, the studio anchors took over. Ackerman flipped to another channel just as they were completing a story on the knockout homicide as well.

"Not good," Leya said.

The three of them turned to her.

"The story is viral on Facebook."

"Has anyone posted a video of the actual assaults?"

"It doesn't look like it," Leya said. "These guys are being disciplined. I'll give them that."

Chapter 33

Andrew Miller stared at his computer.

He still had work to do, but he couldn't focus. His heart raced, and he felt like he needed to hit something, anything. Why was it coming back to him so often now?

For a moment, he considered talking with his therapist, but he pushed that idea away. Talking with her always made him feel worse about himself, the incident, and life in general. No, he knew what he had to do. He had to deal with it. Struggle through the feelings and come through the other side. Like he had done previously.

The office phone rang. His eyes shifted to it, but he let it continue to ring. It was now after hours. *Let it go to voicemail and then check it*, he thought. Besides, he didn't feel like talking with anyone.

He slipped out of his chair to the floor and got into the push-up position. He slowly started going up and down. He needed to find his center, the place where he felt at peace. His mind ran over the confrontation in the street before working its way back to the haunting incident.

When his arms weakened and finally ran out of strength, he stood and stretched. His chest was tight, and sweat had formed on his brow.

He pressed the palms of his hands into his closed eyes.

Africa, he thought.

He didn't want that moment in his head again.

Chapter 34

Spokane Police Officer Glenn Novak watched the activity at Riverside Avenue and Division Street. Known in the community simply as "bar row," it was a popular destination for the drinking crowd. It was also a hotbed of low-level criminal activity at closing time. Fights, drug dealing, and drunken driving were easy to spot. The night had been slow to that point, so Novak figured he'd sit off the corner and observe. He was bored and wanted to get into something interesting.

That part of town had changed dramatically over the previous decade. Several upscale bars had moved into the area, replacing the dive joints. The crime was still there, though. It just involved a more upscale crowd now.

It was nearly 1 a.m. when three young women in short dresses stumbled out of The Globe, a popular nightclub. They were followed by a well-dressed male patron who stopped them on the sidewalk. The women laughed as the guy made his pitch. His arms waved wildly as he spoke. Novak wondered if he was trying to get all three to go home with him or just one. The officer laughed inwardly when he thought he'd have better luck getting all of them rather than to peel a single woman away from her friends.

A group of street kids approached from the east end of the block. One kid—tall, black, gray T-shirt, white shoes—stepped in front. He had an exaggeratedly cocky walk with swinging shoulders and arms that whipped to the side. His cohorts laughed in response.

Novak turned his attention back to the three women and the lone man. The women had left him standing on the sidewalk as two of them helped the third drunk-walk in her high heels. The man playfully hollered after them. The women giggled and turned back to him with some sort of encouragement.

It was then that the cocky street kid passed in front of the well-dressed drunk and sucker-punched him. The man immediately crumbled to the ground.

"Shit!" Novak yelled. He immediately activated his in-dash camera.

The street kids jumped and danced around the fallen man. They soon began kicking him.

Novak grabbed his microphone and keyed it. "David four thirty-four."

"Four thirty-four," dispatch replied.

"Four thirty-four," he said. "Assault in progress. Riverside and Division. Start units."

He dropped the car into gear, activated his lights, and pulled through the intersection. The street kids saw the patrol car and bolted in opposite directions.

The tall black kid ran north, and Novak followed along in his patrol car.

"Four thirty-four, I'm in pursuit of a black male. Late teens. Northbound on Division. He's turned east now onto Spokane Falls Boulevard. He's on foot. Wearing a gray T-shirt, jeans, white shoes. Victim is down in front of The Globe. Start medical."

"Four thirty-four, copy."

A couple of blocks later, the kid realized the futility of outrunning a patrol car and stopped. He raised his hands and turned around.

Novak put the car in Park, jumped out, and yelled, "On the ground!"

The kid shook his head but did as directed. After Novak handcuffed him, he keyed his microphone. "David four thirty-four, one in custody. Also…"

"Four thirty-four," the dispatcher said. "One in custody. Go ahead."

"Four thirty-four, there were other suspects with the one I detained. Responding units grab anyone that's running in the area and bring them back."

"Four thirty-four, copy."

ROUND FOUR

Chapter 35

Leya Navarro, Marci Burkett, and Quinn Delaney sat quietly in the chief's conference room. At 8:47 a.m., Captain Gary Ackerman walked into the room with a folder in hand.

"The chief may join us. Look alive if he does."

The three eyed each other but remained silent.

"Hear about last night's assault?" Ackerman asked. "No? Well, there was another one." He opened his file and tossed a copy of the report to each of them. "I need you to assess if you think this is part of your case."

"Why?" Quinn asked.

"I assume you saw the national news?"

Quinn nodded, as did Leya. Marci shook her head.

"Yesterday," Ackerman said, talking directly to Marci, "there were two reported cases of the knockout game outside of Spokane. One in Jacksonville. The other in Toledo. That's what made national. Who knows what didn't?"

"Damn," Marci said.

"The one in Toledo was caught on a high school camera. The one in Jacksonville was posted on Facebook. The media ran them both. It's ramping up again, and the copycats are out."

"Why the push on this one?" Marci asked, tapping the new report with a single finger. She wasn't reading it. "Why not let us investigate it like any other?"

Leya finished reading the first page and had already flipped to the second page of the report.

"The mayor is grilling the chief right now," Ackerman said. "A couple of councilmembers called him on his way into the department this morning. The press made repeated calls to him since last night. He needs feedback on this latest attack, and he needs it *now*."

"You know how this works, sir," Marci said. "We shouldn't rush an investigation for political expediency."

"I'm not asking you," Ackerman snapped. "Review the case. Tell me what you think. Patrol caught two of the related suspects last night, and they've been booked. We have partial footage of the attack from a dashcam, which I'll have sent to your computers. Read the report and let me know what you think now. After that, go talk with arrestees."

"We should interview them before we make that determination," Marci said.

Quinn leaned forward. "I agree."

Ackerman turned his attention to Leya, whose focus was still on the report. He said, "You're not a detective, Navarro, so I'm not expecting some cover-your-ass maneuvering. Give me a patrol assessment. What's your gut say?"

Leya looked at the detectives, who observed her in return. "I support what they're saying," she said.

A small smile hinted at the edge of Marci's lips, but Quinn kept his face impassive.

Ackerman lifted his hands in resignation. "Teamwork. I can appreciate that. Priority one is to get in the box with those arrested and find out if it's connected. If it's not, let me know. Remember, the chief is part of our team as well. Don't let him twist in the wind on this." He stood and walked out.

When the captain was out of earshot, Leya turned to the detectives and said, "It's not related."

Quinn pulled the report to him and started to read.

Marci laid her hand over her copy of the report but focused on Leya. "Tell me why."

"No one filmed the event. Also, after the victim was on the ground, the entire group kicked him. This is unlike the previous six assaults. It's not the pattern."

Quinn looked up. "I'll buy that assessment, but we don't rule this incident out until we're sure."

Leya said, "I'll let you guys handle that part. I did my part with Ackerman. Now, I'm going back on the street."

Chapter 36

"There are a lot of police out," Critter said as they walked through downtown. Henry and Stick were along to witness his glory that day, which looked doubtful now. "Why so many?"

Henry said, "It's 'cause of us."

"You think?" Critter asked.

They were standing on the corner of Main Avenue and Washington Street. They'd already seen five different police officers walking on foot. There were also two officers patrolling around on bicycles. Somewhere Critter knew there were officers in cars. There always were. Cops love riding around in their cars.

"How many people have we knocked out?" Henry asked.

"Six?" Critter said.

"Gremlin didn't knock that bitch out," Stick said with a snicker.

"But we've hit six people," Henry said.

"Yeah," Critter said.

"That's bound to bring heat."

Critter walked southbound then. Henry looked at Stick, shrugged, and followed. Stick dropped in behind them.

In a moment, Henry asked, "Critter, what are you going to do?"

"I dunno."

"What do you mean?"

"I mean, I dunno," he said, waving his arms as he spoke, but still walking ahead of the other guys. He stopped and turned around. "Does it seem smart to keep playing this game with so many of them running around?"

Henry shrugged. "Prolly not, but what about the scratch? If you don't play, you got zero chance of winning."

"I got zero chance if I'm in jail."

"But don't you wanna outsmart the cops?" Henry asked.

"I guess."

"You don't sound convincing."

"Why are you busting my balls, man?"

Henry said, "See any cops?"

Critter scanned the area. They were now at the corner of Washington Street and Riverside Avenue. There were no cops in sight. "No."

"Stick, you smell bacon?"

The thin man smiled. "There's no pork on the stove."

Henry lifted his chin toward a covered parking lot. "There's a lot of nice cars in there and no cameras. I've boosted from there before. All you gotta do is wait for some hotshot to show up. Then knock his ass out, and we walk out of there like we own the joint."

Critter quickly glanced around before looking back at Henry.

"Outsmarting the cops is fun, right?" Henry said.

A grin spread across Critter's face.

Chapter 37

They were at a full run.

Cops had been everywhere, but he took the swing, anyway.

Denver wanted to get on the board and had Shaggy and Gremlin as his witnesses. They'd noticed the cops wandering through the streets of downtown. It seemed like they were multiplying like cockroaches. They laughed at that idea—cops and cockroaches. You can stomp on one, but they keep increasing. It's nature's way of protecting the damn things. The three of them kept moving farther and farther toward the edge of downtown until they didn't see any more.

A well-dressed man stepped out of The Spokane Club, a private institution for richie-riches. Three other men followed him.

As they approached the club, Denver told his friends about it. He washed dishes there for a couple of weeks after his senior year of high school. That's where all the high rollers in town ate lunch and talked about how to divide the city's spoils. Denver said more than once that the club was made up of the local Illuminati. It made perfect sense to strike a suit there.

"Start recording," he said and moved toward the men who came out. Shaggy and Gremlin did as ordered.

The four well-dressed men stood talking amongst themselves.

Denver walked up to them.

"What's he doing?" Gremlin asked Shaggy.

His scraggly haired friend said, "This looks bad."

When he got near the men, Denver said, "Excuse me, sir."

The four suited men turned. Denver hit the first one squarely across the chin, which immediately sent him to the ground.

The other three men pulled back in horror.

Instead of turning and running, Denver attacked the nearest man by hitting him in the eye. The guy fell to the ground.

The other two men stepped slightly back but continued watching Denver. Fear paralyzed them from doing anything more. He advanced on them, punching and kicking wildly.

When he was done, all four men were on the ground, and Denver stood in the middle of them.

"Shit," Gremlin whispered.

"Let's go," Shaggy said before sprinting toward Denver.

When they got to him, Denver raised his hands, ready to fight further.

"We gotta go, Denver!" Shaggy urged.

Gremlin hurriedly glanced around. "The cops might already be on the way."

The mention of the police brought clarity to Denver. He nodded toward his friends.

As the three ran away, laughing and cheering, none of them bothered to wonder if all four of the men were actually rendered unconscious.

Chapter 38

Officer Leya Navarro had initially responded to the parking garage after the assault had been called in. A white male had been attacked inside the structure and knocked out. He never saw who hit him.

She checked for cameras, but there were none. There was even a large sign at the garage's entry, which announced cameras were not in use, and the ownership would not be held responsible for damage to vehicles. She ruefully shook her head. It was amazing more crimes didn't happen inside there.

While talking with the other responding officers, a second call came in from The Spokane Club. Leya then responded to that location to discover four victims. Although the number of victims didn't fit the pattern, the attack certainly did.

A white male had approached the group, separated one, then knocked him out with a single punch. The attacker struck three other nearby males. None of the other victims fought back. A witness verified the attacker had two friends with him. No one could confirm the associates recorded the attack, though.

Detectives Delaney and Burkett arrived on the scene shortly after Leya. The detectives immediately interviewed the witnesses.

Leya stood back, trying to make sense of it all.

She crossed her arms and studied one of the victims. He wore a dark suit, and his hair cut was expensive. She checked her notes for his age. He was in his early fifties. Ignoring the bloody nose and the bruising already forming around his eye, Leya imagined he was ordinarily handsome.

The other three men were of various ages and body shapes. All had been dressed nicely. One of them, also in his fifties, was being helped into the back of an ambulance. Due to being rendered unconscious and his head hitting the sidewalk, the medics were taking him to Deaconess Hospital for examination.

Something tickled her memory, and Leya walked back to her car. She pulled out the file containing the various assault reports. From each one, she examined the victims' descriptions. The first was an overweight man in a Seahawks shirt, then a homeless man, a woman in a dress, and a man in a light blue polo shirt. The last four had all been white males in suits. She wasn't counting the extra three attacked here at The Spokane Club. She was assuming the attacker was drunk on adrenaline and went after the other three. She knew the adage about assuming—it made an ass out of u and me—but she still assumed, anyway.

She believed she had discovered a new trend within the game.

A black patrol car pulled on the scene. Leya checked the license plate to make sure it wasn't the chief. She relaxed. When Captain Ackerman stepped out, though, she tensed. He wasn't angry. He was way past that. He was furious.

Ackerman trotted over to the suited man in the rear of the ambulance. They spoke for several moments. They shook hands before the ambulance doors shut. Then the captain stalked over to the other three men and the detectives.

Quinn and Marci acknowledged the captain before stepping back to let the captain speak with the other victims. The detectives walked over to Leya as she exited her car.

"What's that about?" Leya asked.

"Ackerman's on the warpath," Marci said. "He must know those guys."

Leya flipped open her notebook. "Any of their names ring a bell? None are on the council, right?"

They watched the interaction between Ackerman and the other men. It had long been rumored Ackerman had business dealings outside of the department. No one had discovered what they were. Had the three of them just stumbled onto the source of that gossip?

Ackerman shook the hands of the three men, then walked over to the three officers. "This is a disaster," he said.

"Who are those guys?" Marci asked.

"Friends," Ackerman forcefully said, shutting down any further questioning. "How could two attacks happen when we have ten officers patrolling the core today?"

"Captain, that's still a lot of ground to cover for a hit-and-run type of crime," Quinn carefully said.

Ackerman glared at him. "No kidding. How does that help me when I have to go before the chief? He's going to have to explain this mess to both the mayor and the council. Tell me you've got something."

"We got something," Marci said. "After the assault, two men ran up to the assailant. One of them was referred to as Denver."

"Denver? You think that's a nickname?"

"That's what we're taking it as," Marci said. "We'll run it through Crime Analysis."

Leya made an entry in her notebook regarding the moniker.

"That's it?" Ackerman asked with frustration on his face. "Four men are attacked in broad daylight, and that's all we get from it? A nickname?"

Anger flashed in Quinn's eyes, and he opened his mouth to say something, but Leya cut him off.

"We've got more than that," she said, pulling Ackerman's attention away from the detective.

The three of them faced her.

"The assaults are now coming two at a time. They have been for the last six—three attacks, two at a time, all within minutes of each other."

"They're trying to divide us," Ackerman said, slowly nodding in understanding.

"That would be my guess," Leya said.

"That's good," the captain said. "That shows some strategy, right? Some method to their madness."

"Are they dividing us by geography to limit our ability to respond?" Quinn asked. "Today's attacks, they're the farthest apart so far. Before, they were only a few blocks away."

"What was different about today?" Marci asked.

The four of them turned toward the heart of downtown. Traffic whizzed by on Monroe Street as it headed southbound.

Leya quickly faced the other three and said, "Our response. We forced them out of downtown. We had so many officers congregating in an area that they needed to move elsewhere to play their game."

Ackerman slapped his hands together. "We pushed them here."

"The other attack that happened," Leya said, "was inside a parking garage. No cameras. A guy was getting into his car and wham! He went down. It was the first time the attack wasn't in the open."

"That's another change to their routine," Quinn said.

"But I think I found something else," Leya said, "something more important. Their game changed a couple of days ago, and we didn't notice it."

"What is it? What did we miss?" Marci asked.

"They changed their targets. I believe they're going exclusively after suits now."

Chapter 39

"The cops were everywhere," Shaggy said.

The group listened intently as Shaggy spun the tale of Denver's attack. No one believed him until he showed the video. Afterward, everyone stared at Denver, even Henry and Bam Bam.

"I lost control," Denver said, his face pale. "I don't know what came over me."

"That was the most amazing thing I've ever seen," Matt said, tapping Shaggy's phone. "Those suits never even fought back."

Stick leaned against the wall, a disapproving smirk on his face. "He's not getting extra points for those other suits, right?"

Bam Bam chimed in with Stick. "Yeah. I thought we talked about this."

Matt held up his hands, quieting the complaints. "Denver's only getting credit for one. That was the deal." Matt pointed to Rabbit. "Add Denver to the list. Don't forget to add Critter as well. That was a nice knockout, man."

Critter smiled.

Several guys chipped in their support of Critter.

"Let's talk about the cops," Matt said. There was a mumbling of affirmation among the group. "You all think they're out because of our game?"

"I'd guarantee it," Henry said. "You can't knock out as many people as we have and not expect the cops to do something about it."

"So, what's the plan?" Stick asked.

"Maybe we should quit while we're ahead," Gadget said. A couple of guys nodded in agreement.

"Do you all want to take your hundred bucks back and go home?" Matt asked the group. "Should we stop the game at the end of the first round and admit the cops have us all scared?"

"I ain't afraid of no cop," Henry said.

"Me either," said Bam Bam, crossing his arms over his thick chest.

The rest of the guys fell in line after the toughest of the group spoke up.

"Then we need to think smarter in this game. That's the challenge, right? Critter found a suit in a parking garage. That was good. Real intelligent." For emphasis, Matt tapped the side of his temple with a single finger. "Denver went to the edge of downtown to get his. There were no cops there. Maybe one of you can go inside a building. That's an option, right? What about an alley? But be aware there might be cameras. There also might be some security sucker you have to deal with. This isn't supposed to be easy, is it?"

Some of the guys chuckled.

Matt flicked his eyes to Rabbit. "How about we double the points when we get to the next round?"

The guys cheered.

"The cops are out, so it's going to be extra challenging. The next round should earn four points instead of two. All agreed?"

The guys were wound tight and cheered louder than before.

"All right, all right," Matt said. "We're back in business. Rabbit, grab the bowl. Who's next up?"

Rabbit looked at the bowl. There was only a single name strip. "Only one name left in round one," Rabbit said and pulled the piece of paper from the bowl. "Craig."

"You're up, brother."

Craig stepped forward. "I'll give my opportunity to another if they let me point out the suit."

Matt glanced at Rabbit, then back to his brother. "What?"

"I'm willing to give up my chance if I can pick the guy."

Matt felt an uneasiness in his stomach. Craig was up to something, but he didn't know what. The guys stared at him, waiting for him to decide. "I don't know—"

"The guy who did this to me," Craig said, pointing at the tape over his broken nose and his blackened eyes, "is a suit."

The group collectively said, "Ah."

Matt's uneasiness grew, and his face warmed. He quickly put together the change in the rules of the game and Craig's sudden desire to join. It was a setup. That's what it had been about. Matt scanned his crew, and each of them was intently watching his brother.

"That's right, a fuckin' suit," Craig said. "And I'm worried if I don't knock him out, he'll turn around and do worse than this to me."

"Then pick another suit," Matt said, his voice flat.

"I want him," Craig said, staring at his brother.

"He's not the only one out there."

The two brothers stared at each other. The room was suddenly quiet. It stayed that way for several moments.

Finally, Henry said, "I'll do it."

"I'm in," Bam Bam said.

The rest of the guys remained silent. The mood of the room had changed. The group wanted to exact some sort of extra revenge on a suit, this specific suit, the one who had hurt a family member.

Matt wanted to say no, to tell Craig to walk downtown and throw his own punch, but he knew to do so would only call attention to himself. He wanted everyone's focus on the game, not the conflict between brothers.

He stared at Craig a moment longer, then relented by lifting his hands. "Anyone else volunteer?"

The rest of the guys knew better than to cross Henry or Bam Bam.

"If you do this," Matt said to his brother, "you get a zero in the first round."

"I understand. The points double the next round. I'll catch up then."

Matt glanced at Henry and Bam Bam. "Two guys then. Fifty/fifty chance. Rabbit, flip a coin."

Rabbit dug into his pocket and held a penny out to Matt. He shook his head, forcing Rabbit to step between Henry and Bam Bam.

Henry immediately said, "Heads." Bam Bam shrugged and stepped forward to watch the toss.

Rabbit flipped the coin into the air, letting it fall to the floor. When the penny landed, it spun for a few seconds before landing tails up.

Bam Bam smiled and turned to Craig. "I got your turn, big brother."

Matt said to Rabbit, "Fill the bowl. Let's start the next round now. Leave Craig and Bam Bam's name out since they're out this turn."

It took only a few moments to draw the next contestant, and Shaggy was selected.

After the group left the house full of excitement, only Matt and Rabbit were left.

"What's wrong?" Rabbit said.

Matt watched the group walking down the street. Several of the guys jumped around his brother. He had a bad feeling about Craig. Suddenly, the game was no longer his, and he didn't like how it felt.

"What's up with Craig?" Rabbit asked.

"What do you mean?"

Rabbit shrugged. "He seems off. Like he's not telling us the whole truth."

Matt watched most of the guys turn the corner and disappear out of sight. Some of the guys headed south.

"I'm going into the back room," he said. "You can stay if you want."

He walked to the end of the hallway and stopped at his bedroom door. Veronica was asleep on the bed. He would wake her up to take his anger, frustration, and worries out on her. He'd feel better after that. He always did. Then she could drift back off to whatever plane of existence she survived on these days.

He turned and saw Rabbit watching him. Matt knew what his friend was thinking—whether he should leave or stay and listen. Matt didn't avert his eyes. Finally, Rabbit lowered his gaze and sat on the couch.

Matt stepped into the bedroom.

Chapter 40

Officer Leya Navarro parked her patrol car in front of the bus plaza and got out. People milled aimlessly about. It was clear they weren't waiting for a bus. Instead, they were killing time and loitering.

She started toward the front door and stopped. At the end of the block were the two security guards she'd met earlier in the week. The big one, Jenkins, was taking notes while the smaller one, Evans, was interviewing a guy wearing only blue nylon shorts, no shirt or shoes. He was dirty, and his long hair looked several days past unwashed.

As she approached, Jenkins noticed her and nodded.

When she finished talking with him, Evans advised the transient to leave.

"What did he do?" Leya asked.

"He was creeping out some of our riders," Evans said. "We don't have anything on him, except he can't ride the bus dressed like that. He needs a shirt and some shoes. Therefore, he's loitering. I explained it to him and asked him to move on."

As he walked across the street, the dirty man glared at the three of them.

"He's probably heading back to his campsite near the river," Leya said.

"Probably," Jenkins said. "We're sort of a transient magnet."

"We're a magnet for all sorts of things," Evans said.

"About that. You keep a database on everyone you contact, correct? Along with any monikers they may have?"

Both security guards smiled at Leya's question and answered in unison, "Yes."

"I'm looking for a maggot nicknamed Denver. Ever run across one?"

Evans and Jenkins glanced at each other and shrugged. Evans said, "We haven't, but it doesn't mean he's not in the system. Maybe someone else has and put him in. Let's go look."

Chapter 41

Bam Bam and Stick were with Craig as they entered the Western Bank building on First Avenue.

"I followed him in here," Craig said. "He works on the fifth floor."

"What's he do?" Stick asked.

"I dunno. Maybe he's an attorney or something. The sign on the office said they were advisors, whatever that means."

"It's suit-speak," Bam Bam said. "They talk in code, so we can't understand what they're doing. They think they're so much better than us. God, I hate them."

"We all do, bro," said Stick. "We all do."

Craig nodded his agreement.

The three of them stepped into an elevator. Bam Bam stabbed the fifth-floor button with his finger.

The elevator played some quiet music as they waited in excited silence. When the doors opened, they stepped out into a common lobby.

"What's his name?" Bam Bam said.

"I dunno," Craig said. "I only know his face."

Bam Bam shook his head in disappointment.

They walked to the west end of the hall. Grayson Advisors, Inc. was printed on the wall next to the entrance. Through heavy glass doors, they could see a receptionist sitting behind a large counter with a granite top. Her head was bowed as she read something.

"He's in there somewhere," Craig said.

Bam Bam looked at him.

"What?"

The big man rolled his eyes. "I can't exactly walk in there on a seek and destroy mission, can I? That's asking for trouble, and everyone would remember me."

"We don't need that kind of trouble," Stick muttered.

The receptionist looked up and studied the three men through the glass entryway.

"Let's go," Craig said and tapped Bam Bam's shoulder with the back of his hand.

As they rode down to the first floor, no one said anything. Each was lost in his own thoughts.

Craig finally said, "Listen, I'm sorry. Let's wait for him in the lobby. He's got to come through there, right?"

"Unless he parks in the garage. That's a different entrance," Stick said.

Bam Bam smirked. "I thought you would have figured this shit out, Craig. Weak, man, weak."

The elevator slowed to a stop, and the doors opened. A man in a suit stood in the lobby, waiting for them to disembark. Bam Bam and Stick immediately stepped off, but Craig held open the door for the man who stepped into the elevator.

"I left something upstairs," Craig said to his friends. Bam Bam and Stick stared at him. Craig tilted his head slightly toward the man now in the elevator.

"Oh, yeah," Stick said.

Bam Bam hesitated, clearly not understanding.

Craig lifted his eyebrows and again tilted his head back.

"Right," the big man said, drawing out the word as he stepped into the elevator.

Stick moved to the corner of the elevator car and pulled his cell phone from his back pocket. His other hand swiped across the lower floor buttons on the elevator's wall. "Sorry," Stick said.

The suit's eyes swept across each of them but hesitated on Craig. He studied Craig's face and the bruising around his eyes.

When the elevator stopped on the second floor, the doors opened, but no one got on or out. Stick lowered his cell phone but tilted it up at the suit.

"Looks like that hurt," the suit said to Craig.

"It did," he said. He tried to sound tough, but his voice shook. He wondered if anyone else noticed.

As the elevator's doors closed, Bam Bam swung a fist at the suit. Unfortunately, it wasn't fast enough. The suit moved at the same time.

He hit Bam Bam as he started his swing. Bam Bam's hand changed trajectory, went over the suit's head, and caromed off the elevator's wall.

An elbow from the suit caught Stick in the temple, forcing his head to bounce against the metal plate that housed the buttons for the floors.

Two punches from the suit—one to the face and the other to the mid-section—hammered into Bam Bam. The big man dropped to the floor. He struggled to stay upright, putting a hand on the ground to steady himself.

Stick slowly slid down the wall of the elevator car when the suit kicked his heel up under the thin man's chin.

The suit then stomped on the hand Bam Bam had placed on the elevator's floor. A crunching sound filled the small car. The big man shrieked.

During the quick melee, Craig stood flat-footed. Frozen. Overcome by fear.

His eyes widened right before the suit punched him squarely in his previously broken nose.

Darkness overwhelmed him.

Chapter 42

Leya Navarro heard the call come over the radio. Three white males were fleeing the Western Bank building. A building security guard had tried to stop them, but they assaulted him as they fled.

Officer Rodney McCrea was already on the scene when she arrived. A couple of other officers were with McCrea. They surrounded the security officer as he explained what had occurred.

"I received a report that there were three guys injured in an elevator, so I went to check on it. I was on the main floor, and I used my elevator key to call each of them to me, one by one. It was the second car I called that had the guys in it. They were messed up all right, but they didn't stick around to tell me why."

"What happened?" McCrea asked.

"I stepped forward to make contact, and a big guy just slugged me. Without a word. Who does that? Then they ran off."

Stepping forward, Leya asked, "Can you describe them?"

The security guard smiled. "I can do better than that. We've got cameras."

***

Along with Officer McCrea, Leya followed the security guard, Rich Newell, back to his office. The other officers cleared the scene to look for any individuals running from the area.

The security office was no bigger than a broom closet, but the guard was quite proud of its setup. Multiple monitors showed rotating camera points of view. Leya quickly noticed cameras were located inside the elevators.

"You've got a lot of cameras," she said.

"This is a first-class building. We take care of our tenants. You'd be surprised how some of the lowlifes try to come in here and steal."

"What about the elevators?"

Newell snickered. "We've caught people doing all sorts of stuff in there. You can't imagine."

McCrea raised his eyebrows. "We can. We've seen it all."

Using the computer's mouse, Newell called up the camera on the second elevator. He slid the time-button back slightly and saw three men inside the elevator. He paused the feed. "That's them."

Leya smiled and shook her head. "I'm going to need a full copy of this video."

Newell nodded. "No problem."

McCrea studied Leya. "What's so funny, kid?"

"The idiot with black eyes and a broken nose." Leya tapped the screen for emphasis. "I arrested him on a warrant earlier this week. He tried to stab some guy at the bus plaza."

"He tried to stab someone, and he's already out?"

"Victim didn't stick around."

"You're kidding me," McCrea said.

"Hand to God. The raccoon tried to stick some suit and got beat for it. Then the suit walked away like he was Clint Eastwood in a Western." Leya flipped through her notebook until she found what she was looking for. "Craig Taylor. That's him."

"Play the rest of the video," McCrea said. "Let's see what happens."

Newell clicked *Play*, and it was only a few seconds before the elevator door opened, and the first guy stepped out. They couldn't see the assault on the security guard.

"Have another angle?" McCrea asked.

"I got one in the lobby."

"Wait," Leya said, reaching out to stop Newell from leaving the elevator feed. "You got a report of three injured men in an elevator, right?"

"Uh-huh."

"They don't look too injured to me."

"Maybe a little roughed up," McCrea added.

"Back it up," Leya said. "Find where they get on."

Newell slid the time-button back and noticed a lot of activity, but he continued back further until the elevator was empty on the screen. Then he pressed *Play*. They watched the three men enter the elevator.

"Can you tell which floor they came from?"

"Looks like the fifth," Newell said.

"How many businesses are up there?"

Newell rolled his eyes up as he thought. "Three."

The elevator arrived on the first floor, and the doors opened. Two of the men exited the elevator, but Craig Taylor remained, holding the door open as a suited man entered. It was only a couple of seconds before the other two men stepped back into the elevator.

"What the hell?" McCrea said.

The guy with red hair pulled his cell phone out.

"Hit pause," Leya said, and Newell did as he was told. She tapped the screen where the phone was. "You see that?"

"He's going to make a call."

"No. He's getting ready to film the attack. They always travel in packs of three. They attack white males in suits. It's the game." Leya nodded to Newell. "Go ahead."

On the screen, the elevator exploded in movement. Two men hit the floor before the suit lifted his foot and stomped down on the big man's hand.

"Damn," McCrea blurted.

Then the suit punched Craig Taylor in the face, sending him crashing to the floor.

"Damn," McCrea repeated, this time slower and with a sense of awe.

With his mouth open, the security guard stared at the screen.

"Play it again," Leya said, leaning toward the monitor. She tapped the screen where the suit was. "What's his name?"

Newell looked up at her. "I don't get it. He's like the nicest guy around. Who knew?"

Chapter 43

Andrew Miller walked through Riverfront Park. His heart rate long ago returned to normal. The sudden surge of adrenaline had worn off, and he was left with its dull after-effects. A headache pushed at the back of his head.

He'd been attacked twice in four days. Why?

His eyes searched people as they passed by. Scenarios ran through his mind, but none of them made sense.

No one would come after him for what happened in Africa. Or would they?

It was stupid to think that. Even if he could come up with some plausible scenario, the attackers they would send after him would be trained and ruthless. The guys in the elevator came at him with fists, not weapons. Besides, they didn't exactly look like they were trained, nor did they behave that way.

Also, he was reasonably sure the guy who attacked him at the bus plaza was in the elevator.

Was it revenge for that—the fight in the crosswalk?

That seemed the most plausible explanation, but that was a lot of trouble for simple revenge.

Andrew found a park bench and sat. Images that he found a way to control were now working their way back into his consciousness.

He lifted his face to the sun, listened to the noises around him, and tried to think it through.

Chapter 44

When Leya Navarro and Rodney McCrea walked through the glass office doors of Grayson Advisors, the receptionist's eyes widened. Leya knew it wasn't because of her. She was dressed in blue jeans and a black T-shirt. Her gun and badge were on her hip, but a sport coat hid the tools of her trade. It was McCrea's uniform that elicited the receptionist's response.

Quickly regaining her composure, she asked, "How may I help you?"

Leya said, "We'd like to see Andrew Miller."

"Is everything okay?"

"Andrew Miller, please."

The receptionist nodded, picked up the phone, and called someone. She talked for a moment, then hung up. "He's not in his office, but he was there earlier. His assistant said she'd find him and send him out."

Leya and McCrea stepped back from the desk so they could talk in private.

"You know something about this guy?"

Leya nodded. "Craig Taylor, the raccoon eyes, tried to stab a guy at the bus plaza."

"You said that."

"The guy he tried to stab…"

"Was the guy in the elevator?"

"Yeah."

"Damn."

"I know, right?"

"You think this whole knockout thing is because of that? Some kind of revenge trip?"

"I'm not sure. I've got to check the timeline on it, but it's strange that Taylor's a part of it."

"And you're sure this was the game?"

"Definitely. Three guys. One pulled out his camera."

"But Taylor never even moved on this Miller guy. He stood there like he was planted in the ground."

Leya shrugged. "I don't know why that is, but he was there for some payback. I'll guarantee that."

A tall, brunette woman walked past the receptionist and approached the two officers. "I'm sorry, but we can't locate Andrew. He must have left."

"Does he normally check out when he leaves?" Leya asked.

The woman shook her head. "No, ma'am. He's free to come and go as he pleases."

Leya looked at the receptionist. "Did he walk past you?"

"Not that I remember. I know he came in a while ago, but that's it."

"Is there another way out?" McCrea asked.

"The stairs," the woman said, pointing down the hall.

Leya glanced at McCrea before asking the two women, "Do you have a home address for Mr. Miller?"

Chapter 45

Stick and Bam Bam ran southbound along Howard Street, toward Edwidge Woldson Park.

The big man was slowed due to his damaged hand, which he cradled next to his body. His breathing was labored.

As soon as they had exited the elevator, Stick hit the security guard. Then the three of them burst from the bank building. That's when they lost contact with Craig. He ran one way, and the two of them ran another. It didn't matter at that point; it had become every man for himself.

"C'mon!" Stick yelled.

Bam Bam shuffled along. His face was wet with sweat.

They hadn't run more than ten blocks, and the big man was in real pain. Stick had never seen his friend this way. It worried him.

"You okay?"

Bam Bam shook his head.

"Your hand?"

"Uh-huh."

They slowed to a walk. Their heads swiveled in search of cops.

"I needa go to the hospital," Bam Bam mumbled. "It's fucked up bad."

"We can't. The cops might be there."

Bam Bam stopped and stared at Stick. "It's not your hand!"

"Dude! I know, I know, but if you go there and get grabbed, what do you do then?"

The big man stared at his hand. It was already swollen and bruised. It looked ugly.

"My mom has all sorts of medical stuff at home," Stick said. "She loves helping people. That's her thing."

"Yeah?"

"We'll tell her you dropped the hood of your car on it."

"She'll buy that?"

Stick smiled. "She ain't that smart. She buys anything I tell her."

"Think she'll have some ice to put on it?"

"Of course, she'll have ice. Just 'cause she's dumb doesn't mean she ain't a good mom. Now, pick it up, and let's get going. I don't want to get grabbed by an eager beaver cop 'cause we're standing around here gabbing like old ladies."

"Old ladies," Bam Bam muttered. He cradled his wounded hand like a baby and shuffled up the hill.

Chapter 46

Officer Leya Navarro tapped Detective Quinn Delaney's shoulder as he hunkered over his computer. "I've got something to show you," she said and held two flash drives up. "Where's Marci?"

Quinn glanced at the empty cubicle next to his. He stood and looked deeper into the detective's bullpen. "Marci!" he yelled.

"What?" a voice came from somewhere deeper in the office.

"Return to your desk. Pronto."

In a moment, she appeared. "What's so important?"

Leya showed her the two flash drives. "I've got something, and I've got names."

They huddled around Quinn's computer as he plugged in the first flash drive. "What is this?" he asked when the file appeared on the screen.

"The day before the reemergence of the knockout game, an assault occurred at the bus plaza. At first, I thought it was unrelated. Now, I'm not so sure."

Quinn double-clicked the file, and a video started. A suited man stood on a street corner before entering a crosswalk where a man in a hooded sweatshirt attacked him. Using his briefcase, he blocked a lunge with some sort of weapon, then punched the man in the face. He immediately kicked the man in the upper leg, which dropped him to the ground. The suit stood over the hooded man; his fist ready for another strike. Then the suit backed away, grabbed his briefcase, and walked on.

"What the hell was that?" Quinn said.

"It was awesome is what it was," Marci said. "Play it again."

They watched the video in silence a second time, but Marci moved in closer, her eyes intently studying the man in the suit. Her face flattened.

"What do you see, partner?"

Marci glanced at Quinn and straightened. "Not sure. Maybe nothing."

Quinn squinted as he studied Marci's face. He knew that look, and it was one he didn't usually see on her—worry.

"We never found the man in the suit," Leya said, "but the guy with the knife—that was a knife the assailant had, by the way—was detained by transit security. I responded and arrested Craig Taylor, the assailant, on a chippy Failure to Appear warrant. Since I didn't have a victim, there was no crime, and the warrant was the only way I could get him."

"The victim didn't hang around?" Quinn said, focusing on Leya. "From a knife attack? That's suspicious as hell."

"It's definitely something," Leya said. "But there's more."

Marci glanced between the two of them and back to the man on the screen. Quinn caught Marci's movements and was about to ask her something when Leya handed him the second flash drive.

"This is an assault that happened a couple of hours ago at the Western Bank building. A suited man entered an elevator and was met by three ne'er-do-wells."

"Ne'er-do-wells?" Quinn asked.

"Play the video," Marci said, her voice anxious.

Quinn looked at her. "You okay?"

"Just play the video."

He turned back to the computer and double-clicked the file icon. A video of the earlier incident came on. The fight between the suited man and the three attackers played.

"Damn," Quinn said.

"I know, right?" Leya added. "The guy is a total badass."

"He reminds me of you, Marci." Quinn looked at his partner, but she was staring right at the screen. "Marci?"

"Detective?" Leya asked.

"That's Andrew Miller," Marci said.

"How did you know that?" Leya asked.

"He's an instructor at one of the local schools. He's very good."

Quinn pointed at the computer screen. "I'll say."

"We got his name and home address from his office," Leya said. "He left work immediately after this incident."

"He didn't stick around after the elevator incident, either?" Quinn asked.

Leya shook her head. "He wasn't home when McCrea and I stopped by. I left a card for him to call me."

Quinn leaned toward the computer screen for a better look at Miller. "I don't get this guy."

Marci said, "I don't know why he didn't come to us, but he probably didn't want to be involved."

"What do you mean?" Leya said. "He's been attacked twice. He's already involved. The first one may have been random, but it's clear from the second attack that they targeted him."

Marci walked over to her cubicle and grabbed her chair. She then dropped into it. "Andrew's a good guy. I've trained with him a few times. He's a skilled fighter, you've seen that. I talked with him once or twice after the events we were at. He's well respected in our circles."

"He's not in trouble," Leya said. "We need him to press charges against Craig Taylor. We've got two incidents on video. If we can get Taylor, we can get into the group that's playing this game."

Marci nodded. "I know who we can talk with."

Chapter 47

"You look pretty."

"Thanks."

"I'm sure your parents will be happy to see you."

Matt reached over and held Veronica's hand. She turned to look at him. Her eyes were a bit unfocused, and her smile crooked, but she did look beautiful. He'd helped her clean up this afternoon. Veronica didn't want to visit her parents, but it was nearing the end of the month. This was part of the game. To keep living free, they had to stay in touch to show them that she was making progress, getting better, and looking for work. If Veronica didn't go to them, they would come to her. It was better this way.

"Remember what we talked about," Matt said.

"I know, I know," Veronica said. "Jobs are hard to find."

"That's right, but you've applied. That's the important part. If they ask where, then make up some places—restaurants and such. Maybe say you applied for a receptionist's job. Those types of things, you know."

Veronica pulled her hand from his and leaned her head against the window. She frowned as Matt continued to drive.

Her parents lived on the north side of town, in an area known as Suncrest. A flat, boring development built sometime in the seventies. Why anyone would want to live there was beyond Matt. It was too far from anything. Only geezers lived that far away from downtown.

When they arrived, Pam and Russell Schuster were at the front door. They had been expecting them. The Schusters looked like they were posing for an advertisement for a lawn furniture set. They wore perfectly coordinated shorts and polo shirt combos. Veronica opened her car door, then hurried to her parents. She hugged and smiled at her mom first, then her father. The act was on.

They'd been through this type of performance before, and there would be fallout later because of it. Veronica would be depressed on the ride home, need more Oxy when they got there, and she'd be closed off over the next few days. Still, if it got them another month of free rent, it would be worth it.

Matt forced a smile as he approached the front of the house. Veronica's parents eyed him with suspicion.

Inside the house, they sat in the living room, Russell and Pam were on the couch with Veronica. Matt was forced to sit in the recliner nearest the television, which was on, although the volume was low.

Her parents immediately peppered Veronica with questions. Veronica did her best to answer them and assuage their fears. As the three of them prattled on, Matt quickly grew bored. His eyes shifted to the television and the news program that had just started. Matt hadn't watched the news in years, not since living at home with his mother, who was a dedicated news junkie.

After the intro, the banner at the bottom of the screen read *More Knockout Game Attacks*.

His heartbeat accelerated, and he leaned toward the television so he could hear what was being said.

"Four new cases of the knockout game have been reported in Spokane today," the reporter stated, "all of them coming against employees who work downtown. Arrests were made in two of the assaults."

"That's horrible," Pam said.

Matt glanced back at her.

"I can't believe people are doing that to each other."

"Me either," Matt said.

Four attacks? he thought. Only two guys had been sent out, so did that mean people were copying their game? For a moment, jealousy hit Matt, but then he realized this was precisely what they wanted. They wanted confusion and anarchy.

He turned his attention back to the screen and racked his brain for who went out today for the game. Craig was supposed to, but he gave his turn to someone else. Bam Bam. That's right. Bam Bam took his turn. Who was the other hitter? Shaggy. Bam Bam and Shaggy. Did they get picked up? If so, would one of them talk?

When the story of the local assaults was over, the news switched to how the knockout game was resurging nationally. Those assaults weren't directed at particularly anyone, just indiscriminate attacks. A woman had been knocked out in Indiana, and in West Virginia, an elderly black man had died because of a punch.

As he listened to the news report, a frown crossed Matt's lips.

Everyone was missing the point.

Chapter 48

Detectives Quinn Delaney and Marci Burkett parked their car on a side street. It was almost 6 p.m., and the parking lot for Spokane Kenpo Karate was nearly full.

Marci opened the front door, stepped in, and bowed. Ignoring the courtesy afforded the studio, Quinn closed the door behind them.

On the mat were roughly twenty teenagers being instructed by two mid-twenty black belts. They were being led through a variety of striking drills.

The hot and humid environment created by sweating bodies irritated Quinn's nose. He was about to comment on it to Marci, but her eyes were wild with excitement. He knew this look. He'd seen it before when they practiced on the mat during in-service training or when she was about to tangle with a suspect. This was Marci's natural habitat.

An older, gray-haired man walked out of the back office and studied the detectives. His black belt had one very thick red stripe on the lower end and three smaller red lines above. He made his way around the back of the mat toward them.

"What's with the red on the belt?"

"He's an eighth degree."

"That means he's been around a long time?"

"It means to show respect," Marci whispered.

When the man approached, she clasped her hands together, thrust them slightly forward, and bowed her head. He repeated the action to Marci. He then eyed Quinn, who nodded with his chin. The instructor did not repeat that action.

"I'm Mr. Shaw. May I help you?"

"Yes, sir. We've met before. I'm Marci Burkett. I train with Mr. Paddington."

Shaw smiled. "Ms. Burkett, I remember now."

"Mr. Shaw, this is my partner, Detective Delaney. Is there a place we can talk in private?"

He nodded and escorted them back to his office.

On the walls were various photos of Mr. Shaw, his students, and other high-ranking black belts. Shaw sat behind his desk, and the detectives sat in the metal chairs in front.

"We're here about Andrew Miller, sir."

Shaw remained silent, studying Marci.

"He's not done anything wrong, Mr. Shaw. We want to speak with him about a couple of assaults that occurred in downtown."

Mr. Shaw put his elbows on his desk and interlaced his fingers. "Do you suspect him of these assaults? I thought you said he'd done nothing wrong?"

"He was assaulted but defended himself both times. These incidents were caught on camera. Neither time, though, did Mr. Miller stay around to talk with the police."

"Is it a requirement to notify a law enforcement authority if you've defended yourself, yet don't need the protection of the police?"

Marci glanced at Quinn, who was about to speak. She quickly said, "Not really, no. He isn't required to call us if he isn't harmed. However, we'd like to know why he didn't."

"Perhaps he had his reasons," Shaw said.

"It doesn't make sense," Quinn jumped in. "He protected himself. He had nothing to fear from us."

Mr. Shaw's eyes had flicked to Quinn but settled back on Marci when he answered. "Maybe there's more to Mr. Miller than you know."

"Can you tell us?" Marci asked.

"It's not my place."

"Are you serious?" Quinn said.

Shaw didn't look at him. His gaze remained on Marci.

Quinn felt his frustration rising but believed this was some martial arts respect thing. He did his best to keep a poker face. It was harder than he anticipated, and his face warmed.

Marci briefly glanced at her partner before turning to the instructor. "Mr. Shaw, would you ask Mr. Miller to call me?" She pulled out a business card from her pocket and placed it on the desk. "As I said before, he's not in any trouble. We believe the people who attacked him have also attacked others."

"I will do that for you, Ms. Burkett."

Marci stood and bowed to Mr. Shaw. He repeated the same process.

Quinn also stood, but he simply nodded. "Thank you for your time."

As they stepped out of the small office, Marci stopped and turned back to Mr. Shaw. "Sir, Mr. Miller started training with you when he was young, right? He told me that when we were at a seminar."

"Yes. He started when he was roughly twelve years old."

"If I remember this correctly, he left for the military after high school. Army, was it? He came back to training with you many years later."

Shaw nodded. "Your memory is excellent. That is why your instructor says you are an outstanding student. And, I would imagine, a formidable detective as well."

"What did he do in the Army?"

Mr. Shaw inhaled deeply and thought. After he exhaled, he said, "That, Detective, is something you'll need to find out on your own, but what he learned there was far more dangerous and destructive than anything I ever taught him."

Chapter 49

Craig was the first one back to the Fifth Avenue house. He didn't know where Stick and Bam Bam had run off to, and he didn't care. How could they not beat one suit? Craig knew why he couldn't; he was an addict. He wasn't at his best right now, but Bam Bam was a beast. He should have beaten that guy easily. And Stick? Well, shit, he didn't know about Stick. But he looked like a scrapper. Besides, the guy was a suit; they're all weak.

At least, they should be.

Craig ran up the steps to the front door and pulled on the doorknob. It was locked. He pounded on the door. Maybe Matt was nailing Ronnie and couldn't hear him knocking.

But Matt had never locked the house because of that. He'd walked in on him before when he was in the middle of balling her. Craig hurried around to the rear of the house. He didn't like being out in the open. The more he thought about what they did, the more he realized how crazy they were—going inside a building where there might be cameras? Hell, there had to have been cameras. It was stupid. And the elevator? That had to have cameras there, too, right? What was he thinking?

He wasn't thinking. That was the problem. He was only focused on one thing, and now he realized that was wrong, too.

The back door was locked, too. Shit.

He looked around for an open window. After a couple of tries, he found an open one on the west side of the house. He dragged a trash can over, climbed on top of it, and slithered in. He fell to the floor. He was inside Matt and

Ronnie's bedroom. He was about to walk out but stopped and looked back at their nightstand. On it was a bottle of pills.

Craig shook a couple free and dry-swallowed them, one at a time. While the pills took their time to kick in, he decided to have a look around. He pulled open the top drawer of the nightstand. Matt's gun was in there. Craig picked it up and looked at it for a moment. Then he put it away. He went through some other drawers for a few minutes.

When the pills finally started to kick in, he stopped and smiled. He walked into the living room and sat on the couch. He only needed a few minutes to clear his head and focus on a plan. For a moment, he wondered what happened with Bam Bam and Stick.

Fuck those guys, he thought and fell asleep.

Chapter 50

"You sure you don't want anything to eat?"

"I'm good," Andrew Miller said.

Candace Ward stared at her boyfriend. "You feeling okay?"

Andrew forced a smile. "Tough day at work."

"You never have a tough day at the office."

"Today was tough," he said. He grabbed the remote and turned on the television. The six o'clock news was about to start.

Candace was a tall woman with long dark hair, the type that shined under lights. She wore a yellow summer dress with printed bumblebees buzzing about. Her left arm was tattooed in a sleeve of images—a cascading waterfall, a panther, and foliage dominated the landscape of her skin. Her lips were a dark shade of red. She was an image of a 1960s housewife mashed together with a punk rock lead singer. On most nights, Andrew couldn't keep his eyes off her. Tonight, he was lost in thought.

"Why aren't you in class?"

"Huh?"

"Class, Mr. Karate Man." She mimed two knife-hands, chopping in the air. "Aren't you teaching tonight?"

Andrew shook his head. "I called Mr. Shaw and told him I wouldn't be in. My heart's not in it."

Her eyes softened. "You did have a tough day."

Andrew nodded. "That's what I've been trying to say."

"Want to skip our date? Maybe hang out alone at home?"

"I'd rather be with you."

Candace kissed him on the forehead. "That's the right answer. How about I make some dinner, and you relax for a bit?"

Andrew nodded absently. Even though the television was silenced, words at the bottom of the screen had grabbed his attention. *Return of the Knockout Game.*

He turned up the volume and leaned forward in his chair.

Chapter 51

Although it was almost 7 p.m., the department was still hectic with activity. Not a single chief nor other high-ranking official had left the building. Captain Ackerman had been busy running from one proverbial fire to the next, getting information, and then relaying it. He felt more like a paperboy than a department head.

When the team investigating the recent wave of crimes arrived, Ackerman inwardly smiled. Finally, he could focus on real police work and lead. Detectives Delaney and Burkett, along with Officer Navarro, were waiting for him in the conference room. His assistant had made copies of the latest assault reports, which he tucked into a folder.

When he walked in, the three of them were cordial, even Burkett, who could be surly at times. He passed out the reports, placed a yellow notepad in front of himself, and picked up his pen.

"You've been to the crime scene on a couple of these, but here are the latest reports from the officers who responded. This is your show. Tell me what you know and what you think."

Delaney pulled the copies of the reports to him.

Burkett said, "Regarding the homicide of Arthur McKee, we firmly believe it was random. We interviewed his wife and co-workers. Nothing stood out. There was nothing wrong in his life."

Delaney looked up from the report he was reading, made eye contact with Ackerman, and nodded in agreement with his partner's assessment.

Burkett continued, "Therefore, we believe it was directly tied into this knockout game."

Ackerman made a note on his pad. "What else?"

Navarro said, "We've identified two suspects so far."

"Two? I thought we only had one. I haven't seen a report on that yet."

"I was working on it when we were called in here."

Ackerman couldn't tell if there was a hint of insubordination in Navarro's tone, or if it was the fact that she was sitting next to Burkett. Whatever it was, he didn't like it. He glared at her, and she continued.

"You're aware of the first suspect who is known by moniker only: Denver. Crime Analysis has no one in the system with that moniker matching the assailant's description. I also stopped by the transit authority's security office to see if they had anyone in their files with that moniker. Nothing."

Ackerman made an entry on his notepad while Navarro continued.

"The second assailant is known to us. Craig Taylor. I arrested him earlier this week for an FTA warrant. He was seen today in an elevator involved in an of an Andrew Miller. We believe that assault was relevant to my contact with Taylor earlier in the week. He also attempted to assault Miller then."

"I don't understand."

Navarro explained the knife attack and then the assault in the elevator.

"Crazy," the captain said.

"You should see the video," Delaney said. "It's impressive."

"What kind of man can do this?"

"He's a fourth-degree black belt," Burkett said.

"Can all black belts do that?"

Burkett shook her head. "A few, but not all. A piece of the puzzle is missing. I'm working on it."

"Is this— What's his name? Miller? Is he part of the problem?" Ackerman asked.

"I don't know," Burkett said, "but they've attacked him twice now. Who knows if they'll continue to go after him."

"When we find Miller," Navarro said, "we can get him to press charges against Craig Taylor. That's our entry point into this group."

Delaney looked up from the reports. "Four new assaults today. One of them we know about involves Miller. That fits our profile. There's a second, another white male in a suit. But these last two, they don't fit the pattern. No one was recording, and the targets were all wrong. Patrol caught the suspects in the last two. Why weren't we notified?"

Ackerman said, "I made the call. I see the pattern you've all identified. The copycats are in lockup now if you want to talk with them, but I didn't want you guys to waste your time. I'm wasting enough time for all of us. I'm answering to the chiefs, the mayor, the council, and the press. Everybody wants answers, but nobody wants to take any responsibility. The ball can't roll further downhill right now, so it's stuck at my level. I'd love to push it to your lieutenant, but then that would be my ass again when he screws up. My job is to run interference and keep you guys in the game. Unless, of course, you still want to go interview the copycats."

Delaney and Burkett looked at each other.

"We're good," they said in unison.

Chapter 52

"Did you see the news?"

Rabbit nodded.

They were standing in the front room, their voices low. While at Veronica's parents' house, Matt had texted Rabbit to check out the news, then meet him at the house.

Matt had just gotten Veronica to bed. She was wound up after visiting her parents, and all she wanted when they got home was to take a pill and go to sleep. He was glad for that because his mind hadn't stopped working since he saw the reports on the various assaults.

"What do you think?" Matt asked.

"I dunno."

Matt walked in circles. "We've got to come up with a plan."

"I thought this was the plan."

Matt stopped and stared at him.

"You said you were bored. That you wanted some action."

"Listen, man, just because I said that doesn't mean I want to get my ass in hot water, know what I mean?"

"I guess," Rabbit said. The confusion was clear on his face.

"How does this blowback on us?"

"Well, you started the game."

"Me?"

"We," Rabbit said. "We started the game."

"Right." Matt crossed his arms and closed his eyes.

"I should let you know about your brother," Rabbit said.

Matt opened his eyes. "What about my brother?"

"He was here when I arrived."

"On the porch?"

"Inside."

"How did he get inside? You're the only person with a key besides Ronnie and me."

"He just was."

Matt walked over to Rabbit and stood directly in front of him. "What was he doing?"

Rabbit pointed at the couch. "He was asleep. He didn't hear me come in."

Matt tilted his head, trying to understand the implication.

"He was out of it, man. I had to shake him awake. He was all fucked up."

"Shit."

"When he realized it was me, he looked around for a moment. He looked scared. Then he got up and ran out of the house."

Matt walked to the back bedroom. Veronica was already asleep. He lifted the bottle of Oxy pills to the light. It was more than half empty. *Dammit*. He shoved the bottle into his pocket.

When he returned to the front room, he said, "If he comes back, keep an eye on him."

Rabbit nodded.

"And when the others show up, peel Gadget off. I want to propose a new plan."

Chapter 53

After putting the children to bed, Leya Navarro sat on the couch with her husband. Ernie rubbed her feet but didn't say anything. After a decade of marriage, Ernie knew Leya would talk about the job when she was ready. Since she got home from the department, she had remained quiet.

Ernie made dinner for the girls, helped them with their homework, and got them ready for bed. When Leya walked in the door, Ernie was on the couch reading a book.

She sipped her wine as the tension eased out from her feet.

They were quiet for some time before Leya said, "Have you seen the news?"

"Lots of news. Anything special I should have noticed?"

"The knockout game."

Ernie rubbed the arch of her foot, which elicited a small moan of pleasure from Leya.

"I saw it. Is that what you're working on?"

"Yeah."

"How do you stop that? Isn't it random?"

Leya took another sip of wine. "We thought it was. Now, we're not so sure."

Ernie didn't respond. Instead, he continued to rub her feet, waiting for her to tell the rest of the story. Five long minutes passed. When she began to snore softly, Ernie smiled.

He gently picked up her glass of wine and put it to the side. Then he lifted Leya carefully so as not to wake her and carried her to bed.

ROUND FIVE

Chapter 54

They were waiting in the conference room when she arrived—Captain Ackerman, along with Detectives Delaney and Burkett. One of the IT guys—the patchouli-smelling kid with the man bun—was seated behind a computer.

"Did you see the video?" Ackerman asked, skipping any formalities.

Leya looked to Quinn and Marci, who both looked worried.

"What video?" she asked, taking a seat next to the captain.

Ackerman nodded toward the man-bun, and he clicked a key on his computer. The screen on the wall came alive. "We captured this before Facebook deactivated the account. However, it was copied and sent out. We also discovered it on YouTube, Twitter, and Instagram. A shorter version of it has been reported on Snapchat. It's like trying to stop celebrity porn," the man-bun said. "Once it's out there, it's out there."

"What is it?" Leya asked.

The video started. A black screen appeared with the words WAKE UP. Then it showed one of the assaults that Leya had investigated. The angle made it hard to identify the attacker, but the victim could be seen before and after. A modulated voice said, *"It's time for the ninety-nine percent to rise up against the one percent. We must stand together and show them who we are. Drop a suit today. We won't be silenced."* The same video was shown again with the poor angle of the attacker.

"When did this first appear?" Quinn asked.

Ackerman looked at his notes. "Two seventeen a.m."

"How'd we find it?"

"I received a call from the chief after the mayor called him. He'd gotten a call from a constituent who chewed his ear. All hell broke loose after that."

"I can imagine," Quinn said.

"Which assault is that?" Ackerman asked.

"Duane Violette," Leya said.

"Not the homicide?"

"Not the homicide," Quinn confirmed.

"Why now?" Marci asked.

"I don't understand the question," Ackerman said. "I mean, I understand what you're asking, but I don't understand the context."

"Wouldn't they have been better served to start this video before they started knocking people out?"

While the four of them contemplated the question, man-bun stared awkwardly on.

Chapter 55

Andrew Miller left Candace's house early in the morning. He slipped out of bed, kissed her once, and was gone. He wasn't even sure she was aware he left.

He drove home, took a shower, and got dressed for work.

His head hurt from a lack of sleep. Dreams of Africa plagued him. He hadn't brought any Ambien with him to Candace's house. He'd been trained to fight through a lack of sleep. One day should barely affect him.

In the bathroom, Andrew tossed a couple of ibuprofen into his mouth. Then he headed to the kitchen and brewed a cup of coffee with his Keurig machine. When the coffee was made, he turned on the television and watched the morning news.

There were further updates about the knockout game, including a disturbing video that had been released overnight.

According to the news report, the video originated in Spokane, Washington. The location in the video had been authenticated. Authorities were trying to verify the IP address where the video had been uploaded. Until then, authorities warned males wearing suits in any metropolitan area to be careful. It seemed to be an overreaction, but there had been six attacks on white males in suits in downtown Spokane alone. Across the nation, the numbers had skyrocketed to almost a hundred.

Andrew looked down at his suit and carefully smoothed his tie. He took a final sip of coffee before leaving for downtown.

Chapter 56

At the Jacobs Java coffee house on Monroe Street, Detective Marci Burkett sat on a wooden bench under a gazebo. She sipped her flavored coffee and watched the traffic pass. The morning sun shone down and warmed her face.

She'd been there for several minutes when a man in blue jeans and a black polo shirt exited the bistro. With an iced coffee in his hand, he crossed the small, landscaped area. He sat next to Marci on the wooden bench but stared straight ahead. He sipped his coffee before saying, "The red fox runs quickly through the meadow."

Marci smirked. "Zane, you are so full of it."

Zane Ingram laughed and turned to face her. "I thought you would like to do this all clandestine-like. Maybe spice up your day."

"My day is already spicy enough. I just want some answers."

He draped an arm over the back of the bench but didn't say anything.

"What?"

"You only call me when you want something related to work. There used to be a time when you called me for—"

"Dude, there was never a time I called you for that."

"A guy can dream, can't he? I've been trying to get you to go out with me for years. What's it going to take—"

She held up her hand, stopping him from continuing. "It won't happen. Can you help me or not?"

"I can, but can we talk about us first?"

"There won't be an us. Not even for a minute. Get over it and be professional."

Zane lifted his face to the sun and closed his eyes. "You hurt my heart."

"There are plenty of girls out there who will buy your spy-with-a-broken-heart routine. Take it on the road."

Zane grinned with his eyes still closed. "I'm not a spy."

"You're a fed. You all smell the same way."

"Ouch."

"Are you going to help me or not?"

"Why do you want this information, Marci?"

"We can only get so far with our security clearances. I know you can get deeper."

"What you asked for is some serious shit, Marci. The FBI isn't here to do local PD's background checks."

"Please, Zane," Marci said, softening her voice. "What did you find?"

Zane opened his eyes and sipped his iced coffee. "How do you know Andrew Miller?"

"He was attacked twice but didn't stick around either time to talk with the police. We want to know why."

"Was he hurt?"

"No."

"Then he didn't need you. Beyond that, you don't need to know about him."

"Don't bullshit me. He ties into something bigger. The guys playing this knockout game are targeting him."

"Yeah?"

"Yeah."

"This took favors," Zane said.

"I'm not sleeping with you."

"I'm not that crude, Marci. I wasn't implying some nasty quid pro quo. What I'm saying is finding out about your guy took work. It took phone calls and calling in markers. There's a reason for that."

"And what reason is that?"

"Your guy is dangerous."

"Dangerous? Like *dangerous* dangerous?"

Zane nodded.

"How dangerous?"

"Like Schwarzenegger in *Commando* dangerous."

"I don't get that reference."

"If you went to the movies with me, you'd get a reference like that."

"Dude, enough. Make with the intel."

Zane slurped his coffee.

"I'm not going out with you."

He shrugged before saying, "Have you ever heard of First Special Forces Operational Detachment Delta?"

Marci scrunched her nose. "That sounds like federal-level gobbledygook."

"You might have heard it referred to as Delta Force."

Her eyes slanted. "That's a Hollywood thing."

"Oh, no, it's for real, but they'd love for you to believe they're make-believe. Back in the day, when the Navy SEALs started, they were also a clandestine group."

"They still are, right?"

"I meant clandestine to outsiders. The Navy didn't want anyone to know they existed. The further in the black hole they were, the better they could operate. Does that make sense?"

"Sure."

"The SEALs were born out of the Viet Nam war. Delta followed in the late seventies and were based on the British SAS. The backstory doesn't really matter, just that Delta was pulled out of the Army and moved under Joint Special Operations Command, just like the SEALs. JSOC is the secret squirrel branch of special operations. The guys who participate in this are better than the best."

"And Andrew Miller was one of them?"

"Was, yes. He enlisted in the Army after high school, went through infantry training, then Ranger school. From what I was told, the guy was a natural. A go-getter who was recruited to Delta where he excelled."

"He's only thirty-eight. Why's he wearing a suit? Shouldn't he still be in the military doing something high-speed and low-drag?"

"What I'm about to tell you is classified, but I'll redact the hell out of it so you can hear it."

Marci tipped her cup toward him. "Redact away."

Zane glanced around before talking. "Miller and his team were on a search-and-extract mission. Their target was in a nasty hotspot in Africa called the Central African Republic. Ever heard of it? No? Doesn't matter, most people haven't. As its name implies, it sits in the middle of the continent. It gained its independence in 1960. In the early part of the new millennium, there was a coup that removed the president. Since then, it's been nothing but civil wars and ethnic and religious cleansings at the level of genocide. Your basic shithole if you know what I mean."

"I'll scratch it from my vacation wish-list," Marci said.

"Good plan. Anyway, Delta was tasked to go in there and extract a high-value asset. They were working with the Night Stalkers. How about them? Heard of 'em? Geez, do you ever watch any movies? Anyway, they're the elite helicopter pilots that work with Delta and other various special operations groups. Miller's team was on an MH-6, one of those little bug-looking helicopters, when it went down. Delta had already grabbed their target and was heading out. The asset was on another chopper, so when Miller's bird experienced trouble, it was determined by command to continue the mission and bring the high-value asset home. Headquarters immediately dispatched a rescue team, which had been standing by. Mission precautions dictated a backup chopper to stand by."

Marci completely turned to face the agent next to her. "Was Miller's helicopter shot down?"

Zane shook his head. "It was a mechanical failure. Murphy's law—if something can go wrong…"

"I understand."

"So, the chopper was going down, but the pilot held it together and made an emergency landing. When it hit, the team was immediately on the move. There were six of them, four operators and two pilots. They destroyed the Little Bird before heading out. That was when the real fight started."

"Did this ever make the news?" Marci asked. "I don't remember hearing anything about this."

Zane ignored her question and continued. "They moved through several neighborhoods, taking fire and fighting back. Finally, a woman allowed them into her home, and the team had a place to take shelter while they waited for help to arrive. She was a single woman with two young boys, one roughly twelve, the other maybe ten. When one of the men asked where her husband was, she said he had been killed in the town's in-fighting. They hardly owned anything. A mattress was on the floor in one room where supposedly the three slept together. Minimal furniture otherwise. No TV, obviously. I don't remember if there was running water, a bathroom."

"You saw a report on this?"

"Like what I'm telling you, it was redacted. Even at my clearance, it was blacked out so heavily I had to put pieces together, make additional calls, dig deeper to get a clear story."

Marci stared at Zane, who sipped the remaining coffee from his plastic cup. It gurgled when he was done.

"It was a trap," Zane continued. "While the six men took up various positions at the windows, looking outside, the two boys ambushed them with rifles. They had them hidden somewhere in a back room. When they initially cleared the house, Miller's team didn't find them. We'll never know whose responsibility it was, although Miller said during the debriefing it was his, that he should have found the weapons. Anyway, when the boys entered the room firing, Miller was the farthest from them. He spun and shot them both, but not until after they had mortally wounded his team."

"Damn," Marci whispered.

"When the mother came running into the room, she saw her children and immediately began screaming. She clutched them to her and shouted at Miller, who was the only other living soul in the room. Knowing her screaming would further alert trouble to their presence, he did what he thought was necessary."

"Oh, God," Marci said.

Zane looked at her. "When help arrived, which was only seconds, maybe minutes later, they extracted the bodies and got Miller out of there. When he returned to base, he wasn't the same. He was sent to a battery of therapists before being medically discharged."

"Had he been wounded?"

"Not during that incident."

"Then why was he released?

"A soldier who won't kill is like a hammer that won't hit a nail. Its use is limited."

"He wouldn't fight anymore?"

"He simply lost the desire to carry a weapon. Not much use on a Delta team for that."

Marci slowly nodded as she realized the impact of Zane's words.

"The Army offered him a variety of therapists and group counseling. Miller went but asked to be released from the team. Something broke inside him that day. No matter what the Army did, they couldn't bring it back. He returned to the home he remembered, but his parents had since moved to Arizona to retire. He finished college, got a job, and made a life for himself."

Zane studied his empty coffee cup while Marci thought about what he just shared. Finally, she said, "You spent a lot of time on this, Zane. Why?"

"The guy is an American hero, Marci. He was put in an unwinnable situation and survived. I don't know if I could have done that. Whatever he's found himself involved in now, I want to make sure your department treats him with respect."

"He's not in trouble, Zane."

"That's good," he said, watching the traffic pass by.

They sat silently for several minutes. Finally, Zane shook his empty coffee cup, rattling the ice around. "Next time you need info, I'm going to make you pay for my coffee."

"The next time I need info, I promise to buy."

Chapter 57

"What do you mean we're stopping the game?" Henry said. "I have a chance to get ahead of Bam Bam now."

The crew was gathered in the Fifth Avenue house. With his left hand bandaged, Bam Bam sulked in the corner. Craig was noticeably absent.

Matt said, "It's too dangerous now since the cops are everywhere. The game has made national news. Others are playing, too."

"But they're not playing for *our* money," Stick said, pointing to the list of names on the wall.

"Yeah, man," Denver chimed in. "We want a shot at that cash."

Matt glanced at Rabbit, then to Gadget before saying, "We released a video last night."

"What do you mean?" Henry asked.

Matt pointed to Gadget, who called it up on his phone. The guys gathered around him, and they watched the video. "Oh," they said when they saw Gadget's knockout punch.

"You're gonna be famous," Henry said.

"The cops saw Gadget's punch?" Critter asked.

"You can't see his face in the video. We made sure of it. And we didn't use anyone else's, so no one can be upset."

"Why did you do it?" Denver asked. "You're telling us to quit playing, but you're poking the bear? I don't get it."

"The game the others are playing isn't the game we're playing. They're hitting women and people like us. Not suits. Not the one percent."

"So, if you get them hitting suits?" Stick asked.

"It muddies the water," Matt said. "The more suits that are knocked out, the less attention is paid to us."

"That's genius," Shaggy muttered.

Matt allowed a smile at the praise.

Henry looked at the other guys. "I don't care. It doesn't change anything. I mean, I still want to play."

Matt's eyes flicked to Rabbit, who stared straight ahead. He knew he sensed it, too. No matter which way they turned, there was real danger.

After several minutes of squabbling, the group collectively agreed they should continue playing. Matt knew better than to fight a united crew.

Henry pointed at Rabbit. "Bring on the bowl, bitch. Let's get this round moving. Shaggy already struck out on his second try."

The crew laughed while Shaggy tried to defend himself. "The cops were everywhere. I never got a chance."

Critter rolled his eyes. "C'mon, man. You had plenty of chances. You didn't take any of them."

The guys laughed again.

Rabbit looked at Matt, who waved his hand in resignation.

When Rabbit grabbed the ceramic bowl, everyone cheered except Bam Bam, who dejectedly looked on as he held his damaged hand.

Matt reached in and pulled out two name strips. "Stick and Henry," he said with no enthusiasm. "You're up. Pick a couple of guys to follow."

He tossed the name strips on the table and walked toward the back of the house, leaving the guys cheering amongst themselves. As he closed his bedroom door, Rabbit was enthusiastically shouting orders.

Chapter 58

Henry got his wish when his name was drawn.

Gremlin and Denver were his wingmen, and they'd left the house immediately. Henry felt like a heat-guided missile launched from a tube. He would destroy the first suit he found.

"Slow down," Gremlin said as he struggled to keep pace with him.

Henry couldn't believe how things had changed since the game started. Were people really playing in other states because of them? How cool was that? Henry made it to the corner of Second Avenue and Howard Street and stopped. His eyes scanned the streets. Gremlin and Denver caught up to him, slightly out of breath.

"Get out your phones. I'm ready to strike," Henry said. Blood pounded inside his head.

Both of his friends dug their phones out.

Henry spotted a guy in a suit and locked eyes on him. He stepped toward him but suddenly stopped.

Is that sonofabitch looking at me?

Is this brazen sonofabitch really making eye contact with me?

Henry glanced back to Gremlin and Denver. "You see this?"

"I think dude wants his ass kicked," Denver said, along with a nervous chuckle.

Gremlin said, "Hey, man, maybe you should reconsider? That guy doesn't look right."

"Start rolling," Henry said and walked toward the suit. He exaggeratedly rolled his shoulders, like a fighter walking toward a boxing ring. When the suit smiled, Henry straightened and stopped showing off.

The hell is wrong with this guy?

Henry thought the guy should know better. Or at least, the guy should be afraid, right?

The suit maintained eye contact with Henry until he was within striking distance. When Henry swung his haymaker, the suit slipped the punch and was no longer there. Henry spun around. The suit just stood there, watching him.

Henry's mind raced. The rules of the game said he couldn't engage unless the victim decided to fight back, and he wasn't fighting back. Henry's body tingled with the anticipation of throwing another punch.

When the suit smiled, Henry muttered, "Fuck it," and drew his fist back for another punch.

The suit kicked him on the inside of the leg, spinning his body and dropping him to one knee. The only thought Henry had at that moment was, *What the—?*

He looked back at the suit as a punch connected with his chin.

Chapter 59

Emile Berger was ready for a fight. He'd watched the morning news warning men who wore suits to be careful about the spread of the knockout game. To be honest, that caution didn't scare him. It did the opposite; it thrilled him.

Life was stale. He was thirty years old, but he already felt like he wanted to quit, pack it all in. He wanted something to shake it up, make him feel alive again.

He was married to a beautiful yet cold wife with two bratty kids. Things had been better before the children, something he admitted aloud once to his wife and was scolded harshly over for days. Emile never mentioned those feelings again, but they remained, nonetheless.

There was a mortgage payment on their house, which was now worth less than what they paid for it. He was still making payments on two cars, one of which was wrecked and parked in the driveway waiting for an insurance decision that had already been delayed three weeks after the collision.

There were mandatory weekend dinners with the in-laws because his wife demanded it, so she could still spend time with her family. He rarely saw his parents because she thought they were too pedestrian. He didn't know what she meant when she called them that, but he was too afraid to ask and risk being admonished for not being smarter.

He worked as a loan processor, where the entire creativity of his day was deciding which box to fill in: A or B, yes or no, approve or deny. Someday, software would make his job moot, and he'd be out of a job, replaced by bits and bytes. He dreaded that day, but still welcomed its arrival because it would put him out of his misery.

How he hated it all, hated them all. He wished he had the balls to tell everyone in his life just to fuck off, the he would leave this town and start over. Maybe go somewhere tropical, be someone new, someone different. Maybe find a girl with cinnamon skin who wouldn't point her finger at him.

Instead, he was the same ol' Emile Berger, the guy he saw in the mirror every morning, the guy whose eyes always looked too sleepy and whose hair was beginning to thin around the temples. He'd be that same guy even if he moved to a new town. He'd be the same guy until he died.

The only thing he loved now was the mixed martial arts class he started attending six months ago. It wasn't a traditional karate school. No bullshit belts. No kiss ass ceremonies. Just hit and get hit. Get it on and train.

He'd never been hit before signing up for lessons. Not even in grade school. To his surprise, he loved mixing it up on the mat. He loved the sweat, the competition, and the camaraderie. He wouldn't and couldn't admit it to his wife, but he loved the grappling part the best, especially rolling around on the mat with the Latin fighter, Manuela. Tall and muscular, she was on her way to becoming a real fighter. He knew he was playing around, working out to pretend he could get in a ring someday. She was there to train, to win real matches. He came in three days a week, one hour at a time. She was there six days a week, and God knows how many hours.

He liked grappling with her whenever the instructor matched them together. She was much better than him. There was no comparison. She only worked with him due to his size versus hers. But he liked it, especially the feeling of occasionally weighing on her. He even liked it when she dominated him. He especially liked that.

He needed to wipe those thoughts from his mind. He had an hour-long lunch, and he was putting himself out as bait, walking the streets, keeping his eyes down but trying to be aware.

The girls in the loan department thought he was crazy for wearing a suit today. He made a big show of how he wasn't going to be afraid of some street thugs. Even his boss, who came into work wearing khakis and a polo shirt, thought he had made a poor decision. His boss was a potato, a gut with legs. Who cared what he thought?

Emile wasn't afraid. Not anymore.

He noticed a thin, redheaded man standing at the corner. Two guys were with him, standing close behind. The redhead eyed him. Emile had seen that look before when he'd been on the mat. Even newbies sized each other up before they sparred. Gladiators probably did it before they battled in the Roman arenas.

He fought back a smile and slowly headed for the man. The redhead said something to his friends and walked his way.

Emile shook his hands and reminded himself to stay loose. Adrenaline surged through him now. It was worse than anything he'd ever felt before. His breathing suddenly became shallow, and his vision became hyper-focused on his opponent.

Relax, he screamed inside his head. Let him punch first. You don't want to get in trouble with the law.

Emile stopped walking, but the redhead continued to approach.

Where is the attack coming from?

The kid was bent slightly forward, his shoulders swayed, bouncing side to side.

Oh, God, what should I be looking for?

The thoughts in Emile's head swirled like a hurricane.
Right hand?
Left hand?
A kick?
Would he kick?
The man's eyes were menacing as he focused on Emile.
Stop looking at his eyes! Emile chastised himself. *Think!*
A panicked thought raced through his mind, which gave him renewed hope. *Most people are right-handed.*
Right hand!
The redhead was almost within striking distance.
Should I strike first?
Blood pounded in his ears.
Hit him before he can hit me?
He couldn't hear anything but his heart and his fears.
No! I could get in trouble for that.
His mouth was dry, and he couldn't swallow.
I don't want to go to jail.
Emile's brain screamed, *Right hand!* which caused his eyes to flick to where his thoughts told him to look.
The redhead hit him with his left hand.

Chapter 60

Officer Leya Navarro responded to the scene of an assault. According to dispatch, a man was down, and there were witnesses. She didn't hold any hopes of getting something useful since the attacker had fled the scene.

When she got out of her car, she saw Officer Ken Jarvis interviewing a young male in tattered jeans and a T-shirt. This wasn't the M.O. she was searching for.

Paramedics were attending to the male who didn't seem to want their services. He repeatedly pushed their hands away.

She paused for a moment and wondered if she should even engage Jarvis. She could get back in her car and just drive away. She had been on her way to contact some of the local school security officers to see if they had ever come across the moniker of Denver. The department was already on heightened awareness for Craig Taylor, but so far, no one had found him.

Jarvis saw her and walked over. "What's up, Leya?"

"I was hoping we'd catch one."

"We did."

Leya looked at the guy sitting on the curb. "What do you mean?"

"This turd attacked some suit. It didn't go his way."

Leya's eyes went from Jarvis to the dirty man sitting on the curb. "You're kidding me."

"Don't believe me? Ask the witnesses." He pointed to several teenagers standing together.

Leya walked over to three teenaged girls. "You saw what happened?"

They started talking at the same time, so Leya held up her hands. "One at a time. You." She pointed to one girl. "Come over here and tell me what you saw."

The two of them walked out of earshot of the others. The girl introduced herself as Melissa Tierney. "Now, Melissa, tell me what you saw."

"I can do better than that," she said and pulled out her phone.

"You recorded it?"

"I was recording my girlfriends. We're sending a birthday greeting to a friend in Seattle. That doesn't matter, does it? What does, is that guy there—" She nodded at the man sitting on the curb. "—headed for some suit, but the suit didn't seem to care. Sort of the opposite if you ask me. I think he wanted to be approached."

When Melissa started the video, Leya moved closer to her and watched. The video started with two of the girls in the frame, then moved to the guys in the background. By stance and walk, it was apparent a fight was about to occur. It was definitely Andrew Miller, and he appeared to be waiting for the three men to notice him. When they did, the large one stalked toward him, his shoulders swinging wildly. That stopped, though, when he realized Miller wasn't moving but just watching him. He then continued walking until he was within striking distance and threw a wild punch. Miller slipped it easily and then watched his attacker, waiting for him to make another move.

Miller could have attacked at any moment, but he chose to wait for the dirtball to punch a second time. Then there was a blur of motion before the man was on the ground. Miller calmly walked toward the two other men filming him. They didn't run but stood there with the camera focused on him. He said something before they turned and ran.

"The hell was that? I couldn't hear what he said. Did you hear?"

"No, there was too much traffic noise."

"Can you send me the video? I'd like to get a copy of it."

"You can get it off my Facebook or Instagram pages. I've uploaded it. It's trending already." Her face lit up with excitement. "I'm getting a lot of likes."

"You *uploaded* it?" Leya asked.

Chapter 61

The two men hid behind the bushes along the edge of a McDonald's parking lot. They watched the female police officer interview a witness. They had no idea Andrew Miller was watching them. He had tracked them after the confrontation with their friend. They had left him behind without a second thought.

Andrew leaned against a support column for the overhead freeway. *Why am I doing this?* he wondered.

Admittedly, it felt good to hit the other man with such ferocity. Surprisingly good. The recent confrontations reminded him of a person he thought buried in the past. He had contained that side of himself for years, ever since that moment in the desert.

What was he expecting to happen now?

He wasn't sure, but he wouldn't go back to the office. This was more fun than numbers and spreadsheets.

He could continue surveilling these two and see where they would go. However that played out, he could then decide on what to do next. That was a choice he liked. It was one that felt natural.

Right now, he felt like a lion watching two unaware hyenas.

The thought made him smile.

Chapter 62

"My name is Detective Burkett, and this is Detective Delaney. We'd like to talk with you about the assault today."

As he studied the lady cop, Henry Ramos leaned back in his chair, which forced the front legs off the floor. "Am I under arrest?"

"No, you're not," she said. "If you were, I would have read you your rights, and that little light up in the middle of the wall would be red. That would mean we were recording this interview, which we're not. We're just talking."

"So I'm free to go?"

"You are, but we need your help. Will you hear me out?"

It sounded like typical cop bullshit, but Henry played along. "My help?"

"We're trying to find the man who assaulted you. He's a suspect in a recent assault at the Western Bank Building. He beat up several guys in an elevator. He might have hurt one of them badly."

Henry dropped into his chair and leaned his elbows on the table. She was talking about Bam Bam, Stick, and Craig. The suit that did him was the same guy? That wasn't a coincidence. He was hunting them.

"Don't forget that one at the bus plaza," the guy cop said.

Burkett snapped her fingers. "That's right. Henry, this same suit, the one that hit you, the one that beat up the three guys inside the elevator, is the same guy who also beat down some dude at the bus plaza."

Craig.

He had that tape over his nose and those raccoon eyes. The sneaky son-of-a-bitch, Henry thought. He knew something wasn't right with him. He must have set the guy off and put him on their trail. When he got done with these cops, he was going to square things up with Craig, and that junkie wasn't going to see straight for weeks.

"You know the guy we're talking about," Burkett said. It wasn't a question.

"No," Henry said, shaking his head. "I don't."

"You nodded when I mentioned the incident at the bus plaza. Didn't he nod, partner?"

There was a knock on the door, and Delaney opened it, clearly irritated by the interruption. A skinny guy with one of those stupid hairballs on his head said, "I got what you've asked for."

"Gimme a minute," Delaney said and stepped out.

"I didn't nod," Henry said.

Burkett shrugged. "That's cool. I thought you might have known this suit."

"Do I look like I would know a suit?"

"Everybody knows a suit."

"Not me."

"My captain is a suit. The mayor is a suit. My attorney is a suit."

"Do you like them?" Henry asked.

The lady cop smiled. "Not really."

"That's why I don't know any suits."

The door to the interview room opened, and Delaney re-entered. He closed the door behind him. He had a computer tablet with him. "I've got a few things to show you, Mr. Ramos."

"Like what?"

"The assault at the bus plaza. Want to see it?"

Henry smiled and nodded. "Oh, yeah."

Delaney tapped the screen, and a video started. He turned the tablet so Henry could more easily see it. Henry's eyes widened as he watched Craig lunge toward the suit. He laughed as the suit countered with a punch and a kick that knocked Craig to the ground.

"Shit!" Henry exclaimed and then laughed.

"You know either of those men?" Burkett asked.

Henry shook his head, still laughing. Delaney replayed the short video for him.

When it was over, Burkett asked, "You sure you don't know him?" She pointed at Craig.

"Did the idiot try to stab that guy?"

"He tried."

"Damn." Henry looked from Burkett, then to Delaney. "The dumbass really tried to stab someone. Why would he do that?"

Burkett said, "You'll have to ask him."

Henry chuckled. "Nice try, Detective, but I don't know him. That's classic, though. What a dumbass."

"Here's the next video," Delaney said.

It was the video the young woman had taken of Henry's confrontation with the suit. When he saw it, his smile faded. He saw his initial punch miss, and then the second punch got interrupted by a kick to the inside of the leg that turned his body. Then he saw the suit's punch, which knocked him out. He rubbed his chin as the video continued to play. The suit walked over to Denver and Gremlin. He didn't hit them, and they didn't attack him.

Pussies, Henry thought.

Whatever the suit said caused his friends to turn tail and run away. When he found them, he was going to kick their asses for not standing up for him. That was three people he owed beatings.

"That's definitely the same suit from the bus plaza, right?" Burkett asked.

Henry didn't see any harm in admitting it. "I guess so."

"Want to watch the video again?" Delaney asked.

Still rubbing his chin, Henry said, "No."

Burkett made a fist and examined her knuckles. "Who were the two guys with you?"

"I was alone. Nobody was with me."

"They were filming you," she said.

"Nobody was filming me. They were probably just there. Like the person who took the video we're watching. They were just there. People on a street corner."

"Final video," Delaney said.

"I think I'm gonna go," Henry said.

"Stay for this last one," Burkett said. "You'll like it, I promise."

Henry stared at her until Delaney got the last video running on the tablet. It looked like it was the inside of the elevator. "The suit we've been talking about—he took out three guys inside an elevator."

As the video played, Henry watched the suit beat up Bam Bam, Stick, and Craig. Near the end of the fight, the suit stomped down on Bam Bam's hand, breaking it.

Henry winced and muttered, "Damn."

Burkett leaned forward. "Brutal, huh?"

"Yeah."

"Notice anything?"

"What?"

"That guy there," she said, tapping the screen where Craig was, "he didn't do anything in the fight. He just stood there. Scared out of his mind."

Delaney backed up the video for a few seconds and started it again. Henry watched Craig stand frozen with fear as the suit attacked Bam Bam and Stick. Then the suit lashed out and struck Craig in the face, dropping him to the floor. The detective stopped the video.

Henry's lip curled.

"That's the guy from the bus plaza," Burkett said. "That's the guy you tangled with."

"I see that."

"Do you know any of the guys in this video?"

Henry shook his head.

"We know that one," Burkett said, tapping the tablet. "That's Craig Taylor. We're already searching for him. Once we find him, we'll get the rest of your group."

Henry tried to keep a poker face, but he blinked several times. Feeling that response, he squinted and cleared his throat.

"We also know about Denver," Delaney said, moving to the corner of the room. "That's another domino. We've got three dominos now. Craig, Denver, and you. Who will be the first to fall?"

"I'm betting Craig," Burkett said. "He's a junkie."

Henry's eyes snapped to her.

"Yeah, we know about his problem. So do you, I see."

"I'm gonna leave now."

"We'd like you to stay just a bit longer," Burkett said.

Henry pushed his chair back and stood. "I don't want to. I'm done."

There was a knock at the door. Delaney opened it to reveal a female police officer in plainclothes. She held up three fingers as she stepped into the room. Delaney nodded in return.

Burkett said, "Henry, this is Officer Navarro. She has something she'd like to tell you."

"Henry Ramos, you're under arrest for the assault of Archie Holloway."

"Who the hell is that?" Henry said.

"You wouldn't know his name since you just walked up and hit him, but I've got two witnesses who say you did it. They just identified you via closed-circuit camera."

Henry's eyes snapped to the unlit light on the wall. He then looked at Burkett. "You said we weren't being recorded."

"We aren't," she deadpanned. "But I didn't say we weren't being monitored."

Chapter 63

Amidst his own grunts of exertion, Matt heard the front door open. He stopped and listened.

"Hmmm, baby?" Veronica mumbled with her eyes closed.

"Quiet," he said.

There was movement at the front of the house.

"Yo, Matt. You here?"

He looked down at Veronica, about to say something, but she had fallen back asleep. *Shit*, he thought and climbed out of bed. "Gimme a minute," he yelled.

As he dressed, he heard muted voices in the front room. While he buttoned his jeans, he realized it wasn't the sound of excitement that had followed the previous knockouts. Something had gone wrong.

He grabbed his shoes and socks before leaving.

Denver and Gremlin stood in the middle of the room. They looked worried. Matt kept his face flat even though nervous adrenaline now raced through him.

He sat on the couch and asked, "What's up?"

Denver's lip curled before saying, "Henry got hisself arrested."

Matt slipped a sock over each foot. "How?"

"He picked the wrong suit to tangle with."

Matt had a shoe in his hand and froze. "The wrong suit?"

"Yeah," Denver said. "Henry took a swing, and the guy lit him up. He was down. We watched from a distance when the cops showed up."

Gremlin nodded when Matt looked at him.

"How is that possible?"

"I don't understand," Denver said, dropping into the bean bag chair. He cradled his head in his hands.

"They're suits. They're supposed to be weak," Matt said, looking to Gremlin for answers. "Some suit took three of us out in an elevator yesterday, one of which was Bam Bam. For fuck's sake! Now, you're telling me another suit took out Henry?"

"Dude was looking for us," Gremlin said.

Matt pushed his foot into the first shoe, then stopped. He studied Gremlin for a moment, then asked, "Why do you think that?"

"He watched us the whole time. When Henry went to him, the guy stayed put. He didn't run. It wasn't right. Henry never stood a chance."

"And that makes you think he was waiting for us? You sound paranoid."

"Then there was what he said," Gremlin.

"He said something?"

Denver looked up at Gremlin. "Show him, man. Everything will make sense then."

Chapter 64

Andrew Miller waited outside the house on Fifth Avenue. After the cops left the scene at Second and Howard, the two men fled. They didn't bother looking behind them as they ran.

Andrew played a game of cat-and-mouse for more than an hour until the two ran inside the house without knocking. He wondered if that was where they lived.

He remained concealed in some bushes down the street at the edge of a vacant office building. His eyes were trained on the house.

He waited and watched.

Chapter 65

The news had spread throughout social media and was all over the midday programs—a suit fought back.

Viewers made disturbing on-line comments. Many stated it was time to take back the country from thugs and criminals. If the cops wouldn't do it, then good men must do it for themselves.

Quinn Delaney sat at his computer and watched the latest Channel 6 News report on the knockout game. Andrew Miller's beatdown of Henry Ramos had quickly gone viral across the nation. Even though the cops knew it was Miller in the video, the news and social media had yet to pick it up. They would soon enough, he knew.

"This is insane," Marci said, looking over his shoulder.

"How people are reacting is what's amazing," Quinn said. "Some call him a hero. Others a villain."

"He's a good person."

"But he's crossing a line. Or at least toeing the vigilante line. Don't you think?"

Marci didn't respond. Instead, she walked over to her cubicle and sat.

When the broadcast finished, Quinn asked, "We good on the Ramos paperwork?"

She said, "Navarro handled the booking and incident report. I'm covering the interview."

Some commotion at the entrance to the department occurred as two officers escorted a handcuffed white male in a suit. He struggled against them and yelled. His skin was tan, and his white hair was mussed.

Captain Ackerman approached the detectives as the man was escorted into an interview room. "Nice, isn't it?"

"What is?" Burkett asked.

"That guy just knocked out some street kid."

"What?"

Ackerman shook his head. "The kid was standing on the corner, minding his own business, when the suit punched him."

"Why did he do that?"

"Said the kid loitered in front of his building every day. He had enough of it."

"Why's he in an interview room?"

"He got the idea from seeing it on the Internet. He thought it was time to start standing up for the good people of the city. Maybe you guys should talk with him before he's booked. I get the feeling we're going to see this some more."

Chapter 66

The crew gathered around Gadget. His laptop was set up on the coffee table. Matt sat directly next to him so he could see the various news sites and social media accounts Gadget had called up. The knockout game, the game they'd reignited, had spread like wildfire throughout the nation.

Everyone watched in silence as Gadget moved from site to site, finding more information.

"Here's another report of a suit being knocked out." The guys cheered. "In some place called Toledo, Ohio."

"Where the hell is Toledo?" Critter asked.

"Where the hell is Ohio?" Bam Bam asked, which led to loud guffaws.

Gadget called up another headline. "In Washington, D.C., some suit hit a homeless person."

"Fucking one percent," Matt said.

They didn't read the articles. They were only interested in headlines. This continued for several sites. So far, the suits were losing the war, but some of them were fighting back.

"So, about our game?" Stick said.

Matt looked up.

Stick's eyes met the eyes of the other guys. "I just thought since I earned my second knockout, I would get the points."

Matt slowly turned his attention back to the news sites. "Rabbit, give this guy his points, so he'll stop whining."

Stick lowered his head as everyone turned their focus back to the screen.

"Is there any mention of Henry getting arrested?" someone asked.

Gadget's fingers danced across the keyboard. "Nope. None."

Matt leaned his head back. The guys were looking to him for leadership, and he was at a loss. What to do? Where to take them?

"Hey, Gremlin, show me that video again. The part where the suit comes up to you."

Shaggy moved from the couch so Gremlin could get in next to Matt. Gremlin called up the video on his phone and moved past the fight between the suit and Henry. Then the suit approached Gremlin.

"Look at his face," Matt said.

"He's pissed," Gremlin said.

"No, he's not," Matt corrected. "He's not anything."

"He's fuckin' scary," Gremlin mumbled.

The guys crowded in to get a better look.

When the suit was directly in front of Gremlin, he said, *"Did you get what you wanted? Keep coming downtown, and I'll be waiting for you. Let's do this again when you're ready. I know I am."*

The video ended.

"That's when we ran off," Gremlin softly said.

"You ran off?" Shaggy asked. "Why didn't you hit him?"

"That's against the rules of the game," Gremlin said.

"Besides," Denver said, jumping to the defense of his friend, "that guy just kicked Henry's ass. You think Gremlin and me could take him? Now we know for sure he was the guy who broke Bam Bam's hand."

Several of the guys turned to Bam Bam, who nodded in confirmation.

"Still think we should have gone after him?" Denver asked.

Matt glanced at Rabbit, then Gremlin, then back to Rabbit. Both smiled. Matt said, "Gremlin, send your video to Gadget. We've got an idea."

"This'll be beautiful," Rabbit said.

Matt smiled as he met the eyes of each of the crew. Then his smile faded. "Does anyone know where my brother is at?"

Chapter 67

When the visitors to the house on Fifth Avenue left, Andrew Miller stepped out of the bushes and stretched. Several hours had passed, and his body hurt from staying motionless for so long. He'd trained for this type of activity years ago, but he hadn't implemented it in a long time. The mental discipline was far more difficult than the physical pain.

The little tan house was where this crew gathered to meet and plan.

He could still see two men moving about inside the house, but Andrew had enough information for now. He massaged his neck as he left the neighborhood.

It felt good to be moving in the summer evening. He decided to leave his car in the parking garage of his office building.

He walked a couple of miles to Candace's townhouse in the upscale Kendall Yards neighborhood.

ROUND SIX

Chapter 68

Burkett, Delaney, and Navarro were watching a video when Captain Ackerman walked into the conference room. The IT man-bun had set up the laptop before their meeting and left.

It was Saturday, but due to recent events, overtime had been authorized for them. The "all-hands-on deck" call had been made to stem the tide of recent assaults. Unfortunately, it hadn't made a difference.

Navarro paused the video when the captain walked in.

"Start it from the beginning. I only saw it once before leaving home."

The video was a twist on the events between Andrew Miller and Henry Ramos. It was made to look like Miller assaulted Ramos. The initial attack and the attempted follow-up swing by Ramos had been removed. Only Miller's inside leg kick and strike across the chin remained. Then Miller was suddenly inside the screen, saying, *"Keep coming downtown and I'll be waiting for you. Let's do this again when you're ready. I know I am."*

A modulated voice announced, "This is the one percent. They own three-fourths of the world's wealth."

The video replayed the kick to Ramos's leg in stuttered fashion to highlight the violence.

"They are arrogant," the modulated voice threatened, *"and no longer fear the ninety-nine percent of us who struggle to survive."*

"I'll be waiting for you," Andrew Miller said again.

The video moved to the punch on Ramos's chin, again playing it in a stuttered fashion. Ramos's head snapped several times, each from the same punch. It was painful to watch.

"They are vengeful and greedy," the modulated voice continued. *"They want everything you have."*

Miller's entire attack on Ramos was now played in slow motion. Henry Ramos collapsed to the ground, and the camera froze on the scene.

"It's time to make your statement. It's time to show your power. Together, it's time we all knock out the one percent." The modulated voice fell silent, and the video went dark.

Ackerman turned to his team. "No one has any real idea where this video originated from except for Spokane. It started with various false social media accounts. They've all been taken down, but the video is already out there. The news has it, so it's too late. Now it's part of the landscape. We have to deal with it."

The three officers glanced at each other.

"The chief and deputy chiefs are meeting with the mayor at his home. Assaults are occurring across the country. I've lost track of how many. The FBI has been called, and they'll be stomping into our investigation soon. Even if we find the guys who started the game, I'm not sure it will matter."

Ackerman's eyes felt gritty. He was worn out from the recent days spent in a bureaucratic pinball machine.

"It will matter, Captain," Delaney said. "When others see we've caught the group behind these videos, things will calm down."

He forced a smile in response to Delaney's encouragement. "Let's talk about the video. What did you guys see?"

"We've seen the actual footage of the confrontation between Miller and Ramos," Navarro said, "albeit from a different angle, so there's nothing new there. What was new was the verbal contact after the fight."

Delaney's eyes drifted to his partner, whose head was bowed, lost in thought. His eyes returned to the captain. "Miller said, 'I'll be waiting for you. Let's do this again when you're ready.' He's in vigilante territory."

Ackerman said, "Burkett, your thoughts? You know this guy. Do you agree with Delaney? Are we dealing with a vigilante now?"

Burkett lifted her head and looked at the others. "Maybe. It certainly looks that way."

The captain drummed his hands on the table as he thought. "Okay, folks, here's the plan. First, keep after Andrew Miller. A car was ordered to sit on his house, so that's covered. We've already asked his place of employment to alert us if he shows up, right? It's the weekend, so we don't have to worry about that. Second, we're still running additional patrols through downtown. That'll continue until things ease up with this game. Finally, you've got two names—Craig Taylor and Denver—that you haven't made any headway on. Gain some ground on those today."

Chapter 69

It's like a scene from a zombie movie, Andrew Miller thought. *Or at least some sort of weird science fiction film.*

It was mid-morning, and no one in the downtown core was dressed professionally. Of course, it was Saturday, so professional business attire would be limited at best, but it was strange to be looking for a suit and not find one in sight.

For that matter, no one was in slacks and a tie. It seemed everyone had dressed down for the day. Sloppiness was a cultural norm now, but this was taking it to a new level. He'd already seen at least six people wearing pajama bottoms and T-shirts. Others who looked like they would be professionals wore dirty jeans and loose-fitting shirts with their hair unkempt.

Did he do this on regular days? He was sure he didn't. Even when he dressed down, he looked clean and put together.

It didn't matter, though, so why spend time ruminating on it? He pushed the thoughts from his mind.

He wore another suit and tie, which caused people to stop and stare. On a regular day, no one would have looked twice. Now, they stared at him with curiosity. Was it because of the suit, or because they recognized his picture from television and social media? The news programs had announced his name this morning.

A few days ago, when people glanced at him following the fight in the bus plaza, his heart had raced. Not anymore.

Today, he was calm. It was the same in the small country of the Central African Republic. Everyone looked at him there, too. Except they had wanted to kill him. He was able to control his response to the adrenaline then, and he felt that level of control returning.

It felt good.

Some of the onlookers were surely questioning why he would subject himself to such danger. Then some were calculating their chances of knocking out a suit so they could join the swelling ranks of those playing a game with no bounty except to hurt someone.

Andrew considered his overall plan of action. He would later go to the Fifth Avenue house and confront the men. They were playing a game with him, even though they didn't realize he was playing it back. Overnight, they released another video of him. He would let them know they were messing with the wrong guy.

Then why go downtown? Why was he walking around drawing attention to himself? What purpose did it serve?

He'd returned home in the early morning and found a patrol car sitting outside his house. It thrilled him to sneak into the back of his residence, change his clothes in the dark, and sneak out again.

It was then Andrew admitted he missed the action of conflict. When he acknowledged that, he knew immediately why he was back downtown.

He wanted clearly defined enemies and objectives. When it went badly half a world away, he'd handled the outcome poorly. Others on the team had gone through similar situations, handled their hurt and disappointments, and moved on.

Why did he react the way he did? Why couldn't he have been better?

Andrew spoke with various therapists, but they never helped him get to where he wanted to be. Maybe because he didn't want to go back there.

Then the new video came out this morning. Candace saw it on Facebook while he was sipping his coffee.

"That's you," she had said with disbelief, her eyes not leaving the video playing on her phone.

Andrew couldn't deny it. Didn't want to deny it. "Yes."

Candace looked up. Her dark eyes clouded with confusion.

"It's a long story."

"You looked angry. I've never seen you that way."

"I was fighting. I'll never be that way with you."

She stared at the image of his face, which was paused on her telephone. He reached out slowly to cover it with his hand, but she pulled back. She wasn't scared, but she looked at him differently.

"Candy," he said, his voice soft and reassuring. "Everything will be okay."

"I'm not sure it will be."

"Please listen."

She quietly walked away toward her bedroom. When the door shut, he knew it was time to leave. The discussion he wanted to have with her would have to occur another time.

Andrew's head was so clouded with thoughts he almost missed the movement of a man approaching him on the sidewalk.

His intentions were immediately apparent.

He was tall, wore a white tank top, blue jeans, and combat boots. Tattoos lined his arms. People on the street moved out of his way, then stopped to turn their attention to Andrew. They knew what was about to happen and waited in horror for the man to hit the suit. Several of them hurriedly pulled phones from their pockets.

Andrew cleared his mind to focus only on the moment. He didn't break stride when the man balled his fists and bared his teeth. When he was near enough, the man dropped into a stance and threw his knockout punch. Andrew blocked it with both hands, chopped the man in the throat, heel-palmed him in the nose, and threw an uppercut into the man's stomach. As the man began to double over, Andrew caught him in the throat with the knife-edge of his hand, which lifted him slightly. He then twisted rapidly and punched the man in the jaw.

The tall man collapsed to the sidewalk.

Another attacker ran across the street toward Andrew. His shoes slapped noisily on the pavement. Andrew turned to him as the man threw a heavy punch. He slipped it to the outside and drilled his attacker in the ribs. The result was a loud cracking sound. The attacker squealed, fell to his knees, and grabbed his side.

"Hey!" a deep, male voice yelled.

Andrew looked down the street. Two uniformed patrol officers ran toward him.

He turned and entered the nearest building. There was an escalator in the lobby, and he bounded the moving stairs two at a time until he was on the second level. He sprinted from the building to the next via the skywalk bridge. Various office downtown buildings were connected by skybridges, allowing access to them without ever leaving a climate-controlled environment.

Andrew sprinted across this glass-enclosed bridge. As he ran, he saw additional officers running along the street toward the area where he just was. When he exited the bridge, he changed direction in the new building when he could and ran southbound, crossing through another skybridge and into yet another building. As he ran, he removed his jacket, tie, and shirt. He untucked his white T-shirt and messed up his hair.

Several blocks away, he dropped back down to street level via an elevator and casually strolled out of a building, carrying his balled-up suit coat under his arm.

Chapter 70

Leya Navarro parked her car in the lot and walked toward Lewis and Clark High School. She'd been on her way there a couple of days ago when she'd been interrupted by an assault downtown. Suddenly, the radio clipped to her belt chirped with activity. Officers were in pursuit of a suit downtown.

There was no reason to run back to her car and head toward those officers. She had no idea if they were chasing Andrew Miller or some copycat. Besides, stranger-to-stranger assaults had become commonplace over the past several days. Unless the pursuit headed her way, there wasn't anything she could do but wait.

With overtime already approved, she set this appointment for the morning. The school security officer had said he would be happy to accommodate her. She continued toward the side entrance.

A couple of minutes passed, and a voice came over the radio. "We lost him."

Leya turned down its volume before texting a phone number she'd been given. A moment later, a trim black man with a receding hairline pushed open the door.

"Officer Navarro?" he asked.

She smiled, and they shook hands.

"Jay Becker," he said. "Follow me."

He led her through the quiet hallways of the school until they came to the Office of Security.

He dropped into a chair behind a messy desk and motioned for her to sit.

"So, Officer Navarro, what can I do for you on this fine Saturday morning?"

"You usually work on the weekend?"

"When I want some quiet time away from the family. I only live a few blocks away, so I can walk over here and putter on paperwork now and then. This is what happens when work is your hobby."

"Have you heard about this wave of the knockout game?"

"Who hasn't? We had our first incident yesterday. One of our quieter kids blasted a fellow student. Supposedly, the two never even had a beef between them. When asked why he would punch another kid, he said, 'His dad is a one-percenter.' Can you believe that? He hit another kid because his dad supposedly has money. Used to be 'my dad can beat up your dad.' Now, it's 'I'll beat you up because of your dad.' What a world."

"Keeps getting better, doesn't it?"

"I don't know about that."

"Do you keep records on all the students? Even past students?"

Becker leaned forward and put his hands on his computer's keyboard. "Definitely. All the district's resource officers feed into the same database. The information is never purged. You'd be surprised how many kids come back onto campus after they graduate. Or drop out, which is more likely in the case of kids who hang out on campus."

"Can you search by a nickname?"

Becker nodded. "What have you got?"

"Denver."

"Sounds like a country boy's nickname." Becker typed the name into his computer and smiled. "Only one Denver in the system. Trevor Bowers."

"Where was he contacted?"

"Here at Lewis and Clark. Multiple contacts several years ago. Before my time. I just arrived at this post a year ago. Used to be up at North Central."

"What were the contacts for?"

Becker leaned toward the monitor. "There's a bunch. Got a disorderly conduct, minor in possession of alcohol, a bunch of trespassings. That last one looks like it occurred after he'd been expelled."

"Do you have an address listed?"

Becker smiled. "Of course. Looks like it's his mom's house. What do you want to bet he still lives with her?"

Leya pulled a folded photo from her pocket. It was a screenshot from the video taken of the confrontation between Andrew Miller and Henry Ramos. She pointed to the edge of the photo where two men stood to record the fight. "Ever seen these guys?"

Becker studied the photo for a moment, then looked up. "Sorry, no. But if you want to leave this with me, I'll send it to the other school resource officers and see if any of them know these guys."

Chapter 71

Veronica Schuster climbed out of the shower and began toweling off. Matt sat on the bed with his back pushed against the headboard.

"We should do some laundry," he said. "Maybe wash the sheets. They stink."

"Uh-huh," she agreed.

"How about we go out and do that today?"

"We have to?" Veronica said. She didn't bother to hide the whine in her voice.

When she dropped her towel, Matt studied her body. She knew she looked frail, nothing like she did when she was in high school. She thought he still found her attractive, but he put less effort into convincing her so.

"We can skip it. I'll wash them later." Matt got out of bed and left the room.

Veronica stared at herself in the mirror and ran her hands along her sides.

Was this the best her life was going to be?

She quietly padded over to the bottle of pills that sat on the nightstand. Matt usually watched how many she took, and she'd already had one recently. She removed another one from the bottle.

What would a second pill hurt?

Chapter 72

The three of them stood in front of the house on Fifteenth. The yard was yellow and burnt, standing out of place in a neighborhood of lush green lawns. Its brown paint was peeling, and the roof shingles were curling. An older-model Toyota was parked curbside.

"What's this guy's name again?"

"Trevor Bowers," Leya said. "This is the guy who assaulted four guys outside The Spokane Club."

Quinn glanced at his partner. "You're hoping he fights."

Marci smiled. "Me?"

Leya watched Marci with something close to awe. She'd heard the rumors about her—about her skills as a fighter, about her tangling with male officers on the department—but she'd never actually seen them on display. She thought it was all rumor and myth, the type of storytelling that goes on inside a police department.

Marci wasn't in her normal pantsuit. Since it was Saturday, she wore a long-sleeve black T-shirt and blue jeans. Black patrol boots were tucked under the jeans.

Quinn nodded to Leya. "You're lead."

She turned and headed toward the house.

On the small porch, Leya stood on one side of the front door while Quinn and Marci stood on the other. Following Leya's loud knock, they could hear footsteps from inside.

A woman in her late fifties opened the door. She wore yellow shorts and an over-sized Denver Broncos T-shirt. Her skin was sallow, and her short hair was unkempt. Upon recognition of the three as law enforcement, a frown appeared on her face. "What's he done this time?" She turned and shuffled away—an unannounced invitation for the officers to follow.

Leya asked, "Is Trevor here, ma'am?"

"In the backyard, vaping. What's he done?"

"We'd like to talk with him."

"Whatever," she said. "If you're gonna arrest him, do it quietly. My show is on." She headed toward another room.

"I'll watch her," Quinn said.

Leya watched with curiosity as Quinn followed the woman down the hall.

"Let's go," Marci said and headed for the back of the house. She pulled open a sliding glass door and stepped outside. Leya was immediately behind her.

Seated on a plastic chair was a mid-twenties white male smoking through a vape pen. "The hell?" he said and quickly stood.

"Trevor Bowers?" Leya asked.

"No."

"How about Denver then?"

"Ain't nobody here by that name."

"Cut it," Marci said. "We want to talk about the knockout game."

Denver dropped the vape pen onto the chair and flexed his fingers outward. "I don't know what you're talking about."

Moving to triangulate the man, Leya stepped away from Marci.

"Sure, you do," Marci said. "You took down four guys at The Spokane Club."

A smile spread across Denver's face. "You think I did that?"

"We *know* you did."

"And they sent two lady cops to get me?"

"One is more than enough," Marci said.

Denver took a slow, deep breath, then suddenly moved, kicking toward Marci. She stepped slightly back at an angle, allowing Denver's kick to miss by inches. When he landed, his face collided with the flat of her elbow. He backpedaled, grabbing his cheek.

"You can't do that!" he hollered.

"Do what?" Marci asked.

"Hit me in the face! Cops can't do that. That's against the rules!"

He swung wildly at Marci, but she was gone before he got near her. By the time Denver realized he'd overcommitted, Marci had kicked him in the back of the right knee, dropping him to the ground, reducing his height. She wrapped one arm around his throat with the other locking it in place. Her legs wrapped around his waist and dragged him to the ground.

Denver clawed at her arms as she clamped the vise tighter around his throat. He thrashed around, but her legs tightened around his midsection. His movements became frantic as he reached back to her face. Marci tucked her head behind his, where he couldn't reach her.

She never released her grip, and soon his flailing became less pronounced. Eventually, his hands lowered to the ground.

"He's out," Leya said.

Marci continued to apply pressure.

"He's out," Leya repeated, her voice louder.

"I know," Marci rasped, her voice husky from excitement and exertion. She squeezed once more for good measure, then shoved Denver away.

While she stood and dusted herself off, Leya applied a set of handcuffs to the now snoring man.

Quinn walked outside.

"What are you grinning for?" Marci asked, her voice returning to normal.

"When we heard yelling, mom got worried her son was gonna hurt you." Quinn studied the unconscious man on the ground. "He didn't hurt you, did he?"

Chapter 73

Matt, Rabbit, and Gadget sat in the front room. Gadget's laptop was open as he gave the latest scoop on the social media response to their video.

"It's viral," Gadget said, laughing. He didn't bother to hide his excitement. "I've never been a part of anything that's taken off like this. It even made the national news."

"Get out!" Matt said.

Rabbit looked worried.

"I'm serious," Gadget said. "All the morning news shows had it on. My mom is freaked out by it. She thinks the country is tearing itself apart. Oh my God, I so badly want to tell her I made it."

"You didn't, did you?"

Gadget made a face. "I'm not retarded."

"This is bad," Rabbit said. "Really bad."

"You worry too much," Matt said.

"I mean it. If this gets back to us, we're screwed."

"There's no way it's getting back to us. Right, Gadget?"

"Not a chance. I uploaded it through several fake accounts. They've burned those accounts now, but the video has been copied and redistributed so many times there's nothing to worry about."

Rabbit shook his head. "Bad. It's bad."

"Quit being a bitch," Matt said.

There was a knock at the door. None of the guys ever knocked, so the guys looked at each other with suspicion.

"Get the door, Rabbit," Matt said.

Rabbit hurried to the door and pulled it slightly open, hiding partially behind it. Standing there was a guy in a suit.

A second later, Rabbit softly said, "Oh shit."

Chapter 74

Andrew Miller kicked the door, smacking it into the face of the short man. He shuffled backward, and his hands immediately went to his forehead.

"Rabbit!" yelled a guy on the couch.

Andrew stepped inside the house and side-kicked Rabbit in the stomach. The guy tumbled back onto a bean bag chair, popping it open when he landed. Little white balls exploded from inside.

There were two guys on the couch. The one holding the computer dropped it on the coffee table and jumped in front of Andrew, his fists held up at the ready. The second guy moved around the table, trying to get behind him.

Andrew took a quick step forward and leaped into the air. He snapped a kick out, landing it on the chin of the guy in front, crumpling him to the floor. Andrew spun around to the man behind him.

That guy lifted his hands in surrender. "I give," he said.

"I don't care."

"Wait!" he said, backpedaling toward the open front door. "I'm sorry. We were just messing around."

"Have you seen what's happened?"

"What do you mean?"

"People are getting hurt."

The guy shrugged.

"Maybe you should understand how it feels."

The guy's eyes widened for a moment, then he smiled.

Andrew paused. *Is he really smiling?* It didn't make sense. Was he going to turn and run out the door?

"Shoot him," the man said.

Andrew glanced back over his shoulder. Standing in the hallway was a skinny woman dressed only in panties and a bra. Using both hands, she held a revolver. It wavered badly as she trained it on him. Her eyelids drooped and her body swayed.

He slowly turned to the woman. "Put it down."

"Get away from him," she said, her words slow and labored.

"I will," Andrew said. "Put it down."

Andrew heard the man step toward him. He kicked backward, hitting the man in the groin and dropping him to the floor.

The gun went off, spinning Andrew around and sending him to the ground.

Chapter 75

Craig Taylor heard the gunshot and hurried across the crispy grass. He'd been hiding in a row of bushes since the morning, waiting for something to happen. He never dreamed it would be this.

He first spotted the suit yesterday purely by luck. He'd been on his way back to the house when he noticed Stick and Gremlin sprinting by. Craig worried something was going on, so he stopped walking and moved out of sight. He was glad he did because a moment later, he saw the suit come into the neighborhood. Then he watched him hide in the bushes for several hours. Craig moved his hiding spot several times. He kept getting further away from the suit, afraid that given enough time, the guy would spot him.

When the suit finally left the bushes and walked away, Craig followed. He was careful and did his best not to be discovered. Maybe the suit would go to a car somewhere. Craig imagined him living up on the South Hill in some richie-rich house. Instead, the suit walked through downtown, across the Monroe Street Bridge, and into Kendall Yards.

By the time they got to that new housing development, Craig knew he was out in the open. He had followed the suit for too long, and he no longer belonged in a neighborhood of hipsters, yuppies, and empty nesters. Craig stopped following the suit and lost sight of him as he walked into the fancy neighborhood. He imagined the guy lived in one of the new houses there. He was happy, though. He was one step closer to finding him.

Craig returned to his brother's house but didn't enter it. Perhaps the suit, or worse, the police, would return soon.

Instead, he took up a hiding place on the opposite side of the abandoned house where he'd waited previously. Even though the pains of addiction were back, he was smart and patient. He now had a bigger goal than himself and his habit. It wasn't even that hard to force himself to sleep for a few hours during the night, though he awoke to fresh pains.

Seeing the suit approach the house a bit ago, Craig knew something was about to happen. He only had to watch and wait a little longer. He wasn't sure how it would happen, but his time for revenge would come soon.

When the shot was fired, he remembered Matt's gun and figured his brother had solved his problem. A moment of regret flashed through him. Craig's revenge had been exacted by someone else. That was okay with him, he quickly realized. His ego had long ago been broken. He only wanted the suit to suffer.

He'd only taken a step from his hiding place when the suit burst from the house, clutching his shoulder. He crossed the street and lumbered toward downtown. Craig understood what had happened then. Someone had shot the suit, and he was now running for help. He would run to the hospital, the cops, or home.

Craig didn't care about the hospital or the cops; those would only bring trouble. If he went there, Matt would be on his own. If the suit didn't go there, though, and went home, Craig wanted to know where that was.

If the suit chose not to go to the cops or the emergency room, he wanted to know why. He hadn't gone to the police so far, so what were the chances he would just go home?

A grin grew on his face. He didn't have to follow the suit. He knew the general area where he was going. He just had to get there before the suit, who was now hurt and slow. Craig could wait for him to arrive and watch to see which house he entered.

Ignoring the cramps in his stomach, Craig Taylor ran with all his might.

Chapter 76

He held his head in his hands. He was in trouble, and he knew it. The cops had him.

Trevor 'Denver' Bowers looked up at Detective Quinn Delaney. The man hadn't said a word since he introduced himself and sat down.

Tears formed in his eyes, and he brushed them away, embarrassed at getting emotional.

The detective smiled. "You have the right to remain silent," he said. "Anything you say can and will be used against you in a court of law."

Denver sucked in some air and ground his teeth together. The lady cop was in the corner. The detective who had beaten him up wasn't in the room. Thank God. He didn't want to face the humiliation of that woman again.

"At this time, you have the right to talk to a lawyer and have them present with you while you are being questioned. If you cannot afford to hire a lawyer, one will be appointed to represent you before questioning if you wish. You can decide at any time to exercise these rights and not answer any questions or make any statements. Do you understand these rights?"

Denver nodded.

"I need you to say that you understand."

He nodded again, but this time said, "Yeah, I understand."

Delaney pointed at the wall. "We're being recorded, both sight and sound. If that red light is on, we're on *Candid Camera*. Got it?"

"Yeah."

"You assaulted my partner, Trevor."

"Bitch elbowed me in the face."

"You tried to kick her. Then you tried to hit her. You want to cry about her getting the upper hand?"

Denver shook his head. "It's bullshit."

Delaney pointed to the lady cop. "She saw it."

She said, "You assaulted her and lost."

"Don't take it too hard," Delaney said. "I've fought with her before, and I've lost."

"Yeah?"

Lady cop raised her eyebrows.

"The woman's tough," Delaney said. "You had a better chance of going after me."

"Shit," Denver said.

"So you're in trouble, buddy. Lots of trouble."

Denver lowered his head.

"By definition, the knockout game is a felony. When you knock out someone, they lose consciousness. That's a temporary loss of a bodily function. Right there, that's Second-Degree Assault, a Class B Felony."

Denver swallowed involuntarily. The detective must have seen that, right? The swallow felt huge, and Denver's hands began to shake under the table.

"And you've got more trouble coming your way," the detective said.

"How's that?" Was his voice shaking?

Oh shit, my voice is shaking.

"We've arrested Henry for one of his knockouts."

Denver's eyes widened for a second, then he recovered. He looked up in the air as if pretending to think. "Henry?" he said. "Henry. Who's Henry?"

"Don't lie," the detective said. "When we put your knockouts together, you're going to have major problems, monumental problems. See, here's the thing. If you did your assaults alone, no big deal, right? Same thing with Henry. No big deal. They're basic assaults. We deal with them, and everybody goes about their way. But this got ugly when you guys started going after people together. Do you know what we call it when a group works together to commit a crime?"

Denver shook his head.

The detective leaned forward and whispered, "Conspiracy."

Denver's mouth opened slightly as disbelief set in. *Conspiracy*, he thought, *that sounds bad.*

"That's right. You and your friends are in a conspiracy to commit assault. How many guys are in your crew?"

The detective quietly sat as Denver counted the guys in his head. When he got to seven, his stomach turned sour, and he felt like throwing up.

"There are a lot of guys, huh?"

"I don't know what you're talking about," he said, then firmly pressed his lips together.

"Here's how a conspiracy charge works," Delaney said. "For every assault charge that one of your friends gets hit with, you'll be charged with a conspiracy charge. It will be one level lower, so you're lucky. For Henry's assault charge, he'll be charged with a Class B felony, and you'll be charged with a Class C Conspiracy charge. Kind of cool how that works, huh?"

Denver blinked several times and felt his face growing warm.

"I don't know exactly how many guys are in your crew, but there's a handful, right? That's a lot of felonious assaults you're going to get tied into."

The cop was fucking with him, and Denver wanted some anger to rise within. If the anger showed up, it would help him get control. Unfortunately, it wasn't there yet, and he was scared. Really scared. So he tried to force his anger by saying, "Are you going to yap all day, or are you going to charge me with something?" His voice shook when he said it, and he knew he sounded like a scared little boy.

The detective smiled. The asshole straight up grinned like he had a handful of aces. "We'll get to charging you in a minute, Trevor."

"*Denver.*"

"What?"

"My name is Denver."

The detective's smile broadened. "So, Denver is your nickname."

Denver blinked several times, not sure if he just admitted to something he shouldn't have.

The detective continued, "There's just one more thing I'd like you to consider—"

"What's that?" Denver interrupted the detective. He felt like he was about to cry and needed to get some control back.

"A guy died."

Denver leaned forward. "What? Who died?"

The detective leaned back and crossed his arms. He remained silent for a moment and studied Denver. "You didn't know a guy died, did you?"

Denver shook his head. "Was it mine?"

"You were responsible for the assaults at The Spokane Club, right?"

"Yeah," he quickly said, realizing too late he'd admitted to an assault. Denver glanced at the lady cop, then went back to the detective. He closed his eyes and sighed. "No one died there, did they?"

"None of the guys you assaulted died. Those guys can identify you, which is why we're here today."

Denver opened his eyes and put his hands together. They were clammy. He rubbed them on his pants but kept his mouth shut.

"We'll circle back to what happened at The Spokane Club in a minute, but let's stay with the idea of conspiracy. I'm excited about this. It's such a cool concept. Maybe not for you, but for detectives and prosecutors, we love it. So check this out. You worked together to commit assaults, and that's a conspiracy. You understand that much, right? You're responsible for Henry's assault, and he's responsible for your assault, and so on and so on. Get it?"

Fighting back the tears, Denver blinked several times. He whispered, "I get it."

"When one of the assaults turned into a murder, guess what happens?"

Denver had trouble swallowing.

"Conspiracy to commit assault gets bumped up to a conspiracy to commit …"

"Murder?"

"Exactly. You're going to be looped into a murder charge. Conspiracy to Murder is a Class B felony, my friend."

"But I didn't kill no one," Denver muttered.

Delaney smiled. "Doesn't matter. You were part of a conspiracy. That's how it goes. Kind of cool, right? The district attorney is going to wrap you up like a Christmas present for the jury. Think about how easy it will be for the jury to understand what you were doing."

Denver looked at the lady cop, who stared at him with dead eyes. She didn't care about his predicament. Maybe he should have called a lawyer at the beginning. He didn't have the money for a good one, but the city would have provided him with one, nonetheless. They had to. It was the law. Maybe the lawyer could help him figure a way out of this.

"You can either start giving me names or piss me off and make me work for it. The first one who talks, either Henry or you, is going to score some additional points with the district attorney. We want—"

"It was Matt's idea."

"What?" Delaney said, with a glance at the lady cop.

Denver shrugged. "The game. It was all Matt's idea."

"What is Matt's last name?"

Denver said, "I don't know. I swear to God, I don't. If I did, I would tell you."

"Where can we find this Matt?"

Chapter 77

Rabbit and Matt stared at Veronica. She sat on the couch and held the gun in her hands. Gadget remained unconscious on the floor.

"Do you think I killed him?" Veronica asked.

"No," Matt said, "you hit him in the shoulder. He'll live."

"He was bleeding so much."

Matt reached for the gun, but Veronica turned her body, not allowing him to take the weapon from her. She kept her eyes on him, though. She looked at him differently now. Not with affection or fear, but with something close to equality.

He knew the gun made her feel powerful. He'd felt the same thing before when he held a rifle for the first time in recruit training.

"Ronnie, give me the gun," Matt said. As an afterthought, he added, *"please."*

She ran her tongue over her teeth and slid back onto the couch. She then lifted the gun's barrel toward him.

Rabbit must have noticed the subtle change in power as he also moved away from Matt. He now looked at him differently, too.

A sourness filled Matt's stomach.

"You make me work for my medicine," Ronnie said.

"What? No. I love you. I've always gotten your pills when you need them."

"You do things to me." Tears formed in her eyes. "Things that aren't nice."

"Ronnie, baby, I don't know what to say."

"Aren't you sorry?"

"Of course I am. I'm just so crazy for you. I don't always know what I'm doing."

"I don't believe you," she said. Her finger trembled on the trigger as she raised the gun.

Rabbit stepped closer to Veronica. "He's lying, Ronnie."

Her eyes snapped to Rabbit.

Matt whispered, "The fuck, Rabbit?"

"He doesn't love you, Ronnie." His voice was soft, like he was whispering into her ear during a date. "You know that, right? You know the truth about him."

"Rabbit," Matt pleaded, anger bursting inside him.

"Did you know he said I could have sex with you?"

Matt pointed at Rabbit. "That's a lie! I would never say that."

Rabbit stepped closer to Veronica. "I would never lie to you, Ronnie." His voice was so sweet Matt wanted to vomit. "You know how I feel about you. How I've always felt about you?"

"The hell are you doing, Rabbit?"

"Shut up!" Veronica yelled at Matt, the revolver shaking in her hand.

"You know, don't you?" Rabbit cooed. "You've always known."

Tears formed in Veronica's eyes.

"If you shoot him, Ronnie, I'll clean it up. Whatever you want to do, I'll support it. It's okay. I'll take care of you."

Veronica's eyes bounced back and forth between Rabbit and Matt.

"Please, Ronnie. I love you," Matt said. He tried to muster some sweetness in his voice, but it sounded hollow, especially compared to Rabbit's bullshit. "I would never hurt you," Matt said, almost robotically.

"I'm here for you," Rabbit said, his voice soft and velvety. "I'll take care of you."

Veronica's eyes turned slightly to Rabbit. She looked like a scared puppy.

Matt hated them both so much at that moment.

Rabbit nodded and whispered, "It's okay, Ronnie. I promise."

When she began to lower the gun, Rabbit punched Veronica across the jaw, and the gun fired.

"Jesus!" Matt said, staring at the wall behind him. A hole had been blasted into the drywall.

Veronica was out cold on the couch. Rabbit yanked the gun from her hand. He studied her for a moment before handing the weapon to Matt. "Sorry for hitting your girlfriend."

"Don't worry about it," Matt muttered. He studied Rabbit for a moment before turning to his girlfriend. "She deserved what she got."

Both men remained quiet, lost in their thoughts.

Finally, Rabbit said, "We've got a problem."

"Yeah."

"The suit knows where you live. How did that happen?"

"Don't know."

They sat in the quiet some more. Matt's eyes drifted to Veronica, then his friend, and back to Veronica. He examined the gun in his hands.

Rabbit was shaking Gadget, who was still unconscious on the floor.

"Rabbit?"

"He's still out. Guy did a number on him. He ain't dead, though. He's breathing."

"Rabbit?" Matt repeated.

The smaller man turned to him and raised his eyebrows.

"You mean what you said? About helping Ronnie kill me?"

Rabbit smiled nervously. "Nah, playa, nah," he said, dismissively waving his hands.

"It sounded like you meant it."

"Ah, hell no, G. I'd never fuckin' do that. I only said that shit, so the bitch would calm herself. She was actin' straight up cray-cray."

A sense of sadness descended on Matt as he watched his old friend. Finally, he said, "Rabbit?"

"Huh?"

"You always talk street when you lie," Matt said as he raised the gun.

Chapter 78

A perimeter was established around the house by the time Detectives Quinn Delaney and Marci Burkett arrived.

When the homicide was first reported, they realized the address was the same as where Denver said Matt lived. He had given them the location, even though he wouldn't give them any names beyond Matt's. He didn't want to get any of his other friends into trouble. Even though he didn't want to be a rat, Denver needed to save his skin.

Quinn called Captain Ackerman immediately and explained the situation.

"Get out there, now," Ackerman said. "If it's part of your case, then you handle it. If not, we'll assign it to someone else."

Leya Navarro was tasked with booking Trevor 'Denver' Bowers into jail and completing the probable cause affidavit. If the homicide were indeed relevant to their investigation, Leya would join them when she was free.

Quinn and Marci stopped at the edge of the perimeter where Sergeant Josh Holtz stood.

"Sergeant," Quinn said with a nod. "What have you got?"

"Anonymous caller reported a shooting."

"Anonymous? Dispatch couldn't pick up a caller ID?"

"No."

"Burner phone?"

Holtz shrugged. "That's what you'd expect. When we arrived, there was a woman, Veronica Schuster, crying on the couch with a gun in hand. Dead kid on the floor."

"Where's the woman now?"

"Sitting in the back of McCrea's patrol car. We've been waiting for you to arrive."

"Anybody in the house?" Delaney asked.

"Once it was cleared, we backed out and secured a perimeter."

Quinn and Marci stepped under the yellow tape and moved toward the front of the house. The second string of caution tape, the inner perimeter, was wrapped around the front porch. They stepped under that tape, climbed the stairs, and entered the house.

They stood in the entryway and surveyed the scene. On the floor was the body of a white male, surrounded by a pool of blood. A popped bean bag chair was near the coffee table, some of its stuffing exploded outward.

Quinn glanced at Marci, who nodded back. They both stepped into the house and carefully moved through the room.

A round had been fired into the east wall. Quinn tapped near it with the end of his pen. Marci grunted her awareness of it.

When he was near the far side of the room, Quinn noticed a piece of paper tacked to the wall. A list of names and numbers was written on it. He leaned in and studied the document. "And here we go," he said, removing his cell phone to take a photo.

"What?"

"Look at this."

Marci moved carefully around the body on the floor until she saw the list. "This was their clubhouse."

"Let's back out and get forensics in here. We'll want pictures of all this."

They carefully walked back to the front door. Marci stopped and pointed at the door frame. "A bullet is lodged in there."

Quinn leaned in and examined the round. He then looked back at the body on the floor. "Three shots were fired. Two in the walls, one in the body."

"Maybe. Or the two in the walls could be from previous incidents," Marci said. "You never know in a place like this."

Sergeant Holtz met them at the outer perimeter and lifted the yellow tape for them to step under. "That was quick."

"This is tied to the rash of recent assaults," Quinn said.

"The knockout game?"

Quinn nodded. "That's it."

"Where's the shooter?" Marci asked, scanning nearby vehicles.

"Over there," Holtz said, pointing to a patrol car.

"Was she advised of her rights?"

"Yes, and she waived them."

As they approached the car, Quinn said, "You should take this one."

Marci nodded and stepped in front of her partner. When she got to the car, she opened the rear door and squatted, so she was at eye level. In the back seat, Veronica Schuster was leaning forward with her head resting upon the plexiglass partition. Her hands were cuffed behind her back. She turned her head to face the detective. Tears streaked down her face.

"Veronica, I'm Detective Burkett. I'd like to ask you some questions."

She leaned back in her seat and twisted her body to look at Marci fully. Veronica wiped her nose on her shirt.

"Why did you shoot that man?"

"I didn't. I mean, I don't think I did. I would never hurt Rabbit."

"Rabbit?"

"Hm-hm."

"Do you know Rabbit's real name?"

Veronica slowly nodded. "Conrad Anderson."

Marci looked over her shoulder to ensure Quinn was making a note of the name.

"Why did you have the gun?" Marci asked.

"Because I shot a suit."

With raised eyebrows, Marci again glanced back to Quinn, then returned her attention to Veronica. "A suit?"

"He was in our house. He attacked Rabbit. Then he was going to hurt Matt."

"Matt?"

"Matt Taylor. My boyfriend. Well, sort of. It's complicated."

"Taylor? Is he related to Craig Taylor?"

"That's his brother."

Quinn muttered, "Wow."

Marci said, "You shot the suit, but his body isn't in the house."

"I know."

"Where did you shoot him?"

Veronica started crying again. "In the arm. I think. Then he got up and ran away."

"Why was he there? The suit, I mean."

"I don't know," Veronica said. "I think it was because of that stupid game."

"The game?"

"I only listened to them talk about it. Knocking out suits."

"After you shot him, and he ran away, what happened?"

Veronica bowed her head, and Marci leaned in to hear her better. "I didn't want to give up the gun. It felt good to be in control of something. You know? It's been so long. But Matt wanted to take it away. I wouldn't let him."

Marci studied the side of Veronica's face. "What happened here?" she asked, pointing to Veronica's cheek. "You've got some bruising started. Someone hit you?"

Veronica shrugged. "I don't know." She moved her jaw around. "It hurts. One minute, Matt was trying to get the gun from me, and Rabbit was there, saying he would help me. He was sweet about it. Telling me he would be there no matter what. Rabbit always had a crush on me. I think he loved me. Not like Matt did, but like real love, kid stuff. Then I woke up, and Rabbit was dead, and Matt was gone."

"You don't remember shooting him?"

"I don't," she said. Tears ran down her face, and her body shook.

Marci shut the door and turned to her partner. "What do you make of it?"

"She's a junkie," Quinn said. "She could have shot him and not remembered any of it because of the drugs."

"Maybe, but it sounds like she had a soft spot for Rabbit."

"You think the boyfriend got the jump on her and killed his friend? Why would he do that?"

"You heard her say Rabbit was sweet on her. Maybe Matt killed him because of that."

"Or maybe she killed Rabbit and just doesn't remember it."

Marci crossed her arms. "We need an Attempt to Locate on Matt Taylor."

Quinn looked around the neighborhood. "Agreed. But somewhere out there is a suit with a gunshot wound. Either he goes to the hospital, or he calls the police."

"That's what you'd expect, right?" Marci said, but she shook her head slowly. "Except when has Andrew Miller done anything we'd expect a normal person to do?"

Chapter 79

It wasn't the first time Andrew Miller had been shot, but it had been years since the one and only time. Also, there was no team medic around to address the wound immediately. The previous round had caught him mid-thigh, tearing up the muscle and requiring surgical extraction.

This time, the bullet had gone through his shoulder. He could feel the exit wound on his back. It was painful when he lifted his arm, but it wasn't excruciating.

Andrew had made it back to Candace's home in the upscale Kendall Yards neighborhood. He was in the bathroom with his shirt off. He leaned against the shower wall with a towel pressed between his shoulder and the tile. He held a washcloth against the front wound.

"You're doing fine," he whispered. "Nothing to worry about."

Despite his lightheadedness, he offered words of encouragement to himself.

"It's a flesh wound—no bone damage. You can move the arm. Get sewn up, and you'll be fine."

The front door opened and closed.

"You're doing fine," he repeated.

"Andrew?" Candace called. Panic was in her voice.

He had texted her when he got to her house and asked her to come home.

"In the bathroom," he called. His voice sounded weak.

Candace appeared in the doorway. She wore black pants and a red blouse. When she saw him, her eyes widened.

Blood was on his chest and on the shower floor. She then noticed his white shirt crumpled in the sink. It was covered in blood. "Oh, my God!"

"I was shot."

"I'll call 911."

"No!" Darkness pushed in on him.

"Why not?"

"Just don't."

"We should call the police."

"Don't," he said, trying to make his voice sound stern, but instead, it sounded like it came from the bottom of a well.

"This is because of that video, isn't it?"

"I'll be okay. Had worse. I'm hurt, but I won't die. You understand?"

"No," she said. "I most certainly don't. I'm going to call."

"Please, Candy, whatever happens, don't call anyone."

"Why should I do that? What's going to happen?"

Darkness overwhelmed him then.

Chapter 80

Craig Taylor stopped more than a block away from the house on Fifth Street. Police cars were everywhere.

He was too afraid to approach and find out what was going on. Instead, he remained down the street in the shadow of a tree and watched the activity.

A woman pushed a stroller his way. She had come from the direction of the police. When she neared, Craig noticed a little fluffy dog in the seat of the carriage.

He asked, "What's going on over there?"

The woman stopped and looked back down the street. "Some girl killed her boyfriend."

"What?"

"Girl shot his ass. The cops just took her away. It's too bad, you know? This used to be a nice neighborhood for normal people. It's full of nothing but junkies and weirdos, now." The woman spat on the sidewalk before pushing the stroller. At the feeling of movement, the little dog yapped once.

He stood on the sidewalk, staring at the house.

Veronica killed Matt? Why would she do that? He loved her.

Craig shook his head. He couldn't believe it. Matt was good to that bitch. Why would she kill him?

It was then he realized he wasn't crying. Why wasn't he? Shouldn't he cry for his brother?

He turned and began walking.

What was he going to do now? Should he tell his mother? Didn't she deserve to know? Screw her, he thought. Let the cops deal with it. He didn't want to see her, anyway. Matt was dead, and Craig's quest for revenge now seemed small in comparison.

Why wasn't he crying? Craig looked up at the sky. Even his stomach cramps had stopped. He was numb. That's what it was. Just plain numb.

When he brought his eyes down from the heavens, he saw something. Farther down the street, a couple of blocks away, someone watched him. He glanced to where the cops were, but no one looked his way. He turned back to study the man, trying to make out his features.

The guy waved at him. At least, Craig thought he did. The guy could have been waving at someone else before he hurried into an area shadowed by the freeway overpass.

Craig moved slowly after the figure.

Chapter 81

When Andrew Miller awoke, Candace Ward held him in her arms. A cold washcloth lay draped over his forehead, and she kept the pressure on both the front and back wounds in his shoulder.

"Hey," he rasped.

"I didn't call anyone," she said. There was no sweetness in her voice.

"Thank you."

"I don't know what you're involved in, and I'm not happy it's inside my home."

Andrew nodded. She'd had time to settle down and mentally adjust to his wound.

"What happens now?" she asked.

"You sew me up."

"You're kidding."

"No."

"Like they do in the movies?" Candace asked.

"Will you do that?"

"No."

"You can do it."

"I don't want to."

Andrew stopped talking. His eyes closed as he continued to lie in her arms.

Several minutes passed, and he thought he might have fallen asleep. When he looked up into her eyes, Candace said, "I'll do it on one condition."

"Which is?"

"When it's done, you leave. While you were out, it became clear this isn't the relationship I was looking for."

Andrew closed his eyes again.

Chapter 82

When his eyes adjusted to the change in light, Craig spotted them hiding in the shadows. Gadget and Matt walked over.

They were under the freeway overpass. The sound of cars and trucks zooming overhead was deafening.

Craig hugged his brother and fist-bumped Gadget.

"What the hell happened, Matty?"

Matt looked to Gadget, then back to his brother. "The suit, man."

"What did he do?"

"He attacked us. Knocked out Gadget," Matt said, thumbing to the smaller man. "He did a number on me and Rabbit. If it wasn't for Veronica, I don't know what would have happened."

"The cops are all over the house. One of the neighbors said she killed you."

Matt shook his head. "She shot Rabbit."

"She did?"

"She was high, man. Flying. You know what that's like." Matt eyed him when he said it. "She was talking about shooting the suit and pulled the trigger without thinking. She killed Rabbit on accident."

"Damn," Craig said and looked back in the direction of the Fifth Avenue house. He could no longer see it, so he turned to his brother. "Why didn't you stick around and tell the cops that?"

"With what we've done? They already got Henry in lockup. Who knows what he's telling them?"

"Henry's stand-up. He won't say anything."

"That's what I've been telling him," Gadget said.

"Besides," Matt continued, "who knows what Veronica will say? She's out of her mind on the pills. She'll lie to stay out of trouble. You know the cops hate us. It's them versus us. They are the enforcers of the one percent."

Even though Craig knew his brother hated the one percent, he'd never heard him complain so much about them.

Matt continued. "Everything finally made sense when we changed the rules. Suits versus nonsuits. Haves versus have-nots. Cops versus citizens. Even when I was a Marine, I was their tool. Their hammer to oppress. The one-percenters say they love the military, but they love us because we follow *their* orders. Don't you get it? Everything makes sense now. I don't know why I didn't see it sooner. I mean, I thought I did, but it's so clear now."

"What are you going to do?" Craig asked.

Matt shrugged. "I don't know. I was going to hide, but where was there to go? I don't want to go to mom."

"That's out of the question," Craig agreed.

"Maybe one of the crew can help us."

"With what money?" Gadget muttered.

Matt glared at the smaller man. "Are you complaining about the drugs?"

Gadget held up his hands in mock surrender. "I'm not saying anything."

"Why don't we go after the suit?" Craig asked.

Matt and Gadget turned to him.

"Let's go after the suit," Craig said softly.

"Why would we do that?" Gadget asked weakly.

Matt studied his brother before asking, "More importantly, how would we do that?"

Craig smiled and touched the bandage on the side of his nose. "I know where the sonofabitch lives."

Chapter 83

Candace finished sewing up Andrew's wounds, then bandaged the affected areas. She did her best to sterilize the needle and to do a good job, but she had no idea if the thread would hold or if the wound would indeed get infected.

She'd sewn plenty of patches in her life, but never a wound. It was something she hoped she would never do again.

Andrew was asleep in her bed. She had placed the bloody towels and shirt in the washing machine. It was doubtful she'd get the blood out, but she would at least try with some hot water and bleach. If it didn't work, she would throw the towels away.

She kept the sewing kit out. She'd have to mend Andrew's shirt when it came from the dryer. He'd need something to wear home.

Now that she mended and put him to bed, she was rethinking her earlier demand to end the relationship. To distract herself from her doubt, she opened her laptop and started her internet browser.

The latest newsfeed popped up with several reports of stranger-versus-stranger assaults. The knockout game was a national fascination. It was bigger than it had ever been before. Now it was being played as everyone versus the one percent. People targeted others for their perceived wealth.

Less than that, Candace thought. Men were being targeted for how they dressed.

She soon found a video that people said had escalated the assaults to a new level. She played it and watched with horror as Andrew struck another man.

He then approached the camera and said, *"Keep coming downtown, and I'll be waiting for you."*

Candace slapped her laptop closed.

Chapter 84

The crew—what was left of it—met in Riverfront Park. They huddled under a large tree near the gondola ride. The evening sun was at the edge of the horizon, and the sky was purplish orange.

Critter, Shaggy, Gremlin, Gadget, and Bam Bam circled around Matt and Craig.

"Why couldn't we drive down here?" Critter asked.

"Because I said so," Matt said. "I'm trying to keep you all out of trouble."

"That's not a good answer," Bam Bam said.

Matt eyed the big man and flexed his jaw before answering. "The cops were all over the house. They're watching my car and Veronica's. Who knows what Henry told them?"

"He hasn't told them anything," Gadget said, a slight whine to his voice.

"If he has, they'll be watching for us and our cars, okay? It's easier to move about on foot through a neighborhood. You get stuck in a car with the cops behind you, and you're done for. You're as good as caught."

"How many times have you outrun the cops on foot?" Bam Bam asked.

"How many times have you survived a firefight in a car?" Matt asked. "Because I'll tell you, I've been in plenty of them on foot, and I'll take that any day over being stuck in traffic. Don't worry about walking to our target, though, because I thought ahead. Shaggy grabbed his dad's truck. Cops won't be looking for that. When we get there, we'll jump out a couple blocks away and make our approach."

Bam Bam glanced at Shaggy before turning his attention to Matt. "We all won't fit in a truck."

"Ride in the back, fat ass." Matt's face warmed, and he ached to fight.

The crew instinctively took a step back.

Bam Bam started to say something but stopped as Stick sprinted toward the group.

"About time," Shaggy said.

Breathing heavily, Stick said, "Denver's been arrested."

"What?" several of the guys said simultaneously.

Stick nodded, then inhaled deeply. "I tried callin' him, but he never answered. So I went by his mom's. She said some cops came by. He fought with them and was arrested."

"Did she say what they wanted?" Matt asked.

"You know how she is. She was none too happy I interrupted her TV time."

"Shit," Matt said, turning in a circle. "Shit."

"That means Henry and Denver are in the can," Bam said.

"I know that," Matt snapped, stopping to look at the big man.

"And Rabbit's dead," Bam Bam said.

"Quit stating the fucking obvious, you retard."

"Hey!" Bam Bam said, stepping toward Matt. He balled up the fist that wasn't wrapped in gauze. "I still got one good hand to whip your ass."

Matt held up his hands in a defensive posture. "Yo… I'm sorry, man. I apologize. I'm upset, and I shouldn't have taken it out on you."

The guys looked at each other. They'd never seen Matt apologize before. No one was sure what to make of it.

Bam Bam nodded and looked around at the other guys. A smile grew with his new sense of power. "It's okay, man, I under—"

Matt kicked Bam Bam in the groin and dropped him to his knees. The big man grimaced and reflexively covered himself with both hands. Matt then kicked him in the head and forced him to the ground. To get up, Bam Bam put his right hand—his good one—onto the ground. Matt drove his heel down onto it.

The big man squealed, rolled over on his back, and held both hands to his chest. He looked like a dying cockroach.

Matt turned to the crew. "Anyone else got a problem?"

The guys watched Bam Bam writhing on the ground.

"Well?" Matt yelled.

They lifted their eyes to him and shook their heads.

"We're going after the suit. Craig knows where he lives. When we get there, we fuck him up. We do this for what he's done to us. We do this for Rabbit." Matt felt the excitement building inside him and did his best to communicate it to the others. He believed they could sense his enthusiasm.

Craig said, "Let's go." The group fell in behind him as he trotted out of the park.

Matt was the last in line. He took a final, disapproving look at the man on the ground.

Bam Bam tucked into a fetal position and whimpered.

Chapter 85

A phone call interrupted dinner. Ernie Navarro raised his eyebrows. "Is this a new thing now?"

"Yeah, Mom?" her daughters chimed in.

Leya pushed away from the table and answered the phone on the fourth ring. "Navarro."

"Leya, it's Josh."

"We've got to stop talking like this, Josh. My husband is starting to complain."

From the dinner table, Ernie stuck his tongue out at her.

"I'm sorry to bother you, Leya, but Riverfront Park security is out with a guy matching one of the suspects from the elevator assault."

"Seriously?"

"We'd given them the photos you wanted distributed, and they just found one."

"What was he doing?"

"Lying on the ground and crying."

"What happened?"

"Somebody stomped on his one good hand, leaving him with no good hands."

"He say anything?"

"He's talking up a storm."

"He say who did that to him? Was it a suit?"

"Said it was his friends."

"His friends?"

"It's a long story, but the gist is they're on the way to kick some suit's ass. He said they know where the guy lives."

"They're going after Andrew Miller," Leya said. "An officer is sitting off his home now. Alert him there's a crew heading his way. I'll change and head in."

Chapter 86

The door gave way as soon as Critter's foot hit the wood. The sound of the door banging against the inside wall was immediately eclipsed by a woman screaming. She stood in the living room and watched with horror as they entered the house.

"Shut up," Stick yelled.

She continued to scream.

"Critter, shut her up," Stick ordered.

He ran around the couch and reached for the woman. At first, she slapped away his hands, but he finally grabbed her and covered her mouth. The woman struggled against his grasp. It thrilled him to have her in his arms.

Stick, Gremlin, and Shaggy stood in the living room. Gadget, Matt, and Craig were on the porch. Before going in, Matt reached up and unscrewed the bulb that lit up the front of the house.

Stick carried a small baseball bat with him. Gremlin had a knife. Shaggy had brought along his mother's taser. They stepped into the hallway.

"Where's he at?" Gremlin asked.

"The fuck should I know?" Stick said. "Critter, ask her where he's at."

Critter lifted his hand from the woman's mouth, but she screamed. He spun her around and punched her in the stomach. Then he grabbed her from behind again and covered her mouth. "Do that again, and I'll really give you something to scream about."

Another level of excitement rose in Critter as a tingle in his groin started. He was pressed tightly against the woman and hoped he wouldn't grow hard. Not now. Not here.

"Go," Stick said, tapping Shaggy on the shoulder. His three friends moved down the hall, leaving Critter with the woman. He watched the hallway and did his best to keep the woman from struggling.

Shaggy stepped in the first doorway and disappeared. While he did that, Stick stepped into the second doorway and quickly checked it. Gremlin moved to the last door at the end of the hall.

"Clear," Stick yelled.

"Clear," Shaggy said, following Stick's lead.

Critter watched as Gremlin froze in the last doorway, then hurriedly thrust his knife at something just inside the last room. It was too late. A man stepped fully into the doorway, landing a blow across his throat. Gremlin dropped to his knees, gagging as the man stepped around him.

Shaggy jumped back into the hallway and was met with a kick to the chest. His finger curled around the taser, sending volts between its two prongs, but doing no harm to anyone. The crackling sound announced its ineffectiveness.

"Hey!" Stick hollered, swinging his bat at the man in the hallway. The bat clipped the edge of the doorframe, which stopped its arc. For a millisecond, Stick stared dumbfounded at the man directly in front of him.

***

Andrew Miller stepped toward the third guy and hit him with a blitz of low kicks and right-handed strikes. His left arm was tucked in tight to his body, protecting his wounded shoulder.

The skinny man collapsed backward into the room and dropped the bat he was holding. Andrew stepped into the bedroom and bent over to pick up the wooden weapon. When he did so, his muscles constricted throughout his body. His hand automatically tightened around the baseball bat.

It was a stun gun contact hit, one where an attacker must hold the weapon against its target. It was also something Andrew had been trained to experience. As he fell and the taser broke contact from the skin of his naked back, Andrew twisted violently and brought the baseball bat across the taser holder's ankle, eliciting a howl of pain. The hairy guy hopped around on his good leg, holding the injured ankle in his hand. Laying on his side, Andrew backhanded the bat across the man's other ankle, dropping him to the floor. The guy lay on his back like a turtle, holding both ankles in his hands.

Andrew then smacked him across the face with the bat, rendering the long-haired man unconscious.

For a moment, the house was silent.

Andrew stood as quickly and quietly as possible, and he strained to hear any movement. When he stepped into the darkened hallway, he could see a man in the living room holding Candace. The man didn't move to flee or attack. He wasn't afraid. Andrew instinctively knew what that meant—there were others in the house. Andrew, still clutching the bat, slowly walked down the hallway.

At the end of the hall, he peeked around the corner.

"Ha!" a small man said and jumped in front of him. He held his fists up in a fighter's stance. It was the guy from the Fifth Avenue house earlier in the day. The same guy Andrew had knocked out with a kick to the chin.

Andrew kicked out again, landing the same attack in the same spot. The small man went rigid and fell backward, hitting his head on the hardwood floor.

There was no more noise.

"Matt! Craig!" the man holding Candace yelled. "He's here!"

Andrew glanced around the corner. Seeing no one there, he walked over to the front door and looked outside.

"Matt! Craig! Now!"

Andrew peeked around the corner again, then shut the front door, locking it.

"Your friends have left," he said.

The man studied Andrew for a moment. "I'm sorry," he said. "Really sorry." He let go of Candace, pushing her away from him. He stepped back into the kitchen. "I didn't want any part of this."

"Yet here you are."

Candace moved behind Andrew.

"You can call the police," the man said.

"We've got plenty of time for that."

"What're you going to do?"

Andrew handed the baseball bat to Candace.

"It's up to her."

Chapter 87

Andrew Miller and Candace Ward were sitting on a bench in the small Kendall Yards park when the police arrived with sirens wailing and emergency lights whirring. Candace stood and pointed to her home.

Several uniformed officers exited their cars and raced toward the house with guns drawn. As additional units arrived, Candace clung tightly to Andrew's good arm. He didn't mind at all.

A woman climbed out of a blue Dodge Dakota. She walked across the street to where they were sitting. A gun and badge were clipped to her belt.

"Andrew Miller?"

He nodded.

"I'm Officer Navarro. You're a hard man to find."

"He's been here all along," Candace said.

An unmarked patrol car pulled alongside the curb. Another female officer got out. When she spotted Navarro, she headed in their direction.

Andrew said, "Huh."

Candace noticed the change in Andrew's demeanor. "You know that woman?"

"This one, I know."

He slowly stood, holding Candace's hand.

"Ms. Burkett," he said, "I didn't know you were a police officer."

"Mr. Miller," she said, "it seems we have many things to talk about."

Chapter 88

They ran along The Centennial Trail, the thirty-seven-mile-long path connecting Spokane to the Idaho border. It passed through the Kendall Yards development where the suit lived.

They had no option but to run. Craig didn't have a car. Matt's car was at his house, which likely had already been swarmed by the cops. Whatever happened to Shaggy inside the suit's house meant the keys to the truck were stuck with him.

When Matt and Craig heard the commotion inside, they knew things were going badly. At that moment, neither wanted to confront the suit head-on. The guy was a wrecking machine. A tactical retreat was the only option.

Angry that a one-percenter had bested him, Matt spat.

How the hell can a suit do all that damage? A suit!

He stopped now and waited for Craig. He was the faster runner and had to prod his brother to pick up the pace continually.

"Let's go, man!"

Craig hunched over as he threw up. They had run on and off for thirty minutes. When he was done vomiting, his brother stood and walked with his hands on his hips. He gulped for air.

Matt was used to running and throwing up. He'd done it frequently during boot camp until his stamina improved. He'd already done it once tonight. It wasn't a big deal.

"We've got to run."

"I can't," Craig rasped.

"If you don't, the cops'll get us."

"Let 'em have me," he said. He put his hands on his knees and sucked for air. "Go ahead. I'm holding you back."

"Stand up," Matt said. He put his hand on his brother's shoulder and helped him upright. "I won't leave you. You can make it."

"No." Craig lifted his face to the night sky. He opened his mouth and sucked for air. "I got nothing left."

Matt watched his brother. He knew this look. He'd seen it before in others when he was in the desert—when guys gave up on themselves.

"Okay," he said. "Let's figure out a plan."

"Your plan… is to leave me behind. I'm good with it."

"You don't leave your buddy behind, and you never leave your brother."

Craig bent back over again and put his hands on his knees. "I'm sorry, Matty. I fucked this up."

Matt glanced hurriedly around before saying. "No, you didn't."

Craig lifted his head and studied his brother.

"I've got an idea," Matt said, "but you're going to hate it."

"As long as it doesn't involve running, I'll say yes."

Matt squeezed his brother's shoulder. "Remember, you said that."

"Why?"

"Because we're going to see Mom."

Chapter 89

Officer Leya Navarro was in the interview room with Detective Marci Burkett and Andrew Miller. Marci had a connection to Miller through the martial arts world, and Leya had worked the case since Craig Taylor's assault on him at the bus plaza. It was right for the two of them to conduct his interview.

Detective Delaney was in another room interviewing Miller's girlfriend.

Leya sat across from Miller at the small table. A yellow notepad was in front of her. Marci stood with her arms crossed and leaned her shoulder against the wall.

"Why didn't you hang around after you were attacked at the bus plaza?" Leya asked.

"Can we focus on tonight?" Miller asked. "They attacked my girlfriend. In her home. That seems to be what matters, isn't it?"

"We have to go back to the attack at the bus plaza. You see that, don't you? It all starts with you and your attacker. His name is Craig Taylor, by the way. He wasn't at the house when we arrived. Did you ever see him?"

"The one in the kitchen called out his name."

"He might have called out for his mother with the beating he got."

Miller broke eye contact with Leya to look at Marci. She lifted her eyebrows.

"Back to the bus plaza," Leya said. "Why didn't you hang around?"

Miller shrugged. "I wasn't hurt. And I didn't want the attention."

Leya shook her head, frustrated. "You obviously got *his* attention. He brought his friends to your place of employment."

"Nothing happened."

"You broke a man's hand," Leya said.

"Three versus one. A guy should remember not to do that again. Don't you think?"

"Why didn't you report that?"

"Because I handled it."

"But you left work immediately. You knew the police would be called. Why didn't you want to deal with us?"

Miller shrugged again.

"Then you went after them. First, on the streets of downtown and then you went to their house, where you got shot. When they attacked you, that could be argued as self-defense. When you went to their house, that's vigilantism. There's no arguing your way out of that."

"Okay."

"You crossed a line," Leya said.

"I understand."

"Aren't you going to give me a reason for doing that?"

Miller thought for a moment, then shook his head.

Leya glanced at Marci, who had been quiet through the opening of the interview. Marci rubbed the bridge of her nose before saying, "Give us a minute."

"What?" Leya asked.

"Please."

Leya stood, confused. In frustration, she slapped the notepad against her leg.

***

After Leya exited the room, Marci sat in the chair across from Miller. She reached over to the wall and flicked off the audio/video recording switch. The red light in the upper wall blinked out.

"We're no longer being recorded or monitored," Marci said.

"You didn't have to do that."

"Yes, I did."

Miller tilted his head, waiting.

"I know about Africa."

He scratched the side of his face. Nothing changed in his eyes.

"I know what happened there."

"You must have a high-security clearance, Ms. Burkett."

"I don't know all the details," she said, "but I know enough to understand something horrible occurred there. Something that changed you."

"I came out okay. Better than my team did."

"I'm not asking you to tell me about it. Quite frankly, I don't care to know. What I do care about is what has occurred here, in my town, in *our* town."

"I care about what's occurred here, Ms. Burkett."

"You can call me, Marci."

"I prefer Ms. Burkett. I like the tradition. Don't you?" Marci nodded.

"Traditions are important. Honor and code are important, as well. I don't need someone to fight my battles, Ms. Burkett. I'm more than capable of taking care of my own… troubles."

"You should have reported the assaults."

"Maybe. I didn't, though. What difference would it have made? So a man attacks me, and I defend myself.

Then I report it, and he's arrested. It goes before a jury, and they hear my training was used against a junkie. The defense will spin that story so that I'm the bad guy. At best, he'd be given time served and some mandatory drug program which he would fail miserably at."

"You don't know that," Marci said.

"What about the assault in the elevator? If I reported that and if it was fortunate enough to make it to court, again, my training would be put up against three guys. Their attorney would twist it to make it look like I was the aggressor. They'd be lucky to spend any time in a cell."

"You're oversimplifying it."

"I took care of myself and walked away. The only point where I crossed a line was entering that house and assaulting those men. I'll accept my punishment for that. Every other time, I was defending myself."

"I don't want you to be punished, Mr. Miller. What I want is for you to help us. I want you to press charges and start cooperating."

They watched each other for a few minutes, the hum of the fluorescent lights the only noise in the room.

Marci ran her tongue under her lip before saying, "You liked it."

"What?"

She leaned back and crossed her arms. "The thrill. The rush. The blood pounding in your ears, your hands shaking, your breath shallow, the cottonmouth. The adrenaline rush isn't bad when you get used to it. If you've been away from it for some time, it's like getting back on a drug."

Miller's eyes drifted down.

"How long has it been since you felt it? I mean, really felt it. Been a while, I'm guessing. I mean, you haven't been in a real fight since you quit, right? It's not the same as being on the mat. Not even close. It never is, even when it gets wild. The mat, it's safe. Too safe. It's got rules. Everyone is essentially friendly, watching out for the other guy, making sure not to hurt each other, making sure to stop immediately if someone taps out. It's not like that on the street. Not like that on the battlefield."

Miller tucked his chin toward his chest as he focused on what she said.

"I get it, Mr. Miller. I really do. I love being on the mat, but it's like kissing your brother. It doesn't move the needle. Know what I mean? My partner gets upset whenever I wade into a donnybrook when he thinks I should wait for his help or get more backup."

Miller looked up. "You're a good fighter."

"I probably like it too much for my job. I know that, but it's who I am. The brass, my supervisors, were happy when I made detective. They thought it would lessen my chances of getting into encounters. It bothers them I still tangle with suspects now and then."

"It's who we are."

"We've been trained to contain that thrill, though. I would imagine your training had you contain it even further until it was a laser that could burn through steel. But you let it get the better of you when you entered that house. You weren't a soldier on a mission, Mr. Miller. Those days are behind you. For better or worse, you're a citizen now. You have a different level of responsibilities, a different level of honor and code you must abide by."

Miller listened to her words, and she could see he was thinking about them, considering them.

"I must also remind you that you're an instructor, which requires you to act and behave a certain way on and off the mat. You have students that look to you for guidance. How do you want them to see you at this moment?”

He lowered his eyes again.

“If you were to advise one of your students at a time like this, what would you say? Would you want them to act the way you did? That’s what your actions will show them.”

Miller lifted his eyes. They studied each other for several seconds. The hum of the fluorescent lights seemed to get louder.

Finally, he said, “You make a good argument, Ms. Burkett.”

She remained silent and watched him.

“Perhaps you should have been a lawyer.”

Marci feigned offense.

Miller nodded toward the switches. “Turn it on.”

She searched his eyes until Miller repeated, “Turn it on. It’s okay.”

She reached over, flicked the recording switch, and the red light reactivated.

“The attack at the bus plaza,” Marci said. “Are you willing to discuss it fully and then press charges?”

“Yes.”

“The attack in the elevator. Are you willing to discuss it fully and then press charges?”

“Yes.”

“The attack on the street?”

“Yes.”

“Are you willing to explain what happened in the house on Fifth Avenue?”

Miller stared at her for a moment.

“Are you—”

“Yes, I will explain what happened.”

"Thank you," Marci said. "Let's start at the beginning."

***

In the neighboring room, Officer Leya Navarro watched with interest. The interview room monitor had gone dark for several minutes. While it was off, she sat silently, lost in her thoughts.

When the monitor came back on, Marci asked, "The attack at the bus plaza, are you willing to press charges?"

Then Andrew Miller responded, "Yes."

Marci asked several more questions, to which Miller answered, "Yes."

"What the hell?" Leya whispered to herself.

She thought about going back into the interview room but decided against it. Marci was on a roll, and it was best to let her play it out.

Chapter 90

"You're on the news," Sharon Taylor said.

Her boys looked up from the kitchen table to the small TV sitting in the corner of the room.

She began to laugh. It was small at first, then grew in volume. She'd been asleep on the couch when they showed up unannounced. Several empty cans of Rainer were on the coffee table, along with an ashtray full of crushed cigarette butts.

"They really are playin' it up, aren't they? Talk about fake news. Gawd, I hate these people."

Sharon leaned onto her black cane. She wore faded pink pajama bottoms and an Oakland Raiders sweatshirt. The tan baseball hat she wore was pulled down to her ears. The sweat ring on it almost reached the faded flag on the front of the cap.

She'd made Matt and Craig peanut butter and jelly sandwiches and tossed a handful of barbeque potato chips onto their plates. Sharon wasn't much of a cook, especially in the late hours of the evening.

"When the cops came by earlier, I couldn't believe what they was sayin'. People all over the country have been copyin' that game, and they say it all started here. They said it was cause of you boys. Can you believe it? National news. Them cops was sayin' my boys started something that's got the whole nation scared to death."

Sharon beamed at the television. The smile faded from her face, and she turned to Matt.

"They also said you had yourself a crew and your boys were runnin' drugs. That true?"

"They made a mistake, Mom."

Matt didn't want his mom thinking he might have any money hidden away. If she knew or even suspected, she would demand he give her some. She was like that. Demanding things just because she brought him into this world. He didn't think he owed her anything because of that, but she had held it over his head since he was little. Even when he was in the Marines, she wanted him to send home a part of his paycheck. When he didn't, she refused to talk with him until he sent her something. He'd like to think he could say no to her, but he knew himself better than that. That's why he avoided her as much as possible.

Sharon leered at her younger son. "The police don't make mistakes like that, Matty. If they say you was doin' it, then you was doin' it. I ain't stupid. I defended you and Craiggy for a lot of years and always looked a fool for doin' so. That's when I realized they was tellin' the truth! Just because we hate 'em doesn't mean we have to be stupid about it. I'll still back you up, Matty, because you're my baby boy, even when you're being a bastard, but you and me both know the cops ain't lying if they said you was dealin' drugs."

"Mom—" Craig said.

"Don't start, Craiggy! You're worse'n he is. I don't know what you're on, but you look like ass. And you smell it, too. If you're goin' to spend a night here, then you're going to take a shower after you eat. I won't have no son of mine smellin' like a greasy shit while sleepin' in my house."

"Mom—" Matt said, but his mother was on a roll.

"How could you do this to me?" Sharon said as she limped away. "What'll my friends think?" She turned to look at them. "You think of that? Well, did you? No, you din't. I guarantee you din't think about what it would do to me. You started that game, and for what? To get yourself caught? What was it for? You ain't getting' no money out of it, are you?"

"We were making a statement." Matt winced at how weak his voice sounded.

Sharon glared at her youngest son before hobbling back toward him. "A goddamn statement! How does making a statement put any food in your mouth? You were going after suits, you dumbass. They got money. You could have at least taken a wallet or demanded a payment or something. Hitting them was a childish idea. A statement? Big fuckin' deal, Matty. You got the whole country to sit up and take notice of how the one percent is holdin' us all down." She lifted both her hands above her shoulders and waggled them, mocking him. "Whoop-de-fucking-do. We all know they's holdin' us down, you retard. So what if you sent a message? There was no money in it for ya, was there? And what's the message you're gonna send when you get caught? Cause you're gonna get caught, you know that, right? All your friends, your so-called crew." She snickered. "A crew, like you're Dean Martin or somethin'. Those boys have been caught, and they're snitchin' you out. They got no loyalty, boy. If you even think so, then you're a fool. Nobody in this world has got loyalty except family. Me and that half-wit sittin' there with a sandwich stuffed in his face are the only idiots in this world who will stand by you through thick and thin."

Matt turned to look at the news just to shut the old broad up. Maybe she was right. Maybe the guys were ratting him out. So what? He no longer cared.

"Whadda you wanna be remembered for, Matty? That you din't make money out of this grand scheme of yours? Or are you goin' to do something that says, this is who you are. This is my real legacy. Because right now, your legacy is you ended up a no-good bum, just like your father."

She limped toward the back bedroom. Her cane angrily thumped onto the floor as she went.

The comment about his father stung. His dad was a loser who'd gone to jail for burglary when Matt was three years old, gotten out shortly after Matt's fifth birthday, and then was shot and killed while robbing a convenience store when Matt was in the second grade. His mom never let him forget how little his old man amounted to in his life. She repeatedly said his father never left a mark on society and chided him about leaving his own legacy.

Was this really it? Would the end of the knockout game be his legacy?

The slamming of her bedroom door brought Matt's thoughts back to the moment.

"I honestly never thought about what it would do to her," Matt whispered.

"Fuck her," Craig said.

"If I knew it would upset her, I would have done it years ago."

Matt and Craig's images were on the television.

"We're famous," his brother said before putting a potato chip into his mouth.

"That wasn't about that."

"Then, what was it?"

Matt watched the television. "I was bored," he said. "And I needed something to distract the guys."

"We're not bored now."

Matt faced his brother. "We aren't that. I thought it was a genius idea, by the way. Making it a message. I ran with it because I thought you really had something there. Then

we lost our way when we went after that specific suit."
Matt studied his brother. "We should have left him alone."

Craig doubled over and sweat beaded on his forehead.

"Coming down?"

His brother nodded.

"Too bad you can't steal some of Veronica's pills again."

Craig looked up with the eyes of a wounded deer.

"I know you stole from her."

"I didn't."

"It's okay. I know."

He winced, then nodded.

Matt turned back to the TV. The story had changed to a reporter interviewing a silver-haired captain. In the background was the house where the crew had fought with the suit and lost.

"It's just you and me now," Matt said.

"What are we going to do?"

An idea grew as Matt watched the television.

ROUND SEVEN

Chapter 91

Officer Rodney McCrea smiled at the woman standing outside the shared entrance to Spaceman Bakery and Lilac City Credit Union. She had been flipping through a magazine, but as McCrea walked toward the front door, she made eye contact and smiled.

Inside, McCrea ordered his black coffee to go. Due to the day, the bank portion of the building was closed. He was the only customer inside the coffee shop.

He had just handled a traffic collision at a nearby intersection. When he was done, he parked his car and walked over to the coffee shop. It was a beautiful Sunday morning, so he took a few minutes to stay outside a little longer. Dispatch wasn't in his ear, demanding he respond to the next incident. He could enjoy a couple of moments to himself.

The barista quickly fulfilled his order. When McCrea stepped back outside, the woman was still there and smiled at him once more.

"Good morning," he said.

"Hi."

She was attractive, with short brown hair and bright blue eyes. She was in her mid-forties and smartly dressed—black blouse, blue skirt, and blue shoes. For a moment, McCrea wondered if she was wearing colored contacts to match her outfit.

"Waiting for someone?" McCrea asked.

"Meeting a friend before work. She's late, as usual. It's such a nice morning. I figured I'd stand outside and get a little sun."

"It is a lovely morning, isn't it?"

The woman's eyes danced, and McCrea brightened.

"Lovely?" she said. "Men don't use that word very often."

"It's a perfectly good word."

"Oh, I agree." Her smile grew slightly larger, which caused McCrea to smile back.

"Can I ask your name?" McCrea asked.

"Harriet," she said. "Harriet Francis. My friends call me Harry. Although, I prefer Harriet even though it's an old person's name."

"I think it's lovely," he said. She didn't smile as much when he recycled the word.

"And your name?"

He pointed to his silver name tag, which read McCrea. "Rodney McCrea. My friends call me whenever they want."

"You are forward, aren't you?" Her smile remained, although the lips were now slightly parted.

"I figure I only have a few minutes before your friend arrives."

She giggled, and they continued talking.

A man approached from down the street, but McCrea paid little attention to him.

Howard Street was busy with foot traffic, and his focus was clearly on Harriet Francis, who he now learned was named after her great grandfather, of course. McCrea was utterly drawn into Harriet's eyes, and he felt himself drifting away on her laugh. She was intoxicating.

He had no sense the man was near. Instead, McCrea had his notebook in one hand and a pen in the other. He'd just written Harriet's phone number down when the man punched him in the side of the head.

Chapter 92

Candace sat at the table and watched her boyfriend make breakfast. He refused to let her help. He cracked multiple eggs with a single hand, then whisked them in a bowl. Carefully, he chopped onions, green peppers, and tomatoes. When he was done, he pushed them to the side.

It had been a long night.

While Detective Quinn Delaney interviewed her, it became very clear how heavily Andrew had gotten mixed up in the recent knockout game. He may not have started it, but he somehow got crossways with the guys involved in it. She knew about his confrontation that made the video, of course. It was all over social media, so how couldn't she know about it? It was also clear she didn't know the whole picture, though.

She'd imagined Andrew was a good fighter but never saw it for real until the videos. Delaney had shown her a video that occurred at the bus plaza, then another that happened in an elevator at his office, and then finally a different angle of the one that occurred on the street.

Candace was shocked by the videos. Not only by the violence she saw Andrew was capable of but that he didn't come home and tell her about it. How could someone experience something like that and not want to tell the world? It seemed wrong and weird.

She was interviewed for over an hour and still had to wait an additional ninety minutes for Andrew to finish his.

Detective Delaney told her that several of the men who entered her house were now at Deaconess Hospital. Andrew was in his right to defend himself and her, but the damage he inflicted on the men would require special attention in his interview. They wouldn't want anyone to claim Andrew had gone too far.

Candace knew he hadn't gone too far with the last intruder.

The man gave himself up, but Andrew wouldn't let him walk out. The man assaulted her in her own home. She felt him growing excited while he clutched her. After he punched her in the stomach, she knew full well how much the moment excited him as he pushed against her from behind.

When Andrew gave her the baseball bat, she knew immediately she wanted the man to feel the fear and hurt he had caused her. She felt powerful when she hit him. It was the first time she'd ever intentionally hit another living thing, and it felt good. It felt right. It felt justified.

She hit him so many times Andrew had to come over and stop her. He held her close and gently pulled the bat from her hands.

When they walked outside, Andrew told her that whenever anyone asked, she was to say he had hit the man.

Candace wanted to tell the detective the truth, not to put that additional burden on Andrew. However, when the time came, she did exactly what her boyfriend had told her to do. When Detective Delaney asked about the man lying injured in the kitchen, Candace told a story of how he attacked Andrew and that her boyfriend defended himself.

She felt terrible for lying to the detective, but she now felt a deeper connection to Andrew. Not because he was protecting her from the possibility of an assault charge. No, it was the actual assault of the man that allowed her to understand something in Andrew. It changed how she viewed him, helped her understand him, even if it was only a small insight.

When he finished the scrambled eggs and toast, Andrew carried her plate over and set it on the table. Then he grabbed his plate and joined her. "Sorry for it being slow this morning," he said.

Candace picked up her fork. "It's perfect."

He took a bite of eggs before asking. "How are you?"

"Shaky."

"It'll get better," he said. "It takes time."

She pushed her eggs around on her plate, not picking any up. "I asked you about the scar on your leg once. You said it was an old sports injury and changed the subject. I figured you didn't want to talk about it."

Andrew took another bite of eggs and chewed slowly, watching her.

"I saw you last night for the first time."

He remained silent.

"Detective Delaney showed me a video. Three videos, actually. You were assaulted in each of them and fought back."

Andrew put down his fork.

"You know what I didn't see in those videos?"

He shook his head.

"Fear. You were never afraid."

Andrew drew a deep breath.

"Then you fought in my house. You beat them. Then I did something I never thought I would do. I became something …"

Andrew covered her hand with his.

"I'm not saying he didn't deserve what I did. I'm glad I did it because…" Her voice trailed off before continuing. "He scared me. They all scared me. But I never saw that in you, not once. You weren't afraid. There wasn't an ounce of fear. I was. I was afraid I was going to die, afraid we would never see each other again, but you weren't. You were something else. If I had to describe what you were, I would say you were… you almost looked… bored. No, that's not the right word. Disconnected. How can that be?"

Andrew moved his chair closer to her. When he sat again, he held her hands.

"Who are you, Andrew?"

"I love you."

"Do you? If you do, you will explain this to me."

Andrew rubbed her fingers for a moment before answering. "There's a part of my life I haven't shared. Not because I don't trust you, but because it's painful. I lived through it. I dealt with it, and then I packed it away. I wanted it left alone. Then that guy attacked me in the crosswalk, and it all started coming back."

"What was it? What happened?"

Andrew inhaled deeply and exhaled. He stared at her for a moment before he began. "There is a small country in the center of Africa."

Chapter 93

The entire block was locked down. An attack on a police officer had occurred, and his weapon had been stolen. Getting overtime approved for Sunday hours would be a no-brainer.

As one of the leads on the knockout game, Leya Navarro responded to the scene, arriving after the other officers, department brass, and detectives had secured the area.

Since Spaceman Bakery shared an entrance with Lilac City Credit Union, security cameras were placed outside the building. Leya walked inside and was greeted by Captain Ackerman. He waved at her from the second floor. She trotted up the stairs, and they entered the backroom of the credit union. Two monitors showed eight camera feeds. One of them was at the front door.

Leya was introduced to the branch manager, Tonya Masterson, who had been called in on her day off.

"Tonya has the footage from the assault."

The manager moved the computer's mouse and double-clicked a button. A window popped up, and a video started. Officer McCrea was talking with a woman outside the entrance. It appeared they were having an intimate conversation.

"That's Harriet Francis," Ackerman said. "She witnessed the attack. She's downstairs now."

"How's Rodney?"

"He'll be okay. They took him to Deaconess for observation."

"In a couple of seconds, a guy is going to enter the frame and hit McCrea."

Just as Ackerman finished speaking, a white male entered the picture and suddenly threw a punch at McCrea. He never saw it coming. As soon as it connected, McCrea's head snapped viciously to the side, and he crumpled to the ground.

"My God!" Leya said.

"It gets worse," Ackerman said.

"How can it?"

The attacker bent over and removed McCrea's gun. It took several yanks, amid rocking back-and-forth motions, but the weapon finally came free. When the attacker stood, he said something to the witness and ran toward the nearby park.

"What did he say?" Leya asked.

"He said, 'They're not as tough as they look.' We're assuming he meant cops."

Leya stared at the screen. "Is there a way to move this back and forth in slow motion?"

Tonya, the bank manager, showed her how to control the video system. Leya moved the video back frame by frame until she had a clear picture of the attacker.

She pulled a folded sheet of paper from her notebook and held it up to the screen. On the paper were front and side profile pictures of a mid-twenties, white male. "Does that look like the same guy?"

Ackerman and the bank manager both leaned in. They glanced between the screen and the piece of paper before they reached the same conclusion. "Yes," they said, almost in unison.

Leya unfolded the bottom portion of the paper to reveal the name of the man.

Matt Taylor.

"That's what I thought," Ackerman said. "His name is plastered over the news, but he assaults a cop and steals a gun. What was he thinking?"

Leya shrugged. "What was he thinking when he started this game?"

Chapter 94

Barry 'Gadget' Wilkerson sat across from Detective Quinn Delaney. He eyed Detective Marci Burkett, who stood in the corner of the interview room with her shoulder against the wall. They'd already started the interview, and Gadget had waived his rights to an attorney.

"When we talked to your buddies," the male detective asked, "they called you Gadget. Why is that?"

"I dunno. I like toys, I guess."

"One of them said you were good with computers. That's how you got the nickname, right?"

Gadget shrugged.

"Don't be modest," Delaney said. "I bet Matt relied on you a lot."

"Sometimes."

"Where is your computer, Barry?"

Gadget said, "I lost it."

Delaney smiled. "Does that sound reasonable?"

"Probably not," Burkett said.

Gadget glanced at the female detective.

"I don't think it sounds reasonable either," Delaney said. "I think we'll get a search warrant for your mom's house."

Gadget's eyes widened.

"That's what I like," Delaney said to his partner. "A poker player."

Burkett smiled.

Gadget's brow furrowed as he looked between the two of them. "What?"

"You need to work on your bluff, Barry. Anyway, we'll get a warrant, search your mom's house, and scoop up the computer. When we get it, I'm sure we'll find the videos you created. Isn't that right? The ones that were uploaded. The ones that caused all the panic."

His eyes darted between the detectives. When he realized what he was doing, he forced himself to be calm and look straight ahead. He stared at the tip of the detective's nose. "There's nothing there," he said, sounding like a robot. *God, that sounded awful.* "Get your warrant."

"When we arrested your crew last night, we took everyone's phones into evidence, including yours."

Gadget's face grew warm.

Delaney watched him for a moment before he said, "Breathe, Barry, breathe."

He let out a push of air and then inhaled. He hadn't realized he was holding his breath. His head pounded now.

"We've seen the videos on everyone's phones. We know the guys were involved in the game. We know you were involved. All we want to know is how it came together and why it started."

Gadget's eyes danced around.

"Right now," Delaney said, "you're trying to figure how to get out of trouble."

Gadget refocused on the detective's nose.

"The problem is there's no clear path for success. The only thing that's going to help you is the thing you least want to do—tell the truth."

Tell the truth? That was the last thing he wanted to do.

Gadget looked at the female detective again, but she shook her head scornfully.

Is she reading my mind? Stop it, he yelled inside his head, *you're screwing with yourself!*

"You can continue to lie and get deeper in the hole," Delaney said, "or you can run through the only door open to you, Barry. It's your escape route. What's it going to be?"

Gadget took a deep breath and said, "There were no drugs."

"We know that. We searched everyone incident to arrest."

"That's not what I meant. There were no drugs to sell. We sold coke. That's what we did, that's how we earned. We all had our little piece of the market, and Matt was our supplier. We were just getting started. Then the market dried up. Matt created the game to give us something to do until the powder came back."

Delaney made several notes before asking, "At first you were going after random folks, then it changed to suits. Why?"

"That was Craig's idea. Matt's brother—you know him? He wanted to join the game and thought the idea was a way to make it better, give it purpose. Seemed like a good one at the time. It's like we all hate suits, you know? Who doesn't? And it was a way for us not to hit women and poor people anymore. Gremlin had to hit a girl once, and I don't think anyone else really wanted to do that."

"Gremlin hit a girl?" Delaney asked.

Gadget glanced at the female detective. She stared at him with dead eyes.

"Craig used you," Delaney said.

"What do you mean?"

"He attacked a suit earlier in the week and lost. The same suit whose house you entered. Craig wanted revenge, and he set the crew to get it for him."

"We knew that," Gadget said. "Didn't matter none. Suits are suits. Because of them, the world is unfair. They've tilted the whole world in their favor. We were just tilting a little portion of it back in our direction."

"What do you know of Rabbit?"

The color faded from Gadget's face. "What do you mean?"

"He's dead."

"I heard that."

"You were there."

He swallowed. "No… I wasn't."

"Veronica Schuster says otherwise. You know her?"

"Yeah."

"My partner interviewed Veronica. Know what she said?"

Gadget's eyes shifted to Burkett, who continued to watch him without emotion. He snapped his attention back to Delaney. Gadget was embarrassed to feel scared of a woman cop.

"Veronica said the suit showed up and kicked your ass as well as Rabbit's and Matt's. She stopped the fight by shooting him."

"Then you know he knocked me out."

Delaney nodded. "Veronica said you were on the floor like a dead fish."

The female cop chuckled, and Gadget's cheeks flushed.

"What happened when you woke up?"

He swallowed with difficulty. Could he get in more trouble if he kept telling the truth? He was already in deep. Wouldn't telling the truth help him? Set him free, so to speak?

"When I came to," Gadget said, "Ronnie was sitting on the couch with the gun in her hand. Matt was standing in front of her telling her she shot Rabbit."

"How was Matt acting?"

Gadget thought about it for a moment, then said, "Fine."

"Were they friends?"

"Matt and Veronica?"

"No. Matt and Rabbit."

"They'd hung out since high school. Like most of us, I guess. Although Matt messed with Rabbit. Teased him, I mean. And Rabbit just took it."

"Veronica swears she didn't shoot Rabbit."

"She had the gun."

"Doesn't make sense," Delaney said. "Veronica said she was upset, and that Rabbit was trying to calm her down. That he was moving toward her. She's still trying to reconcile what happened. But then she goes out—lights out. We found a round in the wall that could correspond with a shot she fired. We'll know for sure when we get the final forensics report, but it sure looks like Rabbit was shot at a different angle than what Veronica is telling us. She's not holding anything back, Barry. She's trying to understand why she would shoot Rabbit."

"He had a crush on her," Gadget said softly.

Delaney glanced at Burkett, then brought his attention back to Gadget. "She told us that, too. Thank you for confirming it."

Gadget nodded.

"There were only four of you in the room. You and Rabbit, Matt and Veronica. You were knocked out cold—"

"Dude kicked me in the face. Like he was Chuck Norris."

"And Rabbit clearly didn't shoot himself. Who was more likely to shoot Rabbit? Matt or Veronica? If she did it, she should pay for the crime," Delaney said. "But if she's innocent, the woman shouldn't take the fall just because someone made it look like she did it."

Gadget shrugged. "I dunno, man. She's a nice girl who's got a problem. You had to see it. The Oxy and all. Matt kept her twisted up with it. I really wish I could tell you she didn't do it. I don't know. All I do know is Matt didn't seem busted up that Rabbit was dead."

Chapter 95

If Gadget hadn't been arrested, it would have been an easy solution. He could have used his computer to find the suit. A few taps on the keyboard and an address would be provided. Gadget was amazing that way.

Even Rabbit might have had an idea of how to find the suit. He was smart when he wanted to be. Matt missed having him around right now. He was regretting the decision to shoot him. It was stupid and short-sighted. He should have controlled his anger.

He realized, though, he couldn't have kept Veronica around forever. She was bound to leave him sooner or later, especially if she ever cleaned up. But it was the things Rabbit said that bothered him. No, it was worse than that; it made him furious.

If things ever got bad, really bad like they were now, Matt knew Rabbit would never be truly loyal. It was questionable if he would have stood up against the pressure of some cops. He sure as hell wouldn't have been loyal to him over Ronnie.

But hadn't he hit her and taken the gun from her? Rabbit did that for him, right? Matt shook his head, trying to clear his thoughts.

"You okay, Matty?"

He rubbed his eyes and said, "Tired."

They were hiding in a vacant house in the West Central neighborhood. Earlier, they had seen the unkempt lawn and no For Sale sign in the yard. Craig approached the front window and discovered the house to be empty. It only took a quick trip around the rear, a foot against the back door, and they were inside. It was an excellent place to camp for a few hours and get some rest.

Craig looked terrible. He sat on the floor with his back pressed against a wall, his arms crossed his body as he shivered. The temperature inside the house had to be in the mid-80s.

His brother's face was pale, and he looked exhausted. Matt knew Craig was coming down. They'd need to score some more drugs for him soon, or this would be how he'd spend the next several days. Maybe it was for the best, though. Craig needed to clean up. He was a liability now.

Matt stared through the dirty bay window and watched as an occasional car passed by.

His crew was locked up. Some of them would flip. Not all of them, of course. He knew Henry, Bam Bam, and Denver would never flip. They were the strongest of the guys. No cop would ever break them.

Critter and Gremlin, though? Matt was sure those two would sing like little birds. They could be intimidated.

And Gadget? He was a wild card. Matt figured he'd keep quiet until there was no other option remaining for him. He'd calculate his way out, figuring the odds until he knew the right play. He liked Gadget because of his smarts. He wouldn't fault him if he rolled because it would be his only option.

Regardless, a couple of guys talking was all the cops would need to pin everything on him. He was done. In the beginning, maybe he could have talked his way out of some trouble by giving them his drug source. Told the cops how they dealt and where the drugs came from. Matt would never have thought of that before and thinking it now made him ashamed.

Some of his guys might rat, but he never would. Before today, he didn't know what he really cared about. Right now, he was worried about only one thing—the thing his mother had harangued him about: his legacy.

That's why he hit the cop. He was going to leave a legacy. People would remember his name. One way or another, they were going to remember him.

"Why are we going after the suit?" Craig said, his voice small and feeble. "I thought you said that's where we made our mistake."

"Because we can make things right by finishing what we started. You even heard mom say it. We're a laughingstock now. I don't want to be laughed at anymore. Do you?"

Craig looked down. "It's not that big of a deal. I've let it go."

"It is a big deal," Matt yelled. "I was a Marine once!" He thumped his chest with his fist. "People didn't laugh at me then."

Craig looked at him, saying the only thing he could think of, "People aren't laughing at you, Matt. They're scared of you."

Matt walked in circles. As he thought, he pressed his hands against the sides of his head.

"How do we find him?" Craig asked.

"We only know two places where he might be—his work and his girlfriend's house. The news said that wasn't his place, right?"

"It's Sunday, so he isn't going to work," Craig said, staring at the floor. "There are too many people, and they probably aren't at his girlfriend's anymore, right?"

"That's what I'm counting on."

Chapter 96

It was Sunday night, and they were in the backyard. Ernie stood at the grill and flipped hamburgers. The two girls, Rose and Violet, were running barefoot through the lawn, chased by a barking Jack Russell terrier.

Leya sipped her beer as she watched her family. "You sure you don't want help?"

"I've got it," Ernie said. "Relax. You've had a long week."

"Tell me about it. We still have to wrap up the paperwork tomorrow. This report is going to be massive. It'll be the biggest one I've ever been a part of. Not sure about Delaney or Burkett."

"Someone say my name?" a male voice called from the other side of the wooden fence.

Leya stood and hurried over to open the gate, letting Quinn Delaney in. He hugged Leya and handed her a six-pack of Bud Light. "The burgers smell great."

She pointed to her husband. "That's my man, Ernie."

He waved a metal spatula, and Quinn waved back.

"Where's Marci?" Leya asked.

"She said she was on her way. I'd expect her—"

A motorcycle roared into the neighborhood.

Leya's eyebrows lifted.

"Yeah," Quinn said. "That's her."

"She rides a motorcycle? Cliché, don't you think?"

"Don't tell her that."

Marci soon came walking through the side gate, wearing a leather jacket, jeans, and black boots. In her left hand was a motorcycle helmet.

"Sorry I'm late."

Leya smiled. "You're right on time. That's Ernie."

Ernie again waved the spatula.

The two little girls ran up to Marci and stared at her. Leya put her hand on the taller girl and said, "This is Rose. The wild child is Violet."

Violet's eyes were wide with excitement. "You're the karate lady, aren't you?"

Marci looked at Leya.

"I told them how you took down Denver."

Marci bent to meet Violet's gaze. "Yes, I'm the karate lady."

"Wow," she said and put her hand in Marci's. She tugged for her to follow. "Want to see my dog?"

Marci handed her helmet to Leya as she was led into the yard by two laughing and dancing little girls.

Quinn stood next to Leya as she watched her children.

"You have a nice family, Leya."

She beamed proudly at the detective. "Yes. Yes, I do."

Chapter 97

Matt pulled the Honda to the curb in front of a dilapidated rancher in Spokane's East Central. They'd stolen the car after they broke into the suit's girlfriend's home. They had watched the house for a bit to make sure neither of them was there.

Once inside, it took some time, but they finally got the final piece.

They knew the suit's name was Andrew Miller. They'd heard it on the news at his mom's. Inside the girlfriend's house, Craig found a *Sports Illustrated* with Miller's address on it. It was in Spokane Valley, a neighboring city about twenty minutes away.

"Why are we stopping here?" Craig said, doubled up and sweating. They weren't at the suit's house.

"I figured we'd get you some medicine."

Craig's eyebrows lifted.

"Relax while we're here, okay? Don't look so… well, don't look like you do. Suck it up for ten minutes."

When they climbed out, Matt tucked the gun he'd stolen from the police officer into the back of his pants. Craig saw his movement, and his smile faded. He swallowed hard and nodded.

As the summer sun sat in the west, it left the night with an orangish hue.

The house was a small, brown box with a red door and a dirt yard. In the driveway was a shiny Kia Soul. It had custom rims and a racing trim package along the sides. It looked out of place in the neighborhood.

Matt knocked on the front door and waited. The door cracked slightly open, stopped by a brass chain. A white face with brown eyes and a scraggly mustache appeared in the opening.

"Let us in, Milo."

"You got some a few days ago."

"That was for my girl. I need something for my brother."

The eyes moved between Matt and Craig. "You're on TV. You're too hot."

"C'mon, Milo. In and out. No more than five minutes."

Milo studied Matt for a second before saying, "I get it for you, and then you go."

"As you say."

The door closed, and they heard a brass chain being removed. After Matt and Craig stepped in, Matt closed the door behind them.

"He don't look so good," Milo said, grimacing as he studied Craig's bruised features. "What's he need?"

Craig didn't say anything but eyed his brother.

"Whites," Matt said.

Milo smirked. "Doesn't everyone? Every high school kid and soccer mom is trading in the stuff. How much do you need?"

"A bottle."

"Wait here," Milo said and disappeared into a back bedroom.

"I like your ride," Matt hollered as he glanced around the house.

"It's new. Little sucker is a pussy magnet," Milo yelled back.

"What do you need that for?" Matt said, moving into the front room. "Don't you have what's-her-name?

"Not anymore," Milo said, returning from the back with a small orange bottle in his hand. "She was a gold digger. I kicked her to the curb."

"Who you hanging with?"

"Nobody," Milo said.

"You're alone?"

"Right now, all I want is some peace and quiet. Remember what that was like?"

Matt shook his head. "Not in a long time."

"You should try it. Helps the body and rejuvenates the soul," he said. Milo handed Matt the bottle. On the white label was a woman's name he had never heard of.

"Usual price," Milo said, "even though I think I could probably charge you more due to the trouble you guys are in."

"Either way," Matt said. He reached behind his back, removed the gun from his waistband, and lifted it to Milo's face.

"Hey—"

When Matt pulled the trigger, Craig bent over and covered his ears.

Milo hit the floor. The bullet removed most of his face.

After the sound stopped reverberating through the house, Craig straightened and stared at the body. "The hell, Matty?"

"We're rebuilding," he said and handed Craig the bottle of pills. "Only one. No more."

Craig quickly opened the bottle and removed a single pill. He dry-swallowed it as he continued to stare at the body on the floor. Blood pooled around the head.

Matt snatched the bottle from Craig and headed into the back room. When Craig appeared, his eyes locked onto the various items lying on the bed. There were more than a dozen bottles of Oxy along with several baggies of mushrooms and other pills.

On the nightstand was a gun.

Matt snapped his fingers in front of his brother's eyes and pointed to the gun. "That's yours. Make sure it's loaded."

He nodded but continued to fixate on the pills.

"Now!" Matt yelled.

Craig turned his attention to the nightstand, grabbed the gun, and removed the clip. "It's loaded."

"Search the house. Be careful not to leave your fingerprints on anything. He's got money somewhere."

It took them only a few moments to find the old briefcase under the bed. When they opened it, it was loaded with cash wrapped in rubber bands. Craig and Matt smiled at each other.

"How much do you think is there?" Craig asked.

"Enough," Matt said, grabbing the drugs from the bed and stuffing them into the briefcase. When he was done, Matt put his hand on his brother's shoulder and excitedly shook him. "This is how we start over."

Craig looked much better now that the drug was entering his system.

"When we're finished with the suit," Matt said, "we'll head out of town. This will be our stake. It'll be the Taylor boys versus the world."

Chapter 98

He awoke to darkness.

Was that a window breaking?

He lay in bed listening, not hearing anything out of place. He heard Candy's breathing next to him. He felt his own heart beating. He lifted his watch, clicked the illumination button. It read 1:31 a.m.

Andrew Miller lay there for another minute. He was certain the sound had been real and not a dream. He quietly slid out of bed.

"Babe?" Candy mumbled.

"Shhh."

"What's wrong?" she whispered.

"Heard something."

"What?"

"Don't know."

Andrew opened his nightstand and removed a small flashlight.

"If you hear anything," he said, "call 911."

He padded toward the bedroom door and locked it behind him. He then stepped into a neighboring room and listened.

Andrew forced himself to be calm. He couldn't hear anything but believed someone was inside the house. In fact, he knew it. It was the training. Years of it had developed almost a sixth sense to be aware of when someone else was nearby.

Something squeaked then—an unnatural sound in the house, out of place with the usual creaks and groans.

Whoever was in his home was creeping, but they weren't trained for it.

He could hear their breathing now. Quick and labored, not controlled. Adrenaline coursed through their veins. They were inexpert at dealing with its effects.

Someone moved slowly up from the basement. They had gotten into the house through one of the small basement windows.

He entered the hallway, stepping over the creaking boards he knew by heart and moved to the top of the stairs.

I'm in the fatal funnel, Andrew thought.

If the person inside his house had a gun, Andrew was at high risk because he stood in the middle of the hallway. This went against all his training, but this was his house, and it was dark. The attacker wouldn't know his way around.

Andrew carefully walked down a couple of stairs, stepping over the noisy one. He put himself at the height of someone coming around the corner.

He could hear the breathing of the other person in the house. It was ragged and fast—excited. As the man cleared the basement stairs and turned into the hallway, Andrew punched him twice before a gun fired.

Candace screamed from the bedroom.

The man fell backward into a second man as Andrew retreated up the stairs, down the hall, and into a bedroom.

He now had new information. There were at least two men in his house, and they were armed.

Several rounds were fired down the hall, hitting the door to the bedroom where Candace hid. She screamed again.

He strained to hear what he thought was Candy's voice. If she was doing as he asked, she was on the phone with the police.

A creak from the stairway focused Andrew's attention. Someone moved up the stairs and into the hallway.

Whoever it was stopped after the creak. He could hear them breathing.

Was one or both moving?

Were there more than two intruders?

Another creak in the hallway and Andrew knew precisely where the other man was now. A single man was outside the room he was in.

He forced himself to be calm. His training was the advantage he had over the armed prowlers.

Slowly, a gun appeared through the opening into the bedroom. The ambient light in the room reflected off the metal of the gun. The attacker had mistakenly led with the weapon too far away from his body.

Andrew grabbed the weapon with both hands and a shot fired across the room. He jerked the attacker's arms under his left armpit before elbowing backward, the flat of his arm connecting with the attacker's face.

The man screamed. Andrew elbowed a second time, then twisted the gun violently free, breaking the attacker's finger. The man's screams became shrill.

Andrew spun around and shot his attacker in the chest. The dark form crumbled to the floor.

In the darkness, he crouched near his attacker. He felt the heft of the gun and believed there were still rounds in it. He quickly released the clip, dropping it into his free hand. He couldn't see how many total rounds there were, but even in the low light, he could see two at the top. With one still in the chamber, his worst estimate was the gun had at least three rounds total. He shoved the clip back, setting it with a forceful click.

"Craig?" a voice called out from the darkness, and Andrew knew who it was.

"He's dead," Andrew said, his voice calm. He strained to hear more movement, but there wasn't any. "I have his gun."

"Craig!" Matt Taylor hollered.

Andrew could hear Candy's murmuring in the other room.

"You don't have to die," he said. "You can stop this."

"Why are you doing this to us?" Matt hollered.

Andrew was surprised by the question. It made no sense. The only thing he could say was, "The cops are on their way."

"Why did you have to ruin everything?"

"Leave now, and you'll live."

Footsteps now. Matt was near the base of the steps.

"You ruined everything!" he yelled.

Andrew leaned slightly out into the hallway. Shots were fired, which forced him to duck back into the room. Candace screamed from the other side of the bedroom door.

How many shots? Andrew wondered.

He quickly decided there had been four in total.

If Matt walked up the stairs, Andrew could lean out and catch him in the fatal funnel as well. However, doing so would mean he would be putting a portion of himself in the same dangerous position.

He silently stepped away from the door. Since the room had only ambient light, he moved to the darkest corner.

The noisy stair creaked. Matt was on the move again.

A moment later, the floorboard creaked in the hallway. Andrew could now hear Matt's irregular breathing. He was on the other side of the wall to the room, standing next to the door, gaining the confidence to jump in and attack him.

Andrew aimed at a point on the wall just left of the doorway and squeezed the trigger. Drywall exploded, and the man screamed. He lowered his point of aim and squeezed the trigger again. This time, instead of a scream, he heard a thud.

Andrew moved quickly from the corner to the door, exposed only a minimal portion of himself, and pointed his gun at the man lying on the floor.

He stepped into the hallway, reached down, and picked up Matt's gun. Then Andrew sat on the floor next to the fallen intruder and waited.

It was only a few minutes before sirens could be heard.

A couple of minutes after that, Matt Taylor died.

Chapter 99

The phone rang shortly after three in the morning.

Leya reached over and picked it up. "Navarro," she said.

"Leya, it's Captain Ackerman."

She sat up in bed. "Sir?"

"There was a shooting in the Spokane Valley."

"Sir?" she repeated.

"Matt and Craig Taylor are dead. They attacked Andrew Miller tonight."

"Need me out there?"

"Not tonight. Valley PD is handling the incident. But I need you to hook up with their detectives first thing in the morning. Understand?"

"Yes, sir."

"We want to wrap this up as quickly as possible and get the media involved. I've already alerted Delaney and Burkett. Get some more sleep. See you in a few hours."

"Yes, sir."

Leya hung up the phone and stared up into the darkness.

Ernie touched his wife's shoulder. "Everything okay?"

"Everything is fine," she softly said as she stared up into the darkness. "Go back to sleep."

COOL DOWN

Chapter 100

Andrew Miller held Candace Ward's hand as they waited for boarding to begin.

Almost seven weeks had passed since the home invasion by the Taylor brothers. Two weeks after the shootings, Andrew was cleared, and the deaths of the Taylor brothers were labeled as justifiable homicide. He hadn't expected anything different, but Candy worried the entire time.

He'd kept in close contact with Detectives Delaney and Burkett and followed the story in the local newspaper.

The various members of Taylor's crew still awaited trial for their involvement in the knockout game. Several of the players were vying to plea their way out of trouble. According to Burkett, it was a mess that would take a considerable amount of time to resolve.

Veronica Schuster was charged with manslaughter in the shooting death of Conrad 'Rabbit' Anderson. Her family hired Wanda Acosta, who Burkett said was the best defense attorney in the city. The trial was still pending, but neither the prosecutor nor the defense felt they would end up before a jury.

The knockout game didn't stop immediately with the media's announcement of the death of the Taylor brothers and the arrest of the related crew. It mostly stopped the attacks in the Spokane area, though. It seemed no one wanted to chance arrest or the possibility of a victim fighting back. However, in the rest of the nation, the game continued for several weeks until it faded into obscurity. Like its previous incarnation, the game just burned itself out.

Andrew was asked not to return to Grayson Advisors. The owner of the company thought the attention he brought was not the right type of image for the firm. He didn't argue and instead picked up his personal items one day after work with the help of a friendly security guard.

The press hounded him for weeks, wanting to get his side of the story, but Andrew kept to himself and always turned them down. He had said everything he wanted to say to the police. He didn't need to say anything further.

Then one afternoon, about a month after the shooting of the Taylor brothers had made national news, there was a knock on his front door.

Andrew opened the door to see a tall man standing on his porch. He held up a wallet with a badge and an FBI identification card.

"I'm Zane Ingram, Mr. Miller. I was asked to deliver this to you."

Ingram handed him a manila envelope.

"That's it?"

"That's it," Ingram said, then he offered his hand to shake, which Andrew did. Ingram stepped off the porch, walked across the front lawn, and drove away.

Inside the envelope were two tickets to Ronald Reagan airport and a letter from the Director of the FBI Academy at Quantico. He read the letter, then reread it. Then he went into the backyard, where Candace was sunning herself.

When he showed her the letter, she said, "They want you to be an instructor?"

He shrugged. "They want me to interview for a position."

"What do you think? You want to do it?"

Andrew leaned over and kissed Candace. "Only if you'll go with me."

Now they were waiting in the Denver Airport waiting to catch a connecting flight. "If they offer me the job, they'll pay to relocate us."

"They won't pay to relocate me," Candace said.

"They will if we're married."

"Andrew Miller, you are seriously not asking me to marry you while we're waiting in an airport."

He smiled and was about to comment when a voice came over a loudspeaker and announced, *"Now boarding flight 1589 to Washington, D.C."*

Chapter 101

Detective Quinn Delaney leaned back in his cubicle to look at his partner. She was typing something on her keyboard and hadn't noticed his movement.

"Marci."

She looked at him.

"Another one pled."

"Huh?"

"Trevor Bowers, the guy you choked out in his mom's backyard, just pleaded guilty."

Marci swiveled her chair to face Quinn completely. "Tell me they got more than the first one."

Barry 'Gadget' Wilkerson had been the first to plead guilty. In exchange for testifying against his friends, he was only charged with a single count of Second-Degree Assault, a Class B felony. The multiple conspiracies to commit assault charges along with the conspiracy to commit murder were dropped. He had yet to be sentenced.

"He agreed to four counts of Second-Degree Assault. No conspiracy charges."

She shook her head. "That's all they could get? His assaults were a slam dunk. We had witnesses for those. We broke our backs putting those cases together, cross-referencing every conspiracy charge—"

"I know."

"—and the prosecuting attorneys do what? The least amount of work they can do without getting called out for it. Low-hanging fruit, that's what they're after."

"I'm sure they'll get more from the others as they go along," Quinn said. "They're working toward Bam Bam,

Billy Bell. He's the one they need to make sure to hang the murder rap on."

Marci smirked. "They should all get that charge hung around their necks."

Quinn lifted his hands in mock surrender. "I agree."

"The prosecutor needs to make an example of them, so this sort of thing doesn't happen again. Playing the odds, taking the easy convictions, it's weak. We don't get to do that. Why should they?" Marci's face was red with frustration.

"It's the way the rules are."

"Yeah, well, it sucks," Marci said. "They suck."

Quinn reached into his desk and pulled out a granola bar. "You hungry?"

A smile hinted at the edges of Marci's mouth.

"Shut up," she said and snatched the bar from his hand.

Chapter 102

Leya Navarro parked her car in a specially marked location for law enforcement vehicles at the Spokane Transit Authority bus plaza.

She'd been dispatched there following an assault between two intoxicated males in front of the plaza. Security personnel had detained the men and were waiting for an officer's response.

Before exiting her car, she notified dispatch via her computer that she was on the scene. She paused for a moment and exhaled. By reading the report, she already knew it was mutual combat. Neither person would press charges against either.

She would go inside, contact the security guards, interview both combatants, then release them. Even if it didn't go as she expected, she would cite them for misdemeanor assault and release them. The jail was full and wasn't going to take a couple of drunks for Fourth Degree Assault.

This was the nature of patrol work, Leya knew.

It was mostly boredom, filled with the same routine calls and paperwork she'd completed over the years, punctuated with moments of sheer dread. It was those moments of dread, though, that called for the hypervigilance most cops were known to have developed. Until recently, she loved being in the patrol car, even despite the tedious calls like she was about to handle now.

It was rare a patrol officer got to engage in the type of continued investigative work she'd done with Detectives Delaney and Burkett. That was fun and mattered in a way she hadn't experienced before. When she was done with that case, it felt like there was a hole left behind. Every day on the job since had not been as enjoyable as she once remembered it being.

She always thought she would be career patrol, a lifer like Rodney McCrea or Ken Jarvis, but now she knew what she wanted.

The next time the detective's test came around, she was going to take it.

Leya smiled at that thought. Then she pushed it away, put on her patrol face, and exited the car.

There were two drunks she still needed to handle.

Did You Like the Book?

I love when friends and family recommend a book for me. I'll often give it a read just because the recommendation came from someone I trusted. That's probably how we all are.

If you enjoyed this story, I'd truly appreciate it if you would tell your friends and family or leave a review at where you got the book.

All writers need feedback on their work—not only to help other readers discover them, but so they know they're delivering the goods with their stories.

Thanks for reading and hope to see you again!

About the Author

Colin Conway is the creator of the 509 Crime Stories, a series of novels set in Eastern Washington with revolving lead characters. They are standalone tales and can be read in any order.

He also created the Cozy Up series which pushes the envelope of the cozy genre. Libby Klein, author of the Poppy McAllister series, says *Cozy Up to Death* is "Not your grandma's cozy."

Colin co-authored the Charlie-316 series. The first novel in the series, *Charlie-316*, is a political/crime thriller that has been described as "riveting and compulsively readable," "the real deal," and "the ultimate ride-along."

He served in the U.S. Army and later was an officer of the Spokane Police Department. He has owned a laundromat, invested in a bar, and run a karate school. Besides writing crime fiction, he is a commercial real estate broker.

Colin lives with his beautiful girlfriend, three wonderful children, and a codependent Vizsla that rules their world.

Find out more about Colin at colinconway.com.